'I'm asking
you marry m

'Of course, if you ca~~n't bear the thought of being~~
married to me, you'l~~l just have to say so.~~ Daniel's
voice became deeper, ~~huskily.~~ But if the way you
kissed me just now is any indication—would it be
such a hardship?'

Charisse shook her head. It wouldn't be a
hardship at all, if he meant just the sexual
component. But marriage entailed a whole lot
more than that.

How could she put her reservations into words?
She wanted nothing more than to be with him, to
share their delight in watching Kristy grow, to
have him by her side in sickness and in health.
Increasingly, she couldn't bear the thought of life
without him.

But what would he do once he learned her secret?

Dear Reader,

I always think of standing in the cold watching fireworks when I think of November, but in this month's novels, we have our own special fireworks and I hope you'll agree that these books are all hot, hot, *hot!*

Dangerous To Love is an irresistible title and sexy spy Dan Reese lives up to all it promises in Sally Tyler Hayes's action-packed **HEARTBREAKER**. Then there's *Clay Yeager's Redemption* from Justine Davis; it's another one of her **TRINITY STREET WEST** books with a cynical and fascinating ex-cop hero.

Also, take care not to miss *The Mother of His Child* and *Cattleman's Promise* from favourite authors Laurey Bright and Marilyn Pappano; these stories are compelling and dramatic emotional rollercoasters. Both novels start with huge surprises, and just look at how things turn out…

Happy reading!

The Editor

The Mother of His Child

LAUREY BRIGHT

SILHOUETTE

SENSATION

*All the characters in this book have no existence outside the imagination
of the author, and have no relation whatsoever to anyone bearing the same
name or names. They are not even distantly inspired by any individual
known or unknown to the author, and all the incidents are pure invention.*

*Silhouette, Silhouette Sensation and Colophon are
registered trademarks of Harlequin Books S.A., used under licence.*

*First published in Great Britain 1999
Silhouette Books, Eton House, 18-24 Paradise Road,
Richmond, Surrey TW9 1SR*

© Daphne Clair De Jong 1999

ISBN 0 373 07918 4

18-9911

*Printed and bound in Spain
by Litografia Rosés S.A., Barcelona*

LAUREY BRIGHT

has held a number of different jobs but has never wanted to be anything but a writer. She lives in New Zealand, where she creates the stories of contemporary people in love that have won her a following all over the world.

Other novels by Laurey Bright

Silhouette Special Edition

Deep Waters
When Morning Comes
Fetters of the Past
A Sudden Sunlight
Games of Chance
A Guilty Passion
The Older Man
The Kindness of Strangers
An Interrupted Marriage
A Perfect Marriage
Summers Past

Chapter 1

"Charisse!"

In the act of placing a packet of cornflakes into her supermarket cart, Charisse Lane turned to the source of the masculine coffee-and-cream voice. Not many people got the pronunciation of her name so right—Shah-*reess,* with the accent on the second syllable. Some of her friends still stumbled over it.

So she was surprised to find herself staring at a total stranger.

A handsome stranger, quite a few inches taller than her own above-average height. Sorrel-brown hair was disciplined by a medium-short cut, emphasising the slightly angular planes of his face, with narrow cheeks and a determined mouth above a strong, clean-shaven chin. His eyes were an unusual grey-green, flecked with amber about the irises and fringed by long, dark lashes.

Something about those eyes made her uneasy—perhaps the intent way they were staring at her, with a mixture of disbelief and challenge and a curious kind of anger. Not the way men usually stared.

Charisse's spine straightened in instant reaction, and she lifted a hand to push a strand of flyaway dusk-dark hair away from her cheek, her own deep-sea blue eyes questioning and wary. ''I'm sorry?'' she said.

Other Saturday shoppers skirted round them, children clamoured and carts clanged metallically, while a muffled announcement came over the speaker system, yet Charisse had the strangest impression that she and this man were locked in a little island of silence laced with a startling tension.

''Charisse,'' he repeated, coming closer so that she took an involuntary step back, stopped by the shelves behind her. ''It *is* you.''

Caution kicked in. She didn't know him and he was rather formidable, his size and stance very nearly threatening. Charisse's hand tightened about the metal handle of her shopping cart, ''I think you've made a mistake.''

A frown appeared between his decisive black brows. ''No.'' The word was flatly unequivocal. ''You answered to your name.''

''I didn't answer.''

''Responded, then,'' he argued. ''You certainly recognised it. Why deny it now?''

''I haven't denied it,'' she said, ''but I don't know you.''

A flicker of uncertainty entered his eyes, then disappeared. He said, his voice going hard and gritty, ''I don't believe you.''

Anger heated her cheeks and she tilted her chin to a defiant angle. ''That's *your* problem.'' She turned and blindly reached for another box of cereal that she really didn't need, presenting her back to him.

When she made to push the cart on, he placed a lean, determined hand over one of hers and stopped her.

Adrenaline surged through her in a hot tide, every tiny hair on her skin rising. Her astonished, furious gaze flew to his purposefully set face. Gritting her teeth and keeping her voice low, she said, "If you don't take your hand off mine this instant, I'll yell for security and charge you with assault."

After the merest flicker of apparent surprise the unsettling sage-green eyes held hers, now only inches away. She could smell the masculine scent of him, a mixture of clean fabric, soap and male warmth.

"Perth, Australia," he said rapidly, "five years ago. Two New Zealanders who met in a strange city on the other side of the Tasman Sea—not to mention across the entire continent of Australia. I never thought I'd find you again back here in Auckland."

With a jolt of appalled shock it dawned on her why his eyes had so disturbed her. Because they were so familiar.

Fingers clenched on the metal bar under her hands, she was suddenly cold and disoriented. Her voice thinned. "I've never been to Perth."

The man's eyes narrowed. *"Never?"*

"No," she said desperately. "Never."

Abruptly he let her go, thrusting his hands into the pockets of the casual jacket he wore over jeans. "I don't understand. Why are you doing this?"

Why? Because he had frightened and confused her. And because she knew now, with incredulous and sickening certainty, who he was.

Instinct told her to run.

She didn't, of course. She stood her ground and kept her voice cool and even, despite the anxious pounding of her heart. "I told you, you've made a mistake. Whoever you met in Perth, it wasn't me. Now, I have to go."

Although she'd only got half of what she'd meant to buy, she almost mowed down an elderly shopper in her haste to get to the checkout, scarcely pausing to make sure the woman was unhurt as she flung a guilty apology in her wake.

She could feel the man's gaze on her all the way but forced herself not to look back.

In the car park she threw the groceries hastily into the boot of her shabby secondhand car. She was inserting the key in the driver's door with shaking fingers when she sensed someone at her shoulder, and whirled round, her eyes wide and defensive.

"I didn't mean to frighten you," the man said patiently. "Here." He held out a white business card. "In case you change your mind."

She looked at the card and saw *Daniel Richmond* scrawled on it in large, looping print. Silently she took it from him and waited for him to leave.

He didn't move for a moment or two, then he made to swing away, glanced into the back window of her car and halted, staring.

Charisse followed his gaze to the child's empty booster seat, the teddy bear and the picture book lying beside it.

A leaden feeling of foreboding settled in her midriff.

Daniel Richmond's head slowly turned until he was looking at her again. "You're married?" he queried, his tone curiously distant. "Or in a relationship. Is that what it was all about in there?"

"It isn't about anything," Charisse denied. "And whether I'm married or not is none of your business, Mr. Richmond."

His accusing stare became baffled. "All right," he said

at last. "I don't intend to harass you. I'm glad to see you're well and...happy?"

Under his searching gaze she almost flinched. It seemed a long time since she'd been truly happy; deep down there was always a continuing ache of grief and loss, an emptiness that nothing—and no one—could fill. But she said, "I'm quite happy, thank you. Goodbye."

He stepped back while she unlocked the door. Then, as she climbed into the driver's seat, he placed his hand on the door, and she panicked. But he only cast her a puzzled look, closed the door behind her and waited while she drove out of the parking space.

She kept peering into the rearview mirror all the way home.

There didn't seem to be anyone coming after her, but she couldn't help feeling jumpy. Her hands, damp with sweat, slipped on the steering wheel.

With relief she turned at last into a quiet cul-de-sac in one of Auckland's older suburbs. The houses were mostly mature bungalows set in neatly kept gardens, and trees grew on the grassed verge. In the long summer evenings children would often play on the wide road, watched by adults who called them to the side whenever a car nosed into the end of the street.

Slowing, she took the car into the driveway between the tall, scarlet-flowering hedge and the painted weatherboard wall of the house. She parked in the garage that had been extended to double its size when she'd had the big old villa divided into two flats, with a double-locked door between them.

Rent from the other half of the house was a major part of her limited income. Maybe when Kristy turned five and went off to school Charisse could get a part-time job that would improve their finances. And one day they might be able to afford to have their home to themselves.

Snowdrops, jonquils and daffodils pushed through the grass under the old plum tree shading a corner of the back lawn. With a pang Charisse remembered her mother planting the bulbs, and her father putting in the lemon tree near the kitchen—the tree that was now taller than she was, and laden with small green fruit promising future abundance.

Her father had laid the tiles for the patio outside the back door and built a trellis to enclose it on two sides, while Charisse and her sister helped with the enthusiastic ineptitude of the very young.

The tiles had weathered with the years, a little mossy under her feet as she carried the grocery bags inside, and climbing vines had long since latticed the pergola roof of the patio. The pink clematis already bore a few starry flowers.

In the kitchen Charisse put away the groceries, noting with relief an unopened packet of macaroni in the cupboard—she'd fled the supermarket before getting to the pasta section.

And she wouldn't dare shop there again. She would have to find another supermarket—preferably on the far side of the city.

Glancing at the stove clock, she saw there was plenty of time before she had to pick up Kristy from her friend's birthday party.

She'd retrieved Daniel Richmond's card from the dashboard shelf of the car before coming inside. Now the small, threatening rectangle of white lay on the table. Underneath the bold black lettering of his name were the words "Geological Engineer."

There were two addresses—an Australian one in Perth

and another on the fourth floor of a city office block in Auckland.

Uneasily she stared at the card, wanting to throw it away and forget about it.

But maybe she didn't have the right to throw it away. And she knew that even if she did, she would never forget this morning's encounter. That chance meeting had changed everything.

What was she going to do?

Chapter 2

Two days later Charisse stood in a wide shop entrance in downtown Auckland, staring up at the fourth floor of a building across the road.

Blue-tinged glass walls reflected other high-rises and the clouds floating above, giving no clue to the building's inhabitants.

Her hand was clutched tightly about the strap of the shoulder bag that held Daniel Richmond's card, and her mouth was dry with nerves.

She'd come here on impulse, unable to banish the memory of an unnervingly familiar, intense grey-green stare, and troubled by guilt and uncertainty every time she thought about Daniel Richmond. But this was probably one of the silliest things she'd ever done. She wasn't even sure now what she hoped to achieve.

This morning when another child's mother had invited Kristy to come home with her daughter after morning kindergarten, Charisse had accepted gratefully.

At home she'd taken out the textbooks for her Open University course in business studies and read the same page over and over without understanding a thing.

Deciding that cleaning the kitchen cupboards would be more productive, she had found herself staring at a packet of lentils, ostensibly trying to decide which shelf to put it on, her mind instead replaying the disturbing meeting in the supermarket for the umpteenth time since Saturday.

Finally she'd given up and changed from her faded jeans and misshapen T-shirt into a respectable if hardly up-to-the-minute skirt, blouse and jacket, and travelled into the city.

But the half-formed plan she'd had was now all too glaringly absurd. She should go away and think about this some more, maybe get expert advice.

Stepping out of the doorway, she came up short. Because there he was—Daniel Richmond—leaving the building with another man.

The casual clothes had been replaced by a business suit, a pristine white shirt and a burgundy tie, but she had no trouble recognising him even at a road-width's distance.

He came down the building's several steps and stood with one hand in a trouser pocket as he talked to his companion.

Within seconds the other man shook his hand and nodded, turning to walk away. Daniel Richmond seemed about to walk in the other direction when for some reason he paused and looked across the road.

Maybe her concentrated gaze had led him to sense someone watching him. Charisse was sure she saw his eyes flash with recognition, and then he strode to the edge of the pavement before a passing van obliterated him from her sight.

Charisse swung about and hurried along the busy pavement, dodging past slower pedestrians, intent on putting as much distance between her and Daniel Richmond as she could.

But it was only minutes before a hand gripped her arm firmly enough to bring her to a halt. And that dark, rich voice was saying her name again. "Charisse."

She tried to look surprised. "Mr. Richmond!"

"What are you doing here?" he demanded.

Charisse lifted her brows. "It's a public thoroughfare." She looked at the people walking around them—one or two shooting curious stares—and then back to his face.

His eyes hardened metallically. "More games, Charisse? You weren't lurking outside my office by accident. Why did you run when you saw me?"

"I didn't *run!*" She wasn't a coward. Thinking better of a course of action was a different thing altogether.

"Have lunch with me," he said abruptly.

"What?"

Someone bumped into her, shoving her closer to the man who still held her arm.

"We're in the way." Moving aside, he took her with him. "There's a café over there—" he jerked his head to indicate it "—where we can sit and talk."

Charisse shook her head. "I don't think—"

"I do—think we need to talk," he told her. "Come on."

She resisted the pull on her imprisoned arm. "You can't make me—"

"No," he agreed. "You can scream and someone will call the cops and then we'll both be taken to the police station to explain to them. Or you can let me buy you lunch and we can explain a few things to each other instead. It's your choice."

Making a scene and involving the police seemed like an extreme overreaction to an invitation to lunch in a public place, no matter how reluctant she was to accept. And he didn't appear to be bluffing.

Charisse managed to hold his storm-cloud gaze with an indignant one of her own. "All right. But I don't have much time…" She stopped there, unwilling to tell him anything further. Let him think she too was on her lunch hour.

"Thank you," he said, as if she'd accepted of her own free will.

She cast him a look of angry scorn.

Surprisingly, he laughed, taking her breath away as his already handsome features turned stunning.

"Sorry," he said immediately, erasing the laughter from his mouth, although it still lingered in his eyes.

He led her into the café and found them a table. "What would you like?"

Charisse had no appetite, but she randomly asked for a filled croissant and a cappuccino, while he ordered a slice of frittata, a piece of chocolate cream pie, and black coffee.

The café was crowded and pop music played over speakers. But their table between her and the man looming at the other side of it was narrow and she couldn't pretend not to hear when he bent his head toward her and said, "Well?"

Her gaze slithered away from the challenge in his eyes, and she moistened her lips, giving a small, helpless shrug.

He asked, "Why were you waiting for me?"

That brought her eyes back to him. "I wasn't!"

"What were you doing then? Spying?"

"No, of course not." But her voice sounded weak even to herself. "I had sort of planned to come and see you, but I changed my mind."

"It seems to be a habit with you."

Charisse shook her head. "No…" Her voice trailed off. The less she said to this man the better.

He leaned back in his chair and surveyed her, a thoughtful frown between his brows.

The waitress arrived with their orders and Daniel looked up and thanked the woman absently. When she'd left he didn't touch the food on his plate, returning to studying Charisse.

Lowering her head, she broke off a bit of croissant, but instead of eating it crumbled the flaky bits in her fingers.

"You know, once I thought I knew you," he said at last.

"You didn't."

"I realise that now."

She looked up, half in apprehension, half in relief. "Then—"

But he was going on, "I found out how wrong I was when you left me in Perth."

"I told you I've never been to Perth."

The faint frown became a scowl of barely reined-in temper, and the seductive voice turned to crushed ice. "Yes, and you lied. Both of us know it, so let's cut the pretence, shall we?"

"I'm afraid you don't understand."

"You bet I don't. I didn't understand at the time, and I don't understand now." He abandoned his pseudolounging posture, leaning toward her again. "On Saturday I let it go—I'd already chalked the whole thing up to experience years ago. Then today you came looking for me—okay, you decided not to follow through. But now I'm curious as hell, and I think you owe me an explanation."

"Actually," Charisse said steadily, "I don't owe you a thing, Mr. Richmond."

He straightened abruptly. "And you can stop calling me Mr. Richmond!" he said without bothering to lower his voice. "My name, as you know damn well, is *Daniel.*" At a nearby table a woman momentarily turned her head, and his voice dropped to a velvety murmur, his eyelids lowering as he leaned forward, holding Charisse's eyes with his. ''I remember you calling it out when you were going wild in my arms—in my bed. You haven't forgotten, though for heaven knows what reason you seem determined to convince me that you have!''

Instant heat rose through Charisse's entire body, flooding into her cheeks. She sat dumb and witless, willing the flush to subside. ''I...I haven't forgotten,'' she managed to choke out, ''because I never—''

He was no longer listening. ''Well, at last we're getting somewhere. You aren't denying any longer that you *are* Charisse Lane?''

''I'm not denying that, no, but—''

''*Is* it still Lane?'' He looked down at her left hand, lying on the table beside her plate. ''I noticed on Saturday you weren't wearing a wedding ring.''

Too late to put her naked hand out of sight. She tried to keep herself calm. ''Look, this is quite irrelevant. The thing is—''

''No.'' He reached over the inadequate space between them and closed his right hand over her left one.

The warmth and strength of his grasp—or rather, her unprecedented reaction to it—startled her into speechlessness. She seemed to feel his touch right through her body, and her skin reacted with an extraordinary sensitivity, every nerve end tingling. Suddenly it was difficult to breathe normally.

Something in his face changed, as if he too had received a small shock, his eyes darkening before he narrowed them. ''It isn't irrelevant,'' he argued. ''We have unfinished business, you and I. And you did come looking for me today. That isn't the action of someone who doesn't care a damn.'' He moved his hand and ran a thumb over her bare third finger, looking down at it. Lifting his gaze, he asked without warning, "Why do you have a child's seat in your car?"

The question panicked her. Her voice a little higher than normal, she demanded, "What does that have to do with you?"

He looked perplexed, and very tense. "I'm interested in what you've been doing, what happened in your life after you...after we parted." He paused. "I'm interested in *you,* Charisse. I haven't been able to get you out of my head since Saturday. Everything we did, everything we were together...it's all come back to haunt me. I know we can't exactly pick up where we left off, but I do want to see you again. And quite frankly, if you're not in a legal marriage I don't care if there's another man in your life—" he halted again momentarily, and his eyelids flickered "—unless," he added slowly, his cheeks tautening, "he's the father of your child."

"I don't have a child." Instantly she wondered if it might have been wiser to stick with her vow of silence. But she couldn't take the words back now. "I have a niece," she added hurriedly. "My sister's little girl." *Careful,* an inner voice cautioned. *Be very careful.*

That transforming smile lit his face. "Then we can see each other again. You do want to, don't you?"

"That's a sweeping assumption—"

"You came after me," he reminded her again. "I can't think of another reason for that. Or am I missing something?"

He was missing a lot. Ready to hurl it at him, to cut him down with his facile assumptions and his too-confident masculinity that simultaneously attracted and infuriated her, Charisse stopped herself in time, an impossible, outrageous idea hazily forming. This might be the chance she needed, and he was offering it to her on a plate.

"We had something quite special, Charisse," he urged. "Something you cut short before we had a chance to see where it might lead us. All I'm asking now is a date, for starters. Dinner…whatever you fancy. Let's get to know each other again. Wouldn't you like to do that?"

She gave him a distracted look, her brain in overdrive, trying to sort out implications, options, pitfalls. Wasn't getting to know him, or at least finding out what she could, the whole reason why she'd followed that crazy impulse to track him down? "I…I don't know," she said. "I need to think about it."

He raised his brows, making her wonder how often a woman was reluctant to accept an invitation from him. With his looks, his very sexy, very male self-assurance, no doubt he'd had more than his fair share of women friends, of lovers.

And now he was intrigued by the prospect of rekindling an old flame.

At the thought, a prickling of antagonism brushed her skin.

His brows drew together, as if he'd seen it in her eyes. "What's the matter?"

"Nothing." She picked up her croissant and bit into it. *Stop talking and start thinking.*

At least eating was an excuse not to speak while she reflected on what she was possibly getting herself into. Because, even though her audacious strategy might work, there were obvious dangers. To Kristy as well as to herself. And Kristy was the one who mattered. If Daniel Richmond found out about her, there would be no going back.

She finished half her croissant and drank her cappuccino

while Daniel demolished his frittata and emptied his coffee cup. The slab of chocolate pie lay untouched on the plate.

"So…" He pushed his cup away. "Dinner tonight?"

"Not tonight." She didn't know if she could find a baby-sitter at such short notice, and anyway, she hadn't yet decided what she should do. Maybe she was mad to even think about seeing him again.

"When? Next week I'll be out of town."

"You're leaving?"

He must have noticed the eager leap of hope in her voice. "No," he said tersely, his eyes cooling. "I'm often out of Auckland, but as it happens, this week I have several meetings in the city so I'll be staying here. Which evening would suit you?"

"I'll let you know."

"If you give me your phone number I'll call you."

Charisse shook her head. "I said I'll let you know."

He regarded her speculatively. "You wouldn't be planning to walk out of here and leave me with no way to find you?"

One part of her wanted to do just that. But there was the nagging sense of obligation that she couldn't escape, knew she would never escape, even if he didn't hunt her down, which probably wouldn't be too hard.

And if he did that, she would have lost control of the situation. Better to keep some measure of initiative if she could, no matter how risky. "I'll contact you," she said. "I promise."

"As I recall, your promises aren't worth much."

"That's not fair!" she said loudly. And then, looking down at the table, she muttered, "People change."

"Tell me about it."

Raising her eyes, she saw the bitter mockery in his voice

reflected in his expression. "I'm sorry," she said awkwardly, astonished at the evidence of repressed emotion.

Maybe he'd been hurt. But he wasn't the only one. And the hurt went on, spreading ripples, encroaching on the lives of people who'd had nothing to do with the original misunderstandings and betrayals.

"Yeah, I guess we're both sorry." He scraped his chair away from the table. "I have to get back to the office."

"Aren't you going to eat your pie?"

"You can have it if you like."

"They'd give you a bag. It's a waste to leave it."

He cast her a look of surprised amusement, then got up and walked to the counter, returning with a paper bag that he dropped the pie into. "Here," he said, holding it out to her.

"I didn't mean—"

Daniel shrugged. "Please yourself."

Kristy would love it. "Thank you," she said with as much dignity as she could muster.

Outside the café she said, "And thanks for the lunch."

"Call me," he said. "You promised, remember?"

Charisse nodded. "I know."

"You still have my card?"

"Yes."

Unexpectedly he leaned down and brushed his lips over her cheek. "Right. I'll see you."

She stared after him as he strode off along the street. Her cheek burned where he'd kissed her, and warmth shot through her veins. Dismay mingled with rather alarming pleasure.

I can't, she thought, with a clutch of near-terror. *I can't see him again.* He was far too attractive, and it was much too dangerous.

But you should find out what sort of man he really is, conscience said sternly. *You owe it to Kristy.*

And for Kristy she would do anything.

Chapter 3

"This is delushus," Kristy declared around a mouthful of chocolate pie. Plump elbows on the table, she swung small bare feet from her chair while she demolished the treat. Her dark, loosely curling hair, so like Charisse's, was tied in two ponytails with bright scarlet ribbons, one of them coming undone. With a pointed pink tongue she licked a smear of cream from her upper lip.

Charisse smiled and didn't correct Kristy's pronunciation. Sitting at the other side of the table, she sipped her coffee, watching the little girl's total enjoyment with amused affection.

"Where did you buy it?" Kristy asked.

"It was given to me."

"Who gived it to you?" At four and half, Kristy's need to know was insatiable.

"A man."

"Who man?" Kristy demanded.

"You mean what man. No one you know."

"You're not supposed to take things from strangers," the child pronounced.

"He isn't a stranger. I said you don't know him. That doesn't mean that I don't."

Kristy thought about that, the fine, smooth skin of her brow furrowing. "Why don't I know him?" She bit into the pie again.

"Well...I only met him recently."

"Is he your boyfriend?"

"No! I don't have a boyfriend—wherever did you get an idea like that? And you shouldn't talk with your mouth full."

Kristy finished chewing, swallowed, and said reproachfully, "You shou'n't ask me a question when my mouf is full, then."

She always had a ready answer. And of course no notion of rhetorical questions. Resisting an urge to laugh, Charisse gave her a stern look. "Finish your pie, then you can help me wash up and we'll go for a walk to the dairy." They needed milk, and although the corner dairy two blocks away was expensive, she should probably buy cheese, too. On her aborted trip to the supermarket she hadn't got as far as the cheese.

"Felicity's mummy's got a boyfriend," Kristy announced. She wasn't easily deflected from a subject.

"Well, that's nice for Felicity's mummy, but I don't need one." Felicity's mother had been solo for almost a year, Charisse knew, since her husband left her for another woman.

"Felicity's got a daddy, too." Wide, clear grey-green eyes fixed a direct stare on Charisse, making her heart falter.

She'd known this would come up sometime. But why

today? "Lots of children don't have daddies," Charisse said gently. "You're not the only one, darling."

"Lots of kids do-o!" Kristy affirmed.

"Yes, well, I'm sorry, but I can't just produce a daddy for you." She hoped that one day she might love someone who might like being a daddy to her delightful little girl, but she wasn't going to make any half-promises to a vulnerable child.

"Why don't I have a daddy?"

"Well…everyone has a daddy somewhere, but yours lives in Australia, and that's a long way from here." It wasn't a lie, she told herself.

"A long, long, *long* way, like heaven?"

"Not so far as that. But quite far." Brushing aside an attack of the guilt that had become all too familiar in the past few days, Charisse added lightly, "So you'll have to put up with having just me for now, I'm afraid."

Kristy swallowed the last of the pie. "You're my bestest mummy," she confided, and climbed down from the chair to come round and twine her arms about Charisse's waist. "I love you."

Charisse lifted the warm, cuddly little body onto her lap. The appealing scent of soap and shampoo and Kristy's own uniquely childish smell filled her nostrils as she bent her head to drop a kiss on the soft, near-black hair. "I love you, too," she murmured. "More than anything in the world."

Nothing must harm this child. And no one could be allowed to come between them. Not, at least, until Kristy was grown-up and able to make her own decisions and deal with the possible hurts of making the wrong ones.

But meantime they had a whole childhood to negotiate, and protecting Kristy didn't give Charisse the right to deprive her of her birthright, did it?

There was no point in going on stewing about this and not doing anything. Tomorrow she'd phone the Children's and Young Persons' Service and make some discreet enquiries.

"Really, it all depends," the social worker replied to her carefully worded query. "A single mother is presumed to be the sole legal guardian, unless the father was named on the birth certificate. In that case he would have certain rights if the mother died or became incapacitated or was judged unfit to raise a child. If he wasn't named and hadn't been maintaining the child he'd have to provide some kind of proof that he's the father."

"And then?"

"As I said, it depends. In a dispute between parents—or between a parent and whoever has charge of a child—the court would decide who should have guardianship."

"If the child was well and happy surely the court wouldn't interfere?"

"That can't be assumed," cautioned the voice on the other end of the phone. "They'd weigh the circumstances and the relative rights of the parties. The interests of the child are supposed to be paramount, but I have to say that often Solomon would have a hard time deciding what that is. And sometimes surprising decisions are made. I couldn't second-guess a judge's opinion."

Solomon, Charisse recalled with a shiver, had suggested cutting the disputed child in half. Not so different, she couldn't help thinking, from some of the custody arrangements she'd heard of. One child at the kindergarten swapped homes at the end of every week.

"I see. Thank you." Charisse put down the receiver, feeling sick. If only she had anticipated this she might have averted the problem, but nobody could have expected Daniel Richmond to turn up here and accidentally find her. And she had to deal with things as they were, not as they might have been.

She phoned him later that afternoon, having delayed as long as possible. Kristy was sitting entranced in front of a children's TV show that Charisse could count on to keep her quiet and still for all of thirty minutes.

A warm, efficient female voice informed her that Mr. Richmond was in a meeting, and asked could she leave a message? Tempted to hang up and tell herself she'd tried, Charisse gave her name adding, "I'll call back later."

"Oh, Ms. Lane!" the woman said. "I'll tell him you're on the line."

When Daniel's memorable voice said, "Charisse?" she guessed from the slightly fuzzy tone that he was using a mobile phone.

"I didn't want to disturb your meeting," she said hurriedly. "It's not important."

"*You're* important, Charisse." He really had a sinfully sexy voice, even when it was less than clear, and the way he said her name was a seduction in itself. "Thanks for getting in touch."

A little spiral of warmth uncurled in her midriff, and she took a quick breath. Even when she couldn't see him this man had an alarming effect on her senses.

Steady, she warned herself. She mustn't get in too deep, here. After all, wasn't that how Kristy had come about? Not that she'd be without Kristy for the world...

Daniel asked, "Are you free tomorrow evening?"

Bite the bullet. "I think so."

"Don't sound so eager." His voice was dry.

"I'm sorry," she said stiffly. "It's just a bit difficult to...arrange." Although her tenants were always willing to keep an eye on Kristy, and had readily agreed to do so before, she didn't like to take advantage of that too often.

"Can I pick you up about seven-thirty?" Daniel asked.

"No! No, I'll meet you."

"I'd rather—"

"*I'd* rather meet you," she added firmly, forestalling any more persuasion. "Anywhere in town."

There was a short silence. "All right. We'll have dinner. Do you have a restaurant you particularly like?"

"No." She hardly frequented restaurants. "Nothing too fancy and expensive though," she added cautiously.

"I'm paying."

Charisse wasn't going to argue about that; her budget didn't allow for eating out. "Thank you. But I prefer an informal atmosphere." And so did her wardrobe.

She would drive into the city, she decided, and suggested a meeting place near a big central car park and on a busy, well-lit corner.

After she'd hung up she discovered she was shaking, and inwardly scolded herself. She'd arranged to have dinner with a man, that was all. A man she intended getting to know, but without revealing too much about herself, and especially about Kristy.

That shouldn't be difficult. In her experience most men were only too happy to spend a few hours with an attractive woman, talking about themselves.

It wasn't quite that easy. The restaurant Daniel took her to—recommended, he said, by someone at the office in Auckland—was surprisingly quiet although nearly full. They were given a corner table, and when they'd ordered wine and their meals he turned an intent gaze on Charisse and said, "So tell me what you've been doing since you came back to New Zealand."

"Oh, this and that," she muttered. "You know…jobs are hard to get. I was a waitress for a while. In a place pretty much like this."

He smiled. "You'd have had experience, but of course, when we met you were only doing it as a holiday job. I remember you were interested in some kind of tourist promotion work. Did you ever follow that up?"

"Well, I—um—had a job in a hotel." She'd been a conference organiser there, enjoying high pay and interesting work, but it hadn't fitted with having a child to care for, and she'd been forced to give it up. "Now I'm…ah… moving into business research."

A waiter approached with a bottle of wine, and she thankfully sat back in her chair, glad of the interruption.

When he'd gone Charisse asked brightly, "And what are you doing in New Zealand? Aren't you based in Australia—er—still?"

He nodded. "And I still get sent to various parts of the world when necessary. We're involved in the development of a new hydroelectric facility, working in partnership with a New Zealand outfit. Being a Kiwi myself, I was the obvious one to send."

"How long do you expect to be here?"

"About four more months."

She filed that away to deal with later. "A dam?"

"Right. I have an office in the client company's premises, but a lot of the time I work out of Auckland, overseeing the geological side. Now that the preliminary surveys have been done and excavation has begun, my job is to liaise between the two companies and deal with any problems that come up on-site."

"What does that entail, exactly?"

He told her, and she listened with one part of her mind,

another part frantically trying to form some kind of contingency plan.

She discovered she'd finished a whole glass of wine by the time their first course arrived, and although she let the waiter refill her glass she didn't touch it again.

Daniel returned to questioning her, and she replied with a mixture of truths and evasions before deflecting him to another subject. She wanted to ask about him—his life, his family and background. That could be a minefield. He'd expect her to remember some of those things from five years ago.

But she stored away every nugget of information he let slip.

She gathered he had a sister on Australia's Gold Coast, and a brother in New Zealand—somewhere in the South Island. He talked a little about his mother but made no mention of his father. "And your parents?" he asked, watching her. "How are they?"

"My parents both died over two years ago," she answered steadily. "In a road accident."

His eyes clouded. "I'm very sorry. That must have been rough for you...and your sister. I know you were close to them."

He'd never met her parents, but she read genuine sympathy and concern in his expression, and to her horror hot tears blurred her vision. "I...yes," she gasped, and grabbed at her table napkin to wipe her eyes.

As she lowered it, his hand closed over hers. "Hell! I didn't mean to upset you, Charisse."

"No, it wasn't you. I...I'm a fool."

"There's nothing foolish about grief. I'm just sorry I reminded you."

"You weren't to know." She didn't want to take her hand from his comforting grasp, but caution made her withdraw it, and he reluctantly let go. "Let's talk about something else." She tried to smile.

"Sure." Still looking bothered, he immediately made some remark about the decor, and within minutes she found herself laughing at a story about a hotel in Hong Kong where he'd once stayed, that he said was decorated in a style he described as neo-Gothic horror mixed with traditional Eastern elements. "I had nightmares for weeks," he asserted, "about being chased around a huge ebony four-poster by vampire dragons."

"You have an interesting job," she said when she'd stopped laughing. "All that travelling."

He gave her a quizzical look that made her remember how careful she should be. "I'm travelling even more these days," he agreed. "But the apartment is still my home base."

"Oh…um…the same place?" she asked innocently.

"The same place. Your parting gift is on the windowsill in the living room." His eyes turned an almost sombre grey.

"Oh…" Something more was needed, surely. "You kept it, then."

"Yes, I kept it. After all, it was the only thing you left me, wasn't it?" The fire was back in his eyes. "I was tempted to smash it at first, but that seemed a shame. Still, I couldn't quite bring myself to put it in the bedroom where I'd see it every morning when I woke. Now I'm used to it, and it hardly even reminds me anymore."

She looked down, blindly pushing at the remains of the food on her plate. "I guess you were…a bit upset."

He made a scornful sound. "Yes, I was *upset*. I'd thought we had something special, Charisse—something we both valued. Only I was wrong, wasn't I?"

A flicker of anger stirred within her. Maybe it had been

special, but not special enough. The "something" he claimed he'd valued so highly had surely amounted to no more than great sex. "Nothing lasts forever," she said to her plate.

There was a curious silence. She put down her fork and turned her wineglass, risking a fleeting glance at him.

Daniel was staring at her. "You didn't give it a chance," he said flatly. "We don't know how long it might have lasted."

"Oh, I have a fair idea," she told him with scarcely concealed irony.

"You mean it was already over for you?" he guessed. "I suppose that makes me an arrogant so-and-so, that I didn't realise it sooner."

"Maybe." Surmising that he hadn't thought any woman could walk away from him, she hadn't been able to help a glimmer of rather malicious laughter entering her tone.

He gave her a straight look, but reluctant humour twitched at the corner of his mouth. "Okay, that's put me in my place."

"Sorry." Though her voice was demure, the inward laughter was still there.

"No, you're not," he accused her. His eyes were alert and speculative, even surprised. "Go ahead," he invited generously, "enjoy yourself." But the look on his face warned her there would be retribution. And what form the retribution might take.

Her breath caught. This was dangerous—not because she feared him physically, but because he had drawn her into a man-woman sparring match, and that could lead to…

To all kinds of things she couldn't allow to happen. She dragged her gaze away from the subtle sexual challenge in his and pushed aside her plate. "That was very nice," she said. "How was yours?"

"Fine." He was still staring at her, looking faintly be-mused, but after a second or two he must have decided to follow her lead. "Shall we look at the dessert menu?"

"Last time you ordered a dessert you didn't eat it."

He inclined his head. "I hope you enjoyed my chocolate pie. You always were partial to chocolate, I recall. Though it never seemed to affect your luscious figure." His glance over what he could see of it was teasing, lazily intimate and yet far short of ogling.

She parted her lips, hesitated. *Careful.* "It was deli-cious," she told him.

The waiter came for their plates and handed them the menus. Charisse asked for a cheese board and coffee, and Daniel closed the menu and said, "Make that for two."

As they picked at the cheeses, he said, "Brie. Your fa-vourite."

It was, but she could seldom afford it these days.

"I'll have the feta," he offered, spearing a piece of it. "Remember the day we went to Lake Monger to see the black swans?"

Charisse ventured a smile and a small shrug.

"I'd never seen you look so beautiful as you did then." His voice lowered. "And afterwards we found that shop stocked with cheeses and wines and grapes. You practically danced around it, filling a basket and agonising over which cheeses we should take back with us to the apartment. You were wearing that blue dress that I liked, with the scooped neck, and when you bent over the chiller to choose, I wanted to grab you right then and make love to you, take those beautiful creamy breasts in my hands and—"

"Stop it!" A piece of ripe cheddar crumbled in her fin-gers. "Don't." She kept her gaze fiercely on the plate in front of her, trying to hide the heat in her cheeks.

"All right," he said after a moment, his voice holding

surprise. "But I can't pretend it never happened. Even if you can...or want to."

"Yes, I do want to," she said, and dared at last to look at him, catching astonished speculation in his eyes. "That's exactly what I want. Could we...could we go back to square one?"

"What do you mean?"

"Can't we pretend that we've just met for the first time? You know, start over with a clean slate?"

"Playacting?" He laughed shortly. "I know you have a penchant for drama, but I don't see the point."

And of course she couldn't tell him. "We need to get to know each other again, you said." She hunched a shoulder.

He looked at her for a long time. Then he asked abruptly, "Why did you leave me like that—without a word?"

"Without a word?" she repeated, shock colouring her voice.

Impatient, he leaned forward, pinning her with his eyes. "Your note," he said dismissively, "gave me no clue. Why didn't you tell me to my face, if you'd had enough?"

She had to say something. "I...I was afraid you'd talk me out of it," she said. "And I missed my family—I wanted to come home."

"You were homesick?" He scanned her face, open scorn in his expression. "You don't expect me to believe that was the only reason!"

"You can believe whatever you want." She kept her gaze on his face. "I don't have to answer to you, Daniel."

He looked baffled, then nodded curtly. "Okay. You don't want to explain. And I happen not to have a thumbscrew handy right now, so I'll wait."

She flashed him an indignant look, and he grinned narrowly back at her. "You want to play one of your games," he said softly. "Okay, Charisse, I'll go along with it."

*   *   *

He insisted on walking her to her car. As they descended
the harshly lit stairwell of the car park, their footsteps echoing on concrete, he said, "Is it safe here for a woman
alone? Couldn't you have taken a cab?"

She didn't point out that taxi fares were expensive. "The
building is well lit, and lots of people come and go all the
time."

"Next time I'll pick you up."

"Next time—if there is one—I'll decide that, thanks,"
she told him. "This is the level I parked on."

He opened the glass door for her and, as she passed him,
said, "I don't recall that you used to be so fiercely independent."

Charisse bit her tongue. "I've grown-up."

"You mean you weren't grown-up before?" He slanted
her a questioning, meaningful smile.

No! she wanted to shout at him, antagonism returning in
a rush. The girl you knew five years ago wasn't grown-up
at all. She was young and foolish, susceptible and ardent
and she gave herself to you without a thought, not even
knowing what kind of man she was so heedlessly entrusting
herself to. But some things turn a girl into a woman overnight.

Silently she shook her head, leading the way across the
cold, hard concrete between rows of cars. "There isn't any
'before,' remember?"

"Oh, I remember." His tone was grim. "Too well."

She turned on him. "We agreed—"

"All right!" Daniel held up a hand. "All right, it never
happened. None of it."

If only it hadn't, Charisse thought. Then everything
would have been so different.

"Isn't that your car?" Daniel pointed.

"Yes." He'd spotted it before she had. He must have taken note of it at the supermarket, perhaps even memorised the registration number.

When she turned the key in the lock he was right behind her, and as she removed it he leaned over, his fingers closing on the chrome door handle. His breath brushed her temple. "Do you kiss on a first date, Charisse?"

"No," she said in a strangled tone. His shoulder was touching hers, and she had a startling urge to turn and let him take her in his arms. "Open the door," she added.

She was relieved that he did, without any argument. "I might have guessed you don't," he said as she eased into the driver's seat.

When she glanced up he was smiling with what looked like genuine amusement. Even affection.

She slid the key into the ignition. "Thank you for dinner."

"Thanks for coming. When can I see you again? I've discovered a jazz club in Auckland that you might enjoy." His eyes gleaming with mockery, he added smoothly, "If you like jazz, that is. Of course, I've no way of knowing."

Of course he did know—or thought he did. "Yes," she said, quelling a flutter of fright at what she might be plunging into. "I do like jazz."

"Are you free on Saturday evening?"

"I...I'm not sure yet."

"Can I call you?" He still hadn't shut the door. "If you trust me with your telephone number."

He could look it up if he was determined enough. There weren't that many C. Lanes in the phone book.

She gave it to him, and watched him write it in a small leather-bound book. She wondered how many other women's numbers were in there, with addresses in all parts of the world.

"Thanks," he said. "I'll be in touch." Then he closed the door and stepped back.

Charisse used her key to enter by the side door, and momentarily leaned against the solid kauri panels before walking slowly into the small, cosy sitting room.

A slim, brown-haired woman in her thirties looked up from the book on her lap. "Hi! How was your evening?"

"A bit nerve-racking," Charisse admitted. "Thanks so much for looking after Kristy, Brenna. Is everything all right?"

"No problems. I read her two stories and then she snuggled down quite happily."

"It's really kind of you to look after her."

"Rot. I've told you, anytime. You don't use my services often enough. When you first rented to us I thought one reason might have been so you'd have semi-resident baby-sitters on call."

"Heavens, no! I needed an income, and I knew we could live quite comfortably in the smaller rooms and the sun-porch in this part of the place. It made sense to rent out the bigger rooms in front."

She'd had to use some of the modest legacy her parents had left to get the extra bathroom and kitchen put in, but it had been worth it. "You and Baz have been great tenants," she told Brenna. She'd chosen them because they'd seemed likely to be tolerant of a child next door, but Brenna and Baz were actively kind to Kristy, even fond of her. Brenna had been a kindergarten teacher before she resigned to help Baz set up his home-heating business. In the next year or two they planned to start a family and buy their own home, but Charisse hoped the friendship they'd established with her would endure.

"You're a great landlady," Brenna assured her. "Why

was the evening with the old friend nerve-racking?'' she asked curiously.

Charisse hesitated. The situation was complex enough without dragging other people into it. ''Oh, well,'' she said vaguely, ''you know, when you haven't seen someone in a long time there's not much to talk about.''

''I'm sorry it was disappointing.'' Then Brenna grinned. ''Kristy's got it into her head you've acquired a boyfriend.''

''Is she still on about that? There's a little girl at kindergarten whose mother has a new man. Felicity's father left last year, but he still sees the children, and she talks about him a lot.'' Charisse gave a wry smile. ''I think Kristy's a wee bit envious of Felicity having two men in her life. She has no idea of the possible complications of the family situation.''

''Sounds like at least Felicity's dad is making some effort. Too many men just waltz off leaving the woman holding the baby—or babies. If they weren't ready to be responsible for a family they had no right to have one at all.''

True, Charisse thought, but she tried to be fair. ''It isn't always the man's fault.''

''A lot of them take sex where they find it and beggar the consequences,'' Brenna argued. ''It's usually the woman who has the responsibility in the end. Though I shouldn't be preaching to you, of all people.''

''That's okay. You're right, but every case is unique.''

''I hope I haven't hurt your feelings,'' Brenna said anxiously. ''I think what you're doing is wonderful.''

Charisse shook her head. ''I don't have a choice.''

''You did. But I know what you mean. You couldn't give Kristy up now, could you?''

''No. No, I couldn't.'' The very thought chilled her with fear.

*   *   *

By Friday she'd made and discarded plans to move to another part of the country without leaving a forwarding address, and others even less feasible. It wouldn't be fair to anyone—least of all to Kristy.

She waited on tenterhooks for Daniel to phone, and when he did she steadied her voice and agreed that she'd see him the following evening.

"This time," he said, "let me pick you up."

"I have my own transport."

"I know, I've seen it." He sounded a bit curt.

Defensively she told him, "It may not be a Rolls but it runs perfectly well." She had bought her car with the insurance money from her parents' vehicle, but it wasn't nearly as good as the one that had been wrecked in the accident. The insurance company had declared that to be overvalued, so she hadn't had a lot to spend.

"And you have to find somewhere to park it," Daniel said. "I don't like the idea of you walking about the city alone at night."

An insidious warmth crept into her soul. It seemed such a long time since anyone had shown her that kind of protectiveness. "I can look after myself," she said, reminding herself more than him. She'd been doing it for years—not only herself but also Kristy.

Which reminded her that, as Brenna had obliquely pointed out, there was a limit to this male instinct to care for a woman. She shouldn't let herself be deceived by it.

"Let me fetch you," he coaxed. "It's much more sensible."

Afraid of arousing his suspicion if she continued to refuse, she finally gave in and agreed to his collecting her from the house.

* * *

"I might be asking you to baby-sit Kristy more often," Charisse told Brenna the next evening, "but you must say if it's inconvenient."

"It's no problem. If we open the connecting door between the flats I can easily peek in on her."

"Let me do something for you in return, though. Ironing or mending, maybe?"

"Don't be silly. How often have we asked you to let tradesmen in to fix the dishwasher and the TV and whatnot while we're at the shop? Does this mean you've met someone?"

"Well, yes," Charisse confessed. "I'd like to…to get to know him better."

"That's great. I'm really pleased for you, Charisse! You deserve a bit of fun."

Charisse hesitated, wondering if she had the right to ask someone else to aid and abet her in deception. "I haven't told him about Kristy."

"I understand. Some men would be put off if they knew you had a child in the background."

Charisse stared in silence. That excuse hadn't occurred to her.

"But," Brenna added, "if he runs a mile when you do tell him, it'll be his loss. And there are plenty of fish in the sea for a bright, beautiful woman with a lovely little girl like Kristy."

Charisse swallowed. "The thing is," she said, "I'd have to be very sure that any man I bring into her life isn't going to hurt her…or abandon her."

Brenna's expression was approving. "I know what you mean. I've seen it happen after a marriage breakup. When the dust settles Mum gets a new boyfriend and everything looks rosy, the kids bond with the new guy, and then the relationship goes sour and the kids are worse off than ever. It breaks my heart.''

''Kristy's never had a father.''

''Mmm, and I'd say she's about ready to identify her missing daddy with the first likely looking male who comes along. You get to know this guy before you decide if you want to introduce him to Kristy.''

After she and Brenna had unlocked the door between the flats, while Brenna read a story for Kristy, Charisse waited in the front room of the house until a sleek burgundy car drew up outside and Daniel's tall figure got out.

''I'm off,'' she said to Baz, buried behind the newspaper.

''Right. Have a good time.''

She hurried to the door and had closed it behind her as Daniel got the gate open.

He smiled as she came down the broad wooden steps, and she saw him glance behind her at the lighted window of the house before his eyes returned to her. ''You look lovely.''

A conventional compliment that shouldn't have made her breathless. It was too long since she'd dated, she decided. And too long since a man had put a light hand on her waist, as Daniel did, guiding her to his car. The pleasure she derived from that was out of proportion to the casually courteous touch.

She had made a clear-eyed decision to avoid sexual and emotional entanglements while she concentrated on giving Kristy the loving stability and attention the child needed. Maybe that was why she was so aware of the man who sat beside her now. Because she had become unused to male company.

She remained aware of him as they listened to the jazz bands vying with each other in the crowded club, and occasionally exchanged comments on the performance. While his attention was on the stage she studied Daniel covertly, telling herself that it was because she needed to know as much about him as she possibly could.

As they left the building, Charisse almost bumped into someone she knew and she had to introduce him. The woman, a longtime friend since before Kristy's advent into her life, gave him an interested look and secretly raised her brows at Charisse.

"Sorry, we don't have time to chat," Charisse told her, ruthlessly sweeping Daniel away. "Catch you another time," she tossed over her shoulder.

Daniel suggested coffee and she agreed. "I mustn't be too late, though," she said unthinkingly.

He looked at her quizzically. "Someone waiting up for you?"

She hastened to cover up. "I just don't like to be out late at night. Um…I have to work."

"On Sunday?"

She'd forgotten what day it was. "Don't you ever work on Sunday?" she parried.

"Yes. I remember you complaining about me being called out on a Sunday." He paused. "At least I would, if I hadn't agreed to forget everything that happened five years ago."

"Well, then," she said lamely, "you're not the only one. Who works Sundays, I mean."

After they were seated in a café, with steaming coffee and a couple of slices of cake before them, Daniel said, "I somehow had the impression you don't have a job right now."

"Um…did you?" What a tangled web. She wasn't good at deception. In fact she'd never told so many lies and half-truths in her life.

"You seemed unwilling to talk about it and I thought

you were oversensitive about being unemployed. I guess I was wrong.''

"I…I'm in market research,'' she told him. She sometimes conducted telephone interviews on a casual basis for a market research firm. The work was irregular and the pay minimal, but she was grateful for the extra money. "I work nights and weekends.'' Well, occasionally she did. "It's all highly confidential.'' And that, she hoped, would stop him probing. "And I'm doing a business studies course by correspondence, which takes quite a lot of time.''

"You mentioned moving into business research,'' he reminded her. "Do you plan to set up on your own?''

"Maybe, eventually.'' It was a half-formed dream rather than an ambition, but talking about her studies as future plans kept them away from riskier conversational shoals.

After a while she deftly turned the topic back to him, reflecting that she was getting quite good at this, and to her great relief he didn't pursue the subject of her present work.

They did, however, discuss a wide range of other things until Charisse finally glanced at her watch and gathered up her jacket and bag. "I've had a lovely evening, only it's getting late.''

Daniel drove her home in silence, but after drawing up outside the house he caught her hand as she made to open the car door. "Charisse?''

She looked down, then met his gaze. The light was dim and she could hardly see him.

"Ask me in?'' he suggested.

"No, I'm sorry.''

Daniel sighed. "Well…at least kiss me good-night?''

Of course she should have known this was coming. "I…I'd like to be friends,'' she pleaded, against her own instincts, against the powerful attraction that she'd been fighting all evening—and before. ''We agreed we need to get to know each other.''

''Don't friends kiss?'' he asked softly. ''Like this…'' He leaned over and touched his lips to her cheek. ''Or this…'' The other cheek. She sat very still, trying not to breathe.

''Or…'' He kissed her forehead, his lips lingering on her skin, until she felt heat rise through her body.

This was unbearable. ''Don't,'' she whispered, closing her eyes.

She could hear his breathing, feel its warmth on her temple. The night thickened around them, and she smelled the faint scent of soap and clean masculine skin.

He moved back, and when she opened her eyes he had one hand on the steering wheel, gripping it hard. ''Okay,'' he said. ''Friends.''

Then he turned and got out, snapping the door shut. By the time he reached the other side, she was already climbing out.

''Thank you.'' Fleetingly she met his eyes. ''I had a nice time.''

Daniel glanced at the darkened house. ''There was a man with you,'' he said, ''when you came out to meet me. The lights were on and I saw him inside.''

''The house is shared,'' she told him.

He nodded. ''It's a big house. How many flatmates do you have?''

Charisse hesitated. ''Two.''

''I wondered if you didn't want me to come here because you were involved with someone.''

He'd said he didn't care if she was, provided the man wasn't the father of her child. That was an irony he had no idea of.

''I'm not involved with anyone,'' she told him. Maybe she shouldn't have admitted it, but there were enough unavoidable deceptions between them. Adding another could only complicate matters further.

"Thank you for telling me," he said. "Good night, Charisse." He opened the gate for her.

"Good night." She went through the gate. "You needn't come any further."

He gave a slight smile, his eyebrows arching. "I guess not."

But he waited, watching her go round to the side of the house. Would he wonder why she didn't enter by the same door she'd used before?

People often used a back door when they came home from an outing, she assured herself, taking out her key.

She had the door open and had switched on the light before she heard Daniel's car drive away.

The following day she wasn't at all surprised to get a phone call from the friend she'd seen at the club, full of unabashed curiosity.

Deflecting questions as best she could, Charisse wondered how long she could keep her secret. She was playing an incredibly hazardous game, but the stakes were high.

Chapter 4

Surprisingly, Charisse enjoyed the several evenings she subsequently spent with Daniel, despite watching every word she said. The simmering resentment that she couldn't help feeling for him faded, and she almost forgot why she was seeing him. Even the constant ache of grief that she'd become accustomed to magically disappeared for hours at a time.

When he invited her to join him and some friends on a yachting weekend she turned him down, pleading pressure of work and her latest study assignment. She couldn't abandon Kristy for two days.

One evening when they had a date, he turned up early and Baz let him in. Brenna came to tell Charisse he was there. She quickly flung on her jacket, kissed Kristy good-night and, heart pounding, hurried through the connecting door. She whisked him out of the house before he had a chance to do more than exchange pleasantries with Baz.

Daniel hadn't told her where they were going, but had

suggested she wear something pretty. She'd put on a cream
sheath with a narrow gold belt, adding a thin gold bangle
that had been a twenty-first birthday gift from her parents.
The dress was several years old but it was fairly dateless;
she'd altered the hemline last time she wore it.

He took her on a dinner cruise on the harbour. The food
was delicious and wonderfully presented, and the view of
the city lights and the arched harbour bridge was spectacular.

There was dancing on board, but after the first experience
of being held close to Daniel on the minuscule bit of space,
his thighs moving against hers, his cheek brushing her temple, Charisse made the crowded floor and the instability of
the boat an excuse not to dance again. His nearness was
too disturbing, too likely to topple her resolution to avoid
getting physically involved.

He gave her a quizzical look but didn't argue. Later they
leaned on the rail as the boat swished its way back to the
shore. Other couples in the shadowy light were standing
close, arms about each other.

Daniel put a warm hand over hers, and although she
knew she shouldn't, Charisse let it stay there. His fingers
were strong and firm, and when one thumb began a small
stroking movement she felt her skin tighten with a wave of
desire that she was afraid to let him see.

A curved streak of lightning seemed to lift from the water and disintegrate in golden splashes, and there was a
murmur of excitement among the passengers. ''Dolphins!''

More light-streaked dim shapes appeared, leaping in and
out of the white foam of the wake, and Daniel's hand tightened on Charisse's. She turned to him in silent delight and
found him looking down at her, his expression absorbed.
Then he smiled back, and she looked away again to watch

the graceful sea creatures playing about the boat before disappearing into the darkness.

Just as the vessel slid into the dock and the shore lights played over it, Daniel turned, lifted Charisse's hand until it lay over his heart and, with his other arm, drew her toward him.

When he bent his head he let him find her mouth, his kiss a tender exploration, a question rather than a demand. Tentatively she returned it, standing very still within his embrace, savouring the taste of his mouth and the sensation of safety and warmth enveloping her.

The boat shuddered as it came up against the wharf, and Daniel lifted his head, steadying them with one hand on the rail, his other arm still holding her as he gave a soft laugh. Light dazzled her eyes, and people began moving off, brushing past them.

"I hope you don't mind—it seemed a fitting end to the evening."

She smiled slightly, shaking her head. "It was nice."

"Nice?" His brows quirked and then he laughed again, and turned her to walk to the gangway.

Driving her home he was silent, and Charisse was wrapped up in her own troubled thoughts.

After drawing up his car outside her house he unclipped his seat belt and twisted to study her. "I had a great time," he told her.

"So did I, thank you. But you don't need to spend so much on me." It hadn't been a cheap outing, and she felt as if she were taking his money under false pretences.

"I can afford it."

"Well, thank you. It was…"

"Nice?" he asked.

"Yes, very—and I don't mean to sound lukewarm."

"About the cruise…or the kiss?"

Charisse looked away. "About…anything."

"We could try the kiss again," he offered hopefully.

She glanced up, to see a glimmer of laughter in his eyes. "I don't think that's a good idea," she said. It had been a romantic setting, and she wondered if he'd deliberately chosen it with that in mind. She couldn't be unaware that he would like their relationship to become closer.

His hand came up and turned her to face him. The smile died as he said, "What are you afraid of, Charisse? It's not like you." He looked puzzled. "Sometimes…"

"What?"

She stirred uneasily and he dropped his hand. "Sometimes," he said slowly, "I'm amazed at the difference a few years can make. You're not the same girl I knew before."

Charisse steadied her plunging heart, and swallowed painfully. "No one…stays the same over five years."

"I suppose not. I guess I've changed, too."

"I'm sure you have." He must have. Surely he was more mature, more dependable? And if so, it made her crucial decision-making even more difficult. "Anyway," she added, "you didn't know me before. You agreed…"

"Yes, well, if you insist we carry on with the act…" He seemed at a loss. Then he leaned over and brushed his lips across her cheek. "I'll see you to the gate."

Kristy was invited to spend a weekend with another family at their beach house. She had stayed overnight with them before and Charisse was confident she would be well looked after.

On Saturday evening Charisse attended a party with Daniel. The hosts, celebrating their tenth wedding anniversary, had three young children who in the early part of the evening carefully offered bowls of nibbles. A girl not much older than Kristy offered a divided dish of savouries and dips and Charisse smiled at her and took a carrot stick. "Thank you."

Daniel hunkered down to the child's level. "Let's see." He picked out a taco chip. "Which dip do you think I should have?" he asked her.

"The pink one," she answered promptly. "It's nice."

"Okay, the pink one." Daniel dipped the chip and put it in his mouth. "Mmm, you're right. Can I have another?"

She nodded solemnly and watched while Daniel dipped a second chip in the gooey mixture before he straightened.

"You like children?" Charisse asked as the little girl moved on round the room. It was a safe enough question in this context, surely.

"Depends on the child," Daniel answered carelessly. "My brother's kids seem pleasant enough—a bit shy. I can't say I know them well."

"Have you ever thought of having some of your own?" she asked boldly.

He gave her an amused look. "I wouldn't even contemplate it unless I was married."

"And you don't want to marry."

"Did I say that?" He cocked his head in enquiry.

"Something like it, surely, when you…I mean when we…"

"When we were together in Perth?" He looked at her piercingly. "It *is* difficult to keep up this fiction that we've never met before, isn't it? You just proved *you* haven't forgotten. Have you?"

How was she to answer that? Charisse shrugged. "Some of it. Quite a lot, actually."

He frowned. "Deliberately?"

Cautious, she shrugged again. "I've had other things to think about."

"Other men? How many have there been since then, Charisse?"

She turned a startled gaze on him, and was surprised when a flush darkened the taut skin along his cheekbones. "Sorry," he said. "None of my business."

"Absolutely." Still shocked, she turned blindly away from him, and was relieved when their host approached, offering to top up their glasses and staying to chat awhile. They were soon joined by others, and Charisse began to relax. She met some nice people and allowed herself more wine than usual, for once feeling no anxiety to get home at a reasonable hour.

It was late when she said good-night to Daniel at the gate. Perhaps it was the wine that made her say rashly, "Would you like to come to lunch tomorrow? You've given me lunch or dinner several times now. I think it's time I returned the favour."

"No need," he assured her, "but I'd love to come to lunch. Can I bring something? A bottle of wine, maybe?"

"Thank you," she said. "That would be nice."

"Thank *you.*" He bent and kissed her, a warm, lingering but restrained kiss that, weakly, she didn't try to avoid. "I'll look forward to it," he promised, his voice deep and husky.

In the morning Charisse tidied away all evidence of a child's presence from the living areas of the flat, nearly forgetting the bath toys before shutting them in Kristy's room. She even removed the latest artwork from the refrigerator door, reminding herself that she must replace it before Kristy was delivered home that evening.

She hid the tricycle behind her car in the garage and shut the door, then inspected the lawn for playthings, although she always encouraged Kristy not to be careless with them. Eyeing the swing that Baz had hung in the old plum tree by the garage, she decided there was nothing she could do about it, and anyway she had told Daniel she had a niece.

Besides, she could truthfully say there had always been a swing there. Her father had erected the first one for her and her sister, and they'd spent hours playing on it and climbing the tree. When the tree became old and mossy and failed to fruit as well as it had in previous years, he'd wanted to cut it down, and only their pleas had saved it from his chain saw.

Running a hand along a still-strong branch, she recalled those days when she and Gabrielle had been so close, their childish arguments fierce but short-lived, their loyalty to each other equally fierce and much more constant. She wanted Kristy one day to look back on a childhood as secure and happy as theirs.

She prepared a rice and minced beef dish, economical but tasty, and baked a batch of spicy muffins. Then she changed into clean jeans and a pink cotton shirt, brushed her hair and applied some eyeshadow and lip gloss before checking on the food and hunting out wineglasses from the back of a cupboard.

She'd told Daniel to come to the side door, and when he rapped on it she took three deep breaths before going to open it.

"Hi." His lips curved in a smile, and his eyes softened as he looked at her. She stood back to let him in and he held out the bottle in his hand. "I hope it's suitable."

"I'm sure it's fine." Suddenly she was doubting the wisdom of inviting him here. When she ushered him into the little sitting room he seemed to dominate it, making it look even smaller. "I'll put this in the kitchen," she said. "We have to eat in there—I don't have a dining room."

"Fine." He looked about. "This looks very cosy."

"It was my parents' home. Most of the furniture was theirs."

"And now you share with flatmates."

"To pay the expenses," she informed him briefly. "The house is old and takes some maintenance these days. Besides, it's much too big for only…only one person. Sit down while I take this to the kitchen." She waved at the shabby, comfortable sofa.

She had reached the kitchen doorway when she heard a muffled squeak, and Daniel's sharp exclamation.

Turning, she found him standing by the sofa, holding a battered little cloth rabbit.

"Your niece's?" he enquired.

Charisse swallowed her momentary dismay. "Yes."

"It was under the cushion. I was afraid I'd sat on a kitten for a second."

"We…I don't have a kitten. Sorry if it gave you a fright."

He put down the toy on the arm of the sofa. "I don't think I've damaged it."

She gave him a distracted smile. "I'm sure you haven't. It's years old."

He smiled and, instead of sitting down again, followed her to the bright little kitchen.

"Your sister, does she still live in Auckland?"

Charisse's throat closed. "No," she said starkly. "Not any more."

"You don't see that much of your niece, then?"

"Uh…um, yes, actually—quite a lot." She put down the wine bottle with shaking fingers.

"You and your sister were always close, weren't you?"

Hoping it was a rhetorical question, she didn't reply. Daniel had strolled to the bench and was looking out the window. "Who does the lawns?" he asked. "You have a lot of grass out there."

"Baz," she told him, weak with relief at the change of subject. Baz had insisted, although Charisse was quite capable of managing the motor mower. Charisse had thought of dividing the big section and building another flat, but was reluctant to sacrifice the space that gave Kristy and her friends plenty of room to safely play. She didn't like them being on the street.

"Can I help?" Daniel asked, watching her lift the lid of a covered dish.

"Everything's done, thanks. Would you like a drink? Your wine, or something else?" She had a precious hoard of visitors' drinks in one of the cupboards.

"I'll be driving. So thanks, but I'll just have a glass of wine with the meal."

Put that on your mental list, she prompted herself. But she had already noticed he was cautious about drinking and driving.

She'd noticed a lot of other things, too. He was thoughtful and courteous and slightly overprotective. But when she asserted herself he didn't make an issue of it, although sometimes he appeared disconcerted.

He'd accepted her expressed wish to keep their relationship on a casual level, and his good-night kisses never strayed beyond the limits she'd set. But that didn't stop him from giving her an occasional glinting male look that told her she had only to say the word to change the status quo.

No doubt in his mind that was a "when" rather than an "if."

He'd probably always been good-looking, besides having brains, and she'd gleaned that as a youngster he'd played football and cricket, representing his school and later university.

Even his job carried a certain glamour, with worldwide travel and involvement in big, important projects. Everything he did, it seemed, he was successful at.

Including sex, of course, she concluded cynically. But although he might be good at the mechanics of making love, Daniel was wary of commitment. A wariness that might extend to other relationships, she reminded herself. He didn't want emotional entanglements. And that was why she must proceed with caution.

If only he were obviously a brute or a crook, she wouldn't suffer this agony of uncertainty.

"What is it?" He arched a dark brow, and Charisse realised she'd been staring at him.

"Sorry," she said hastily. "I was thinking of something."

"Something worrying you?"

Oh, yes. Ever since he'd come on the scene so unexpectedly. "Just whether I've put enough herbs in the casserole," she lied flippantly.

"I'm sure you have." He came closer to her and, with one finger, lifted a strand of hair from her cheek and smoothed it back behind her ear. "Not that I'd care," he added slowly.

Charisse sidled away from him. "You could open the wine," she suggested. "The glasses are on the table."

He did as she asked, and filled the glasses. "Where are the flatmates today?" he asked her.

"They've gone out." Brenna and Baz had left that morning in their car.

"They seem a nice couple. Not that I've seen much of them."

"They are."

"Do you eat together? There's not much room around this table."

"There's a dining room in the front part of the house." In the other flat. She sometimes missed that room, but when she had more than a couple of guests they ate informally, and if there weren't enough chairs some people were happy to sit on the floor.

She set the rice mixture in front of him and placed a salad bowl beside it. "Help yourself."

He took a generous portion, and after he'd eaten a few mouthfuls told her, "You needn't have worried about the herbs. It's perfect."

"Thank you." She took a sip of her wine. "I aim to please."

Daniel slanted a grin at her. "I'll hold you to that."

She grinned back, unable to help responding to his teasing, but shook her head. He was flirting, and she shouldn't let him.

Something inside her ached warningly. If only things had been different, if she didn't have to watch everything she said, every move he made…

Supposing she hadn't known who he was, even after he recited that rapid-fire reminder in the supermarket and then pressed his card on her with his name?

But then he wouldn't have spoken to her, and she'd never have gone looking for him, and…

Perhaps that would have been better all round.

"You're very pensive." He pushed away his plate.

Charisse had only half finished. "Have some more," she said, evading the query in his eyes.

He did, taking a few more spoonfuls.

When they'd both finished, she brought the muffins in, and he demolished three before declining another. "You always were a pretty good cook," he said. "I remember when you—"

Perhaps he saw her stiffen, because he didn't finish the sentence. After a moment Charisse got up to clear the plates. "Coffee?"

"If you're having some." He got up, too, not quite blocking her way but making it difficult for her to pass him. "Charisse, how much longer do you intend to keep up this pretence?"

"Pretence?" Her alarmed gaze flew to his face.

"Your insistence that we carry on as if we'd never met before."

"I just want time," she said. "To get to know you… again."

"Any relationship needs to progress, Charisse, and whenever I try to move ours along you put the brakes on."

Once or twice she'd let her guard slip before she'd remembered the risks. The trouble was, he was so damned attractive, and she was certainly not immune. But sex, as she had good reason to know, could warp a woman's judgement and blind her to reality. Direly in need of keeping a clear head, she was afraid of losing it completely.

"I don't understand," he said. "You've never been a shrinking violet—" his eyes crinkled at the corners "—but you're not the same girl at all as the Charisse I thought I knew."

Her mouth had dried. "Five years ago—"

"I suppose that's it. You're more mature. You were always unpredictable, and you still keep surprising me, but you're not nearly as playful, in spite of this charade you've insisted on."

"You mean I'm not as much fun?" she queried. She should take note of this—didn't it indicate that he was no more serious about a relationship than he had been five years back?

"I don't mean that," he said slowly. "Losing both your parents so suddenly must have had a huge effect on you. Some of the surface sparkle is gone, but of course you're still fun to be with—I enjoy your company as much as ever. More. And I think you like being with me—even like the idea of making love to me. But you never let go, do you? It's almost as though I scare you." He paused, then drew in a breath and asked soberly, "Have you had some kind of traumatic experience? You weren't attacked, were you?"

Shock brought her eyes back to him. His expression was both troubled and angry. She shook her head quickly. "No, nothing like that!"

"Then it's me." He frowned. "What have I done?"

I don't know, she thought. *Not exactly.* And that was the problem. Maybe she never would know unless he told her. And in five years surely he had changed, too. "A relationship doesn't have to be based around sex," she said.

He glanced briefly up to the ceiling, then back at her. "We have a lot more than that—we always did. We were good friends, Charisse. But I don't believe that any normal man and woman can leave sex entirely out of the equation. You can deny it all you like, but it's there."

"I'm not denying it. I just want to keep it in the background."

"For how long?" he demanded. "I only have a couple of months left—"

"Yes!" she said fiercely, "and then you'll fly off back to Australia."

His eyes narrowed. "And leave you, just as you left me?" He shook his head. "I'm not out for revenge, Charisse."

Charisse gave a small shrug and moved away to put the dishes in the sink.

She was running the hot water when two large hands clamped down on the counter on either side of her. "Is that what you think?" Daniel's low voice asked in her ear. "That I want to get you into bed just so I can walk out on you the way you did to me?"

"Maybe that's not how I see it," she muttered.

"What?" He sounded perplexed. "I'm not sure what you mean."

"There are two sides to every story," she said louder, and turned off the tap in front of her.

"Yes," he agreed after a moment. "So what's yours?" He shifted his body. She could feel his chest at her back, and was acutely conscious of the strength of the arms that trapped her. "Charisse?" His breath stirred her hair.

She couldn't think with him so close. And she mustn't allow him to beguile her into forgetting why she was seeing him at all. No matter that her every nerve was yearning to turn and let him hold her, to discard all caution and common sense.

He had no right to do this to her, tempting her to succumb to a mindless sexual need. She knew exactly where that could lead. Keeping her voice even, she said, "Get away from me."

"For God's sake, Charisse—"

She whipped round, her eyes blazing, hands raised to push against him. He had already removed his hands and straightened, ready to step back, but as her palms encountered firm male flesh covered by cotton shirting he stopped perfectly still. She could feel the beat of his heart, and her eyes widened as tiny flames of desire leaped in the grey-green depths of his.

Time seemed suspended. Then very quietly he said, "Are you sure you want me to?"

Her lips felt stiff. She couldn't move. "Yes," she said finally, forcing the word out.

He looked pointedly down at her hands, still flattened against him, and then he took a step back so that they fell away.

"Thank you," she said shakily, angry and disappointed—and appalled at herself—all at once.

He said tautly, "If we don't talk about Perth at all, Charisse, this relationship is never going to go anywhere. And we might as well end it now. Is that what you want?"

It would certainly simplify things. And yet something strangely like grief, mingled with guilt and alarm, gripped her at the thought of never seeing him again.

Dumbly she moved her head in negation.

His chest rose and fell with a quick breath. "Right," he said. "So tell me why you left the way you did."

Could she confess the truth?

Instinct urged her to confide everything, but rationality warned against being so reckless, so trusting. The trouble was, instinct might lead her astray, because he affected her so powerfully on a sexual and emotional level. She might have been willing to gamble on instinct for herself, but she had no right to do so with Kristy's future.

Tentatively she began. "You never expected that relationship to be permanent, did you?"

"Neither of us did. We were pretty honest with each other from the start, weren't we? But I didn't think it was something you'd discard so easily."

Easily? A stirring of doubt was swamped by anger. "*You* didn't like being discarded, you mean."

His eyelids flickered. He looked almost bewildered.

"Well, did you?" she challenged him.

"No," he admitted finally. "I hadn't expected to be left high and dry with no warning and no explanation. If you wanted out, that was your prerogative, but I think you owed me the courtesy of at least a proper goodbye. I just can't accept your lame excuse for leaving the way you did."

"It was on the cards from the beginning," she argued, "if…I mean, as you just said, it was no more than a casual affair, never meant to be permanent." She moistened her lips. "I…was on holiday—you knew that. Maybe I just got bored."

"Bored." His tone was flat, but his eyes burned with anger.

"I'm sorry if it wounds your ego. I can't put it any more…more delicately than that."

"Bored," he repeated, deeply sceptical. His gaze raked her face, and then his eyes hardened and his expression became one of bitter determination. He closed his hand about her shoulder, bringing her toward him, and his head lowered, his mouth finding hers.

Lately she had sometimes fantasised in that half-waking state before dropping off to sleep, or in the morning when the remnants of dreams remained, about being kissed by Daniel—kissed properly. But none of the fantasies had been like this.

He parted her lips with his, his mouth both persuasive and determined. And frankly passionate. When she raised a hand to push at him he captured it in his, holding it against his heart.

She closed her mouth stubbornly despite the insistent, seductive probe of his tongue, and he caught her lower lip gently between his teeth instead, sending a warm tide of sensation cascading through her body.

I won't give in, she told herself, desperately defying the urge to do so. *I won't.*

Indignation stiffened her will and she remained resistant and uncooperative until he at last lifted his head and looked down at her flushed face and furious eyes. "Damn it, Charisse," he muttered. "Why won't you kiss me back?" He looked angry too.

"Hasn't it occurred to you," she asked him stingingly, "that I don't *want* to?"

His mouth moved in a strange smile. "It occurred, yes," he said. "But there's more to it than that, isn't there? Why are you fighting me…fighting yourself?" Still holding her hand in his, he brushed his thumb across her shirt where the flimsy material covered the tip of her breast. His eyes darkening further, he said quietly, "You're almost as aroused as I am."

Almost? She'd had to clench her teeth to stop the shudder of pleasure that overtook her at his fleeting touch. Staring back at him, she willed her eyes to convey nothing but righteous rage.

He was so close she saw the faint flare of his nostrils as he took a breath. Releasing her wrist, he brought up his hand to cup her chin, and when he kissed her again his fingers and thumb exerted a subtle, insistent pressure until her mouth involuntarily opened for him, and then she was lost.…

Minutes later she surfaced, breathless, from a kiss that had devastated her. Her head was cradled firmly in the angle of Daniel's arm and shoulder as he stared down at her with a fixed expression of gleaming triumph. "Bored, were you?" he asked tightly. "Now…any more lies you'd like to tell me?"

"That was unfair!" Charisse gasped.

One of Daniel's fingers traced the line of her lips, moist from his kiss. "As unfair as what you did to me?"

"You had no right!" She pushed at him again, and this time he let her put some space between them.

His expression became rueful, and his eyes actually fell before the accusation in hers. "No, I didn't," he conceded, almost managing to sound contrite. "But it proved my point, didn't it?"

"All it proves is that you're a Neanderthal!"

He raised stormy eyes, then unexpectedly laughed. "It's something you bring out in me," he said. "I've been wanting to do that for weeks. Although it wasn't meant to be quite so…"

"Primitive?" she suggested waspishly.

"Erotic." His gaze slipped over her, caressingly. "Did it bring back memories for you, too?"

She felt the shrinking of her skin, and an instant coldness spread through her, raising gooseflesh on her arms.

Daniel frowned. "What's the matter?"

"Nothing." Except that for a few treacherous minutes she'd nearly forgotten who he was, why he was here in her home. Shakily she said, "I'd like you to go now."

"Do you mean that?" he asked roughly.

"Yes." Her voice was almost a whisper. "Please, Daniel."

There was a long silence. "All right." His voice grated. "But if I do I might not come back," he said, and waited.

Paralysed with confusion and several kinds of panic, she didn't answer.

The silence lengthened unbearably, and then he swung on his heel and walked out of the kitchen. A few seconds later she heard the outer door slam behind him.

Was history, in some twisted way, repeating itself in reverse? Maybe this time he was making sure he was the one to walk away….

She'd made it plain she wasn't prepared to agree to the

same sort of conveniently loose arrangement he'd enjoyed before, with no strings and no future, so would he simply shrug it off and find someone more amenable? Hadn't he said once, "I chalked it up to experience years ago." And no doubt he'd found consolation elsewhere.

A piercing jealousy shook her. Jealousy that she had no right to feel and that was surely a warning signal. Already she was too involved with Daniel for her own good—or Kristy's.

She had to keep reminding herself of her duty and responsibility. Two things that Daniel Richmond seemed as anxious as ever to avoid.

Numbly Charisse finished the dishes, then occupied herself cutting up one of her old dresses that had torn under the arms, and sewing it into a simple little dress for Kristy. The child grew out of clothes so quickly it was a constant task to keep replenishing her wardrobe.

When the phone rang she tensed, catching her breath, and then flew to answer. But it was only someone from the kindergarten committee wanting to consult about the agenda for the next meeting.

As the day wore on she became more and more despondent. If Daniel didn't contact her again what was she going to do?

Could she allow him to disappear out of her life—out of Kristy's—without his ever knowing what he was turning his back on? Jabbing a needle into the hem she was sewing, she pricked her finger, swore and sucked at the small wound until it stopped bleeding, before continuing more carefully with her task.

Finished, she pressed the new dress and hung it on the handle of Kristy's wardrobe.

Automatically she straightened the collection of mixed objects crowding the child's-height dressing table. Kristy hoarded everything, from her kindergarten art to pebbles and feathers and coloured paper clips.

Among the clutter stood a family-group picture of Charisse's parents, her sister and herself, with Kristy at just over a year old. A happy photo, even the baby held securely in her mother's arms smiling at the camera, all of them unaware of the tragedy that lay ahead.

Tears blurred her eyes and she put the picture down to wipe them away. Crying did no good; she'd learned that long ago. After the accident she hadn't had time to sit and weep. For Kristy's sake she'd had to be strong and capable and go on living, trying to be normal although at times she'd wanted nothing more than to lie down and give up on life altogether.

Having a child to care for had pulled her through that black time. One day, of course, she would have to let Kristy go her own way, give her the freedom to live her own life. But she hoped the bonds that made them so close now would never break. Dismayed and fearful as she had been by the overwhelming and totally unplanned responsibility for a tiny life, if they were separated now her world would end.

Kristy was dropped off just after five, her hosts turning down Charisse's invitation to stay for a cup of tea or coffee, anxious to get their own tired and overstimulated brood home.

Bare feet dangling from a chair, her hair dusted with sand and tumbling around her cheeks and her face shining with remembered bliss, Kristy was counting out a selection of shells on the kitchen table for Charisse to admire when someone knocked on the outer door.

It could be anyone, Charisse told herself sensibly after the first heartstopping moment. A religious caller hoping to convert her, a friend dropping in, or her elderly neighbour bringing surplus vegetables from his garden.

But when she opened the door Daniel stood there, looking handsome and vital and wearing a strangely set expression.

Charisse stood dumb, not knowing what to do.

"I couldn't do it," he said. "May I come in?"

Charisse fought relief mingled with consternation. She'd have to tell him it wasn't convenient, that this was the wrong time. But as she framed the words, she felt a slight warm pressure at her side and Kristy was there, smiling up guilelessly at the stranger. "Hello," she said. "I'm Kristy."

Daniel pulled his gaze from Charisse's and looked down. "Hi there. I'm Daniel." He glanced at Charisse. "Your niece?"

"Yes." For the life of her she couldn't say more.

Kristy looked up at Charisse. "Does you know that man?"

"She certainly does," Daniel assured the child.

"Yes. Kristy," Charisse said hurriedly, "why don't you go and put your shells away?"

"In a minute," the child promised airily, still staring at Daniel. "I've been to the beach," she confided. "Do you want to see my shells? They're pretty."

"I'm sure they're lovely shells." He looked back at Charisse. "I'd like to see them if that's all right."

Kristy reached forward and took his hand. "Come on, then."

For a moment longer Charisse stood her ground, then with a sense of inevitability stepped aside, tacitly inviting him in. Maybe this was fate.

Charisse waited in an agony of apprehension while Daniel admired the shells, Kristy solemnly describing each one as she handed it to him to inspect. When Charisse suggested again that she put them away, she sighed theatrically, making Daniel grin, and placed them carefully back in a plastic bag.

Charisse moved to help her, but the child looked up and said, "No, I can do it mineself!" and kept on methodically clearing them from the table one by one.

"Independent," Daniel commented. "She's very like you."

Charisse swallowed hard. "Yes."

"Except," he said, as Kristy finished her task and looked up, "that your eyes are so blue, of course. Hers are quite different, although there's something…" He frowned, obviously trying to capture the elusive connection, and Charisse held her breath, casting round her mind for something she could say to distract him, but unable to form a single word.

She saw the moment it hit him, when Kristy held up the bag of shells in a dimpled fist. "There!" she said as she surveyed the two adults. Her eyes were wide and clear and unmistakably the same unusual grey-green as his, with identical flecks of amber about the irises. "All finished."

And Daniel stood rock still, the colour slowly draining from his cheeks, leaving them sallow, his own eyes riveted on the child before him.

Then he took a step forward, his hand closing about the back of a chair as if he needed something to keep him upright. "Kristy," he said, his voice hoarse.

Kristy blinked at him uncertainly and clutched the plastic bag to her chest.

"Kristy," he repeated gently, and went down on his haunches, bringing his face to her level. "How old are you, sweetheart?"

"Four 'n' a half. Next birfday I go to school."

Charisse closed her eyes. She heard Daniel ask, "And when is that—your birthday?"

Opening her eyes again, Charisse parted her lips to cry out, *No, don't tell him!* But of course she couldn't say that, and it would be useless anyway—Kristy was already reciting with pride the date that was marked prominently on the wall calendar just behind her. The date that Charisse had taught her because she'd demanded to know when she would be big enough to leave kindergarten and go to school.

And Daniel, Charisse knew, was doing a rapid and, no doubt, accurate calculation in his clever, engineer's brain.

She couldn't see his face. He stood up and placed the other hand too on the back of the chair, and she saw the knuckles whiten.

At last Charisse found her voice. "Kristy," she said, "go and put those away."

"Okay." With another sigh Kristy trotted off with her precious new treasures, leaving Charisse staring miserably at Daniel's hunched shoulders and rigid back.

"Are you all right?" she said.

"Yes. No." The words sounded muffled. He let go the chair and turned like an old man, showing her a face still paler than normal, the skin over his cheekbones drawn taut, and his eyes glittering in a way that made her breath stop with irrational fear. "I feel as though I've just been kicked in the gut," he told her, his voice turning raw. "Why the *hell* didn't you tell me about her?"

Chapter 5

"I'm sorry you found out this way," Charisse said feebly.

"*Sorry?* It's a bit late for *sorry!* Had you any intention of telling me—ever?"

"Yes, of course, if—"

"*When?*" Daniel demanded. She had the feeling he was refraining from shouting at her only through a great effort of will. "When would you have told me?"

"I...I hadn't decided, but—"

His impatient movement forward brought him looming over her and made her retreat a step. "You hadn't decided?" he repeated. "That's why you never invited me in before, isn't it?" he accused. "Because you didn't want me to meet Kristy. To find out."

"Yes," Charisse admitted.

He stared at her as if she'd grown horns. "I don't believe you had any intention of telling me the truth," he said. "You've been lying to me all this time. Why should you suddenly decide to enlighten me about the existence of *my daughter?*" He blinked as if saying the words had somehow shocked him into realisation. "My...child."

Charisse tilted her chin. "I wasn't sure you'd *want* to know! You'd made it plain enough you had no desire to be saddled with a family!"

His mouth thinned. "Well, it seems I have one whether I like it or not." A thought seemed to strike him and his face went oddly rigid. "Was it intentional?"

For a moment she didn't know what he meant. Then she said, "Of course not! Do you think any woman would be crazy enough to deliberately get pregnant by a man she knows has no intention of facing up to his obligations?"

The skin about his lips went white. "I was never given the chance!"

"Well, lucky you!" She glared at him, an old resentment surfacing, and her voice rose. "You didn't have to make the choice and cope with the consequences."

"That had nothing to do with luck," he argued savagely. "It was a direct result of *your* decision to keep me in the dark."

"That wasn't—"

"Mummee!"

They had forgotten to keep their voices down. A small, warm body collided with her knees and plump arms clung.

"It's all right, Kristy," she said, her hand on the soft curls. "We were just talking."

Kristy's face, hidden against Charisse's leg, turned toward Daniel. "You shou'n't talk so *loud* to my mummy too!" she reproved him.

If Charisse hadn't been so tense and bothered she might have laughed at the expression on Daniel's face. Taken aback didn't even begin to describe it.

Daniel said almost humbly, "I'm sorry, Kristy. I didn't

mean to frighten you. Or your…*mother*.'' He looked back at Charisse. ''I just got a…a big surprise.''

''Don't you like surprises?'' Kristy didn't release her hold on Charisse, but turned her face up to him more fully.

''That depends,'' he answered, ''on what kind of surprise it is.''

''Wasn't it a nice surprise?'' she asked him, wide-eyed.

He stared down at her innocent, enquiring expression. ''I guess so,'' he said slowly. ''It's just that I wasn't expecting it.''

Kristy chuckled and loosened her hold to face him. ''That's what a surprise is, silly! If you're 'specting it, it's not a surprise.''

Charisse found her voice. ''You mustn't call grown-ups silly, Kristy.''

''That's all right.'' Daniel was looking at Kristy as if he couldn't take his eyes off her. ''Some of them can be— very silly.'' His gaze swept momentarily upward to Charisse's face.

Kristy finally let go Charisse's leg. ''*This* is a surprise,'' she said, daintily holding out the skirt of the remade dress for Daniel's inspection. Charisse had been too upset to notice she'd put it on. ''Look, it's a new dress.'' She twirled one way and then the other, showing off, then turned back to Charisse and raised her arms for a hug. ''Thank you, Mummy.''

Charisse bent to return the hug, receiving a kiss as well. ''You'd better take it off before tea,'' she instructed. ''You don't want to get it dirty.''

''Can I wear it tomorrow?''

''Yes, all right,'' Charisse agreed distractedly. ''But go and change now.''

''Can't I keep it on till teatime?'' Kristy begged.

"No," Charisse answered firmly. "Take it off and hang it up, there's a good girl."

With another of her exaggerated, long-suffering sighs, Kristy reluctantly trudged off.

Daniel's gaze followed her all the way across the sitting room until she disappeared into the passageway. A spark of amusement lit his eyes, although his mouth remained in a set line. "She's...enchanting," he said.

Charisse felt a stirring of trepidation. He was falling in love with his daughter before her eyes. And what that might eventually mean didn't bear thinking about. "I don't want her hurt," she blurted out.

He turned his gaze back to her, a frown raking between his brows. "I wouldn't even think of it."

"Then you won't tell her who you are."

She might have thrown cold water over him, the way he reacted, his face suddenly pinched. "She has a right to know who her father is!"

"That doesn't give you the right to tell her!" Charisse flashed.

"Why not? *You* haven't done it, obviously! What *did* you tell her? That she was found under a gooseberry bush?"

"Don't be stupid. She knows her father lives far away."

"Well, thanks!"

"You *should* thank me." Charisse reacted to his sarcasm. "I could have told her that he was a self-centred jerk who wasn't prepared to take responsibility for his actions and would probably have wanted her aborted." It was what she'd believed for a long time, after all.

"That's bloody unfair and you know it!"

"Maybe." And of course she would never have said it to Kristy. "I've thought lately that possibly it wasn't entirely true,'' she admitted, a little embarrassed at her outburst.

''Am I supposed to be grateful for that?''

''You're not supposed to be anything—except concerned for Kristy's welfare, if you have any…any paternal feelings at all.''

''Paternal…?'' He shook his head impatiently. ''I don't know what I feel. I never even knew she existed until now.''

Charisse refused to feel guilty about that. ''You needn't worry about it,'' she advised him. ''We've managed perfectly well so far, and we will in the future. Only—'' her voice wobbled and she cleared her throat ''—I'd like you to leave me some way to contact you if you ever change your job, because Kristy might want to know one day, and she has the right.''

He glared at her. ''You expect me to just walk away from her?''

''I don't expect anything. If that's what you want to do—''

''You don't have the faintest damn idea what I want!'' His voice turned glasspaper-harsh although he was obviously making an effort to keep it low. ''You think that I'd happily turn my back on my own child?''

''What *do* you want?'' she challenged him, glancing aside to make sure Kristy was still out of range. ''To introduce yourself as the daddy she's never had, spoil her rotten for a couple of months, and then disappear back to Australia? How do you think she's going to feel about that?''

That silenced him for long moments. ''No,'' he said at last. ''That would be cruel.''

''I'm glad you realise it.''

"Of course I realise it! But I refuse to just bow out and leave you to it now that I do know about her."

"Not even if it's in her best interests?"

"In whose opinion?" Daniel enquired scathingly. "Yours?"

"Yes, mine! I know her better than anyone else."

"Because you didn't bother to tell me about her. It's hardly my fault I've never got to know her, is it? You can't stop me from seeing her, Charisse. You don't have the right."

Did he mean morally or legally? Charisse felt her stomach lurch as she recalled her conversation with the social worker. She was on very shaky ground here. "It isn't a question of rights," she argued huskily. "Not yours or mine, anyway. Kristy is the one we should be thinking of."

"Yes," he said. "I have to agree with you there. But I can't pretend this never happened, Charisse. And I won't. Every child has a right to know its own parents. Both of them."

It was, after all, the reason she had followed up the address on his card in the first place, and got herself and Kristy into this situation. She tried to swallow her resentment and her burgeoning fear. "I intended to break the news to you once I was certain I could trust you. I know you don't believe that—" she could tell by his face that he didn't "—but why do you think I would take the risk of seeing you otherwise? I had to be sure it was the right thing for Kristy, but if I'd never had any intention of telling you about her I'd never have agreed to meet you after that morning in the supermarket. That's why I went looking for you in the first place."

He seemed to suffer a small shock at that, his expression changing. Then his eyes narrowed and she could almost see his brain ticking over. "That's the only reason you came looking for me?"

"Yes. I decided that as you were here it wouldn't be right to deprive Kristy of the chance to know her father."

"Five years late. You weren't in any hurry, were you?" he accused. "If I hadn't found you I'd never have known you'd had my baby. What the hell took you that long?"

Charisse paused, hoping her voice wouldn't shake. "I had to find out if you'd changed in that time. I needed to know what kind of person you really are…now."

He looked at her frowningly. "And so you kept on seeing me, and telling me lies?"

Her gaze fell away. "I'm sorry." She'd tried very hard not to tell outright lies, but she couldn't deny she'd set out to deceive him. "It seemed the best thing to do, until I could be confident about you, confident that it wouldn't do Kristy more harm than good to know you."

She could feel his fixed stare and was relieved when Kristy came back into the sitting room, dragging a large, battered teddy and a gangly rag doll. "I put my shells on the dressing table," she announced. "I 'ranged them all nicely, Mummy, so you mustn't touch, please!"

"I don't know where you found the space," Charisse commented, moving away from Daniel and into the larger room.

Daniel followed, and again his attention was drawn to his daughter. "And who are your friends?" he asked, squatting down to her level once more.

"Here's Big Daddy Ted," Kristy told him, handing over the toy, "and this is Annabelle." She hugged the doll to her.

"Annabelle," Daniel repeated. "That's a pretty name."

"They're going to town to shop. Do you want to play shopping with us?"

"Um..."

"Daniel has to go," Charisse intervened. "You could play shopping in your room, Kristy."

"I want to play here," Kristy said firmly as Daniel rose to his feet and deposited Big Daddy Ted on the sofa. "Can Daniel stay for tea?"

"Not today. Maybe another time. I'll see you out, Daniel."

When she fleetingly met his eyes he looked as if he might argue, but instead he said quietly, with only a hint of sarcasm, "Thank you." Turning, he added, "I'll see you again, Kristy," and then to Charisse's great relief he made for the door.

Kristy trailed after them, still cuddling her doll.

With his hand on the doorknob, Daniel turned to Charisse. "I mean it," he said, his voice low and tense.

She could hardly stop him seeing Kristy again, short of barring the door and keeping the child inside. "I understand. But..."

With Kristy right there beside her leaning against her thigh, she couldn't finish the sentence. Only her eyes pleaded with him not to give away her secret yet.

He watched her broodingly, then gave a curt nod. "We have to discuss this—soon."

"I know."

"After all, I must have some rights. I'll be taking legal advice," he warned grimly.

A wave of fright set her trembling. Once he knew the whole story how would he react? But she couldn't possibly tell him everything now, in front of Kristy. Trying not to let her agitation colour her voice, she pointed out, "I haven't denied you access." Glancing at Kristy, who was trying to plait Annabelle's woolly yellow hair, she added,

"And I promise I won't, as long as I'm sure you're not…not doing any damage."

He followed her glance down at the child, then met her eyes again, his own a deep grey now and very concentrated. "I appreciate that you're concerned," he acknowledged. "Surely we can work something out." Hesitantly he reached out a hand to Kristy's bent head, but dropped it before touching her. "Goodbye, Kristy."

"Bye," she said carelessly, and returned to her task.

"I'll be in touch," he repeated to Charisse, and wrenched open the door.

When she'd closed it behind him, Charisse leaned back against the cool wood, letting out a breath.

Kristy regarded her curiously. "What's the matter, Mummy?"

"Nothing." Charisse straightened and tried to look capable and in command. "I'm a bit tired."

"I'm tired, too," Kristy informed her. "But I'm hungry first. Can we have tea soon?"

"Yes, soon." Then she could get Kristy bathed and into bed, and take some time to sort out the dramatic events of the day, do some hard thinking, and decide just how much she was going to tell Daniel about what had happened since the abrupt end of that brief, torrid affair in Australia.

And if he was planning to see a lawyer as he had warned her—at the thought, a nasty black lump settled in her chest—then maybe she should, too.

Consulting a lawyer didn't make Charisse feel any better. It cost more than she could afford and gave her no hope of a way out of her dilemma.

"If you had legalised the situation earlier," the stripe-suited woman told her, "you'd be in a much stronger position, but at this late stage…" The lawyer shook her head.

"I'm afraid it could turn into a nasty custody battle. For the sake of the child, I suggest you and the father try to work out an amicable arrangement, and then have me draw up an agreement."

"That would be legally binding?" Charisse asked anxiously.

"Well, a court would have the power to overturn it if it came to an argument, but a properly composed written document would give you and the child some protection from arbitrary action by the other party—like removing her from your home or taking her out of the country."

In short, Charisse thought bitterly as she left the office, feeling more frightened than ever, she was too late. All she could do now was tell Daniel the whole truth and hope…

Just thinking about it made her feel sick. He'd been furious that Kristy's birth—even her conception—had been kept from him. Supposing when he found out what else Charisse had been hiding he was even more so? What if he wanted to claim his daughter, take her away?

Stark, paralysing fear chilled her bones and made her steps falter.

Already Daniel had shown signs of feeling drawn to Kristy. A kind of instant connection, she guessed, simply from knowing she was his own flesh and blood, that—however unwittingly—he'd helped to make this small human being.

If that developed into real affection he might well want to have her with him in Australia.

Panic swept over her again, and she clenched a fist at her midriff, trying to contain it.

He'd told Charisse he wouldn't harm Kristy, but love wasn't always selfless. Sometimes it was greedy, and sometimes blind. She couldn't be sure that Daniel wouldn't convince himself Kristy would better off with him. And when had he ever shown himself capable of selfless love?

If a court was asked to arbitrate, Daniel could probably afford really good legal help; and financially he would be able to provide Kristy with things Charisse could never give her.

No one had the right to wrench a child from her familiar surroundings, from everything she knew, did they? Wouldn't a judge understand that there were more important things for a child than money?

Charisse hoped so. And maybe it wouldn't come to that.

She picked Kristy up from the kindergarten and took her home for lunch. Watching the little girl demolish a sandwich and a banana, she felt the gnawing anxiety inside her grow with every minute.

Kristy swallowed the last mouthful, finished a glass of milk, and said, "Why are you looking at me?"

Charisse forced a smile. "I like looking at you."

Kristy wriggled in her chair, and smiled indulgently back. "You are a funny mummy too!" she pronounced.

"And you're a funny girl," Charisse answered, leaning across the table to place a tender finger on the tiny nose as Kristy wrinkled it.

The telephone rang, and Charisse went to answer it.

"Charisse." It was Daniel's deep, dark voice. "Are you free tonight?"

"I assumed you'd be out of Auckland by now."

"You hoped, I guess," he said on a note of cynicism. "Are you busy?"

She thought rapidly and discarded the coward's way of pretending she was. "No, but I can't go out."

"Then I'll come to you. After all, you've nothing to hide now, have you?"

She didn't comment on that. He had no idea how much

she was still hiding from him. "All right," she reluctantly agreed. "Will eight-thirty do?" By then Kristy should be safely asleep.

"Fine." He paused. "Thank you."

She didn't respond, and there was an awkward silence. Finally he said, "I'll see you at eight-thirty then."

"Yes." She hesitated. "Goodbye."

It had been a strange, stiff conversation. For the first time since she'd known Daniel he seemed uncertain.

"Who was that?" Kristy asked.

"No one." If she told Kristy Daniel was coming back she'd never get the child to sleep tonight.

"You can't talk to no one!" Kristy giggled.

"It was just grown-up talk," Charisse said. "Nothing that would interest you. Now let's clear this table and then you can help me make some biscuits."

When she opened the door to him at just before eight-thirty, Daniel's expression gave nothing away, as if he'd decided to remain emotionless rather than give in again to anger.

Charisse offered him coffee and he accepted. Within a few minutes she handed him a cup and sat down opposite him with hers, glad of something to hold in her hands.

A plate of fresh biscuits sat on the coffee table between them, but neither of them reached for one.

"I'm sorry you got such a shock," she said formally. "It wasn't the way I intended you to find out."

"We've already covered that," he said, dismissing the apology. "The point is, where do we go from here?"

She tried to sound assertive. "If you want to get to know Kristy I won't object. But we'll have to make it clear to her that you're a visitor, not someone who's always going to be around."

He lowered his cup from his mouth. "A visitor in my daughter's life?"

"I know it's not your fault, but that's how it is, isn't it? You'll be returning to Australia soon, and your job entails travelling. It wouldn't be right to let her think that you'll be…available. I don't want you to make her any promises before you leave, but I'm sure she'll be glad to see you if you're ever in New Zealand again."

Daniel stared into his cup, then raised it and drank again. "And you think I'll be happy with that?"

"It isn't your happiness that counts," Charisse said shortly.

He inclined his head in reluctant acknowledgement, and looked down again at his coffee. "You seem convinced that I'm incapable of facing up to responsibility," he said. "But I can't and won't walk away from this. That's my child in there." He looked toward the doorway leading to the passageway and Kristy's room. "And I'll find a way somehow to be a part of her life."

Charisse took a sip of her coffee. It was hot, potent and steadying. Huskily she said, "If you want to make some financial provision—"

The sudden fierceness of his gaze stopped her. But when he spoke, his voice was carefully neutral. "That isn't what I meant, although of course I'd be glad to contribute. Anything she needs…"

"Thank you. We manage, and I hope when she goes to school I might be able to earn a bit more. But if something comes up…"

His brows drew together. "What do you do with her when you're working?"

"I don't go out to work," Charisse confessed. "I do some telephone interviewing from home occasionally to bring in a little bit of extra income."

He stared at her. "You're quite an accomplished liar, aren't you?"

"I didn't lie about that! I said—"

"All right," he interrupted. "That was unwarranted. Calling each other names isn't going to help, is it?"

"No." But it was an indication that he still harboured a good deal of anger under the surface. And not so far under, either. "The thing is," she said, trying to conceal her anxiety, "Kristy's a happy, healthy, well-adjusted little girl."

"Do you think I want to change that?"

"I know you don't. But lately she's been talking about other children having daddies."

"She has?" His eyes lightened, his expression becoming almost eager. "Then surely she's ready to accept that she *has* a daddy."

"That's just it! If she bonds with you and then you take off as you're going to do, where does that leave her?"

Daniel sat looking at her in silence. He put down his cup and got up, taking a few random steps across the room before turning to face her. "I see what you're getting at," he conceded. "But I grew up without a father myself. I won't leave my own child in the lurch now that I've found her."

"It's…it's decent of you to feel that way."

"And not what you expected," he supplied bitingly.

Charisse gave a helpless shrug. "I understood that you weren't keen to start a family."

His mouth went hard. "All right, I accept this mess is partly my fault. I did make it clear at the time that I wasn't looking for that level of commitment. But then neither were you. I just wish that you'd trusted me enough to tell me you were pregnant and let me share the problem—and the solution. We could have worked something out."

"Like an abortion?"

"No." The vehemence of the denial surprised her. He paused. "If you'd wanted that I suppose I'd have had to accept your decision, but it would have been hard. Probably I'd have done my damnedest to talk you out of it. I most certainly wouldn't have suggested it."

"It was never an option."

"Thank God," he said simply. "She's beautiful. I'm glad you didn't take that way out. And I'm not going to walk away now that I've found her. Don't ask me to."

Her hands gripped her coffee cup. She moistened her lips and opened her mouth. "Daniel—"

"You're obviously a good mother," he told her, "and I fully respect what you've done with Kristy. But I do intend to be a *real* father to her, Charisse, whatever it takes."

Her stomach dropped. Fighting down the all-too-familiar panic reaction, she asked warily, "What do you mean by that?"

"Exactly what I said." He was standing with his hands in his pockets, looking down at her, making her feel disadvantaged. "I have the feeling you'd like me to go away and forget this ever happened. Well, I can't do that. Whatever you believed, I wouldn't have done it five years ago, and I'm definitely not going to now."

Chapter 6

"But you're going away again soon!"

"I know. I have to."

He hadn't changed his plans. Maybe there was a way out even yet, if she could stave off the seemingly inevitable for a few more weeks....

Charisse's mind raced, contradictory thoughts clashing as she tried to sort them into some semblance of logic. Guilt and hope and despair muddled her brain.

"Forget that for the moment," Daniel said. "I'll try to work something out. Is my name on her birth certificate?"

Kristy's birth certificate. For a moment her mind blanked totally, before she shook her head. *Steady.* "That would have required your permission."

"And asking me for permission would have let the cat out of the bag." He eyed her with a disconcertingly assessing stare. "You really were determined to keep me out of this, weren't you?"

"I thought that was what you'd have wanted!"

"Then you took a hell of lot for granted!" His temper was showing again, and she saw him make the effort to control it. "I had a right to be told," he said. "And I have a right to some say in my daughter's future."

"In Perth," she said carefully, "I thought you were very clear that you weren't looking for commitment. That your career was more important than any relationship."

He said nothing for a long moment. "Was I as brutal about it as that?"

"Well…that's what I understood." She drew a breath and moistened her lips. "Was I wrong?"

There was an even lengthier silence. Finally he said, "No, you weren't wrong. I did want you to know in the beginning that I was making no long-term plans. I was trying to get ahead in my career and wasn't in a position to take on personal responsibilities. It was only fair that you knew. And as I recall, you were quite happy with that. You'd come to Australia to enjoy yourself and we were having a good time, so let's make the most of it, you said."

Charisse swallowed. "I…I don't remember saying that."

"Those might not have been your exact words. But that was what you meant, surely?"

What had the exact words been? And had he read into them what he wanted to? "Then why were you so angry when…"

"When you left?" he asked bluntly. "The way you did it made no sense to me. We hadn't quarrelled. In fact the night before you left you were so…passionate—" his voice deepened "—I've never forgotten it. There was something almost magical in the way you made love to me that night. You were utterly beautiful, with a sort of luminousness about you that I'd never seen before. It's haunted me ever since."

Charisse felt her throat close achingly on the threat of tears.

''All the next day,'' Daniel went on, ''I couldn't get it out of my mind, and after work, I bought a huge bunch of flowers for you. When I opened the door of the flat I was looking forward so much to…seeing you, touching you, hearing your voice—and there was nothing. No one there. Just that little scribbled note saying goodbye and good luck. Not even an address to write to.''

Her throat still hurt, making speech impossible. She stared straight ahead, unable to look at his face. ''Did it occur to you,'' she asked when she was able to form the words, ''that maybe your coldhearted bargain had back-fired?''

''Coldhearted?''

''It seems to me—'' She stopped, and started again. ''It seemed to me that you laid down the ground rules from the start. Didn't you ever wonder if it was a bit one-sided?''

''We both understood what we wanted from the rela-tionship, Charisse.''

''Sex.''

''You know damn well that isn't all it was!'' he said. ''Don't cheapen it now. We *liked* each other. We laughed together a lot, we enjoyed the same sort of things—some-times even in bed we just talked. You must remember that. But I enjoyed the sex and so did you. It wasn't *boredom* that sent you away from me. I think we've dealt with that pretty thoroughly already.''

She tried to laugh, but it came out as a strangled sound. ''That's your ego talking.''

''It's plain logic,'' he retorted. ''No woman makes love like that to a man she finds deadly dull, on the eve of walking out on him forever.''

''You know so much about women?'' She heard the acrid note in her own voice and was appalled to realise that it had its roots in totally unwarranted jealousy.

His tone turned caustic. "Once I thought I knew…a woman. She seemed open and honest and ardent. Then she proved I had no idea what was going on inside her head— or her heart."

Charisse clutched her coffee cup and dragged her eyes away from the challenge in his. "Maybe she thought you wouldn't want to know."

His gaze sharpened. "You knew you were pregnant then, didn't you? That night—you knew and you'd already decided to leave."

Charisse bent her head, staring into the depths of her cup.

"And not to tell me about it. Even now you'd rather I didn't know. Are you jealous?" he asked her abruptly.

"What?" Surprise made her blink. Had she been so transparent?

"You've had Kristy to yourself all this time. Do you think of me as some sort of rival?"

"No! I'm just worried about her. About how she might react to having a father and then…not having one."

"I swear I won't let her down, Charisse, if that's really what you're afraid of."

"Do you blame me?" she asked. Although it wasn't the only thing she was afraid of. She didn't know which alternative was worse.

He regarded her thoughtfully. "It was you who left *me*," he jabbed softly. "Now at least I know why."

"Well, that should salve your ego," Charisse suggested somewhat meanly. She felt guilt ridden and afraid and on edge, and hitting out at him was a sort of defence, a relief for her conflicting feelings.

Daniel gave a short laugh. "Not much." He paused

broodingly, then added with apparent sincerity, "I wish I'd been there for you, Charisse."

She was suddenly blinking away tears, and raised her cup to hide them, draining the coffee from it before putting it down on the table. How different things might have been.

"Was your family supportive?" he asked her.

"Yes, they were," she answered when she was sure her voice would be steady. "My parents were upset, of course, and worried. But they always said that whatever happened we—my sister and I—could rely on them for help. They proved they meant it when Kristy came along. They were the most loving grandparents you could imagine. When… when they died she was too young to realise properly what had happened, but she missed them for a long time."

"So you don't want her to love someone else and lose them. That's understandable."

"*Do* you understand?" she asked tensely. "She's already lost so much…"

"Yes, I do," he assured her. "What do I have to say to convince you I want to be a proper father, not some casual visitor?"

Charisse briefly chewed her lower lip. That didn't actually help her at all. But there was no going back now. She would have to deal with whatever arose from the situation.

"You said you were going to see a lawyer," she reminded him, forcing herself to look at him. This was a desperate gamble, carrying the fight into the enemy camp. If Daniel was the enemy…

The slight flicker of his eyes betrayed him, and she guessed that his legal advice hadn't been much more palatable than hers. Of course, it might have been different if he'd been in possession of all the facts.

"Yes," he said shortly. "I have."

Encouraged, Charisse dared an even more dangerous

bluff. "Then he'll have told you that if a child's father isn't named the mother is considered the sole legal guardian."

"He also told me it's not too late to amend Kristy's birth certificate by adding my name to it. All that's required is my agreement."

All? Her heart gave a nasty lurch. No one had mentioned that small but vital point to her. She obviously hadn't asked the right question. What else might she have missed? "And...and mine, surely," she managed to say, not at all sure of her ground.

"Are you saying you'd withhold it?"

Could she? No, of course not. She didn't have the right anyway, and if it came to a legal battle all his lawyer had to do was look up the birth record and that would be the end of it. She breathed quietly, fighting down her sick dismay. "I don't want to tell Kristy yet," she pleaded. "Can't you let her get to know you first as...as a friend?"

His eyes were stormy and she could see he wanted to reject the idea. But after a moment he said, "If you genuinely think that's best, I'll abide by your judgement."

"Thank you." At least she'd gained a little more time.

"You know more about children than I do," Daniel said. "You'll need to tell me if I'm not doing something right."

She had to smile at that. "Kristy will probably tell you herself."

Daniel grinned, although the strain hadn't left his face. "She's quite an assertive little person."

"Takes after her father," she suggested dryly.

The grin broke into a short laugh. "Possibly. But her mother has a mind of her own, too."

She didn't answer that, turning away from him to pick up her emptied cup. "Would you like some more coffee?"

"No. Thanks anyway." The laughter died and he looked at her with what seemed like curiosity mingled, perhaps, with a dash of respect. "It can't have been easy for you, bringing up a child on your own, especially after your parents died. What about your sister?"

Charisse's heart stopped. "My sister?"

"Gabrielle, isn't it? You've hardly mentioned her lately, but in Perth I had the feeling the two of you were unusually close. All those letters you insisted on posting yourself, as if no one else could make sure they got there. And the phone calls. At first I didn't understand why you insisted on having your own mobile and keeping your phone bill separate—not until I found out how much time you spent talking to her. Is she fond of Kristy? Does she help out?"

Charisse remembered those phone calls, several times a week, often brief because of the cost of international calls, but in some measure making up for how much she and Gabrielle had missed each other. And yet, although they'd never been short of topics, some of the most important things had not been said. And now they never would be. "Gabrielle," she said slowly, "was very fond of Kristy. And of course Kristy loved her. But my sister died in the car crash along with my parents."

Shock darkened his eyes. "I didn't realise you'd lost your entire family. No wonder you're so possessive of Kristy."

"Possessive?"

He spread his hands. "That's how it looks to me. I guess I've offended you."

"No." Let him think that was what her reluctance was founded on if he liked. It might keep him from digging further. "I'd prefer the term *protective,* though."

Daniel's quick smile seemed genuine, and sympathetic. "Protective, then. I'm not faulting you for it, just making a comment. I suppose it's a mother's instinct."

Her answering smile was strained. "Maybe."

"You're tired," he said, and abruptly got up. "I know it's far too late to see Kristy, so I'll say good-night. I have to leave for the site again tomorrow, can't put it off any longer, but could we get together next Saturday? Maybe we could take Kristy to the zoo. Would she like that?"

That gave her a few days' reprieve. "Yes," she agreed, resigning herself to the inevitable. "I'm not really keen on animals being locked up, but I think they try to make them comfortable, and I'm sure she'd enjoy it."

"I'll pick you up on Saturday then—about ten-thirty? We can have lunch there."

She walked to the door with him, and he turned as he had last time and asked, "Did you wonder why I came back after you sent me away on Sunday afternoon?"

It had gone completely out of her head. A lot seemed to have happened since yesterday. "Was it important?"

His smile twisted. He looked down at her, his expression oddly undecided. Then he gave a strange little half laugh and said, "It'll keep. Good night, Charisse."

"Good night."

He still didn't move, and she realised he was debating whether to kiss her. Hastily she stepped back. Their relationship had become more complicated than ever. She didn't think that bringing sex into the situation would help matters at all.

Kristy was excited at the prospect of going to the zoo with Daniel. Wearing her new dress, she sat in the back of the car on a cushion with her safety belt firmly fastened, chattering unselfconsciously until Charisse suggested they should let Daniel concentrate on driving.

"She's a good kid," he commented, glancing in the mirror as a conscientiously silent Kristy turned her attention to the passing scenery.

"Usually," Charisse agreed. Kristy was a nice child, although not invariably so obedient. Mostly she was easy to deal with, and Charisse counted herself lucky.

The day was fine but not too warm. Kristy ran from cage to cage and compound to compound, wanting to see everything.

As they watched her, Daniel remarked, "The zoo people are certainly doing their best to provide a natural environment."

"They can't duplicate the wild."

"Some of these animals are almost extinct in the wild. These days zoos are preserving species rather than just giving people the chance to gawk at exotic animals."

"We're still gawking," Charisse pointed out as they stopped to view the monkeys on their artificial rain forest island.

"Providing the funds for research and breeding programmes," Daniel suggested.

She gave him a candid look. "Kristy has an answer for everything, too. It must be a family trait."

Daniel laughed, his gaze going back to the child who stood before them, absorbed in the antics of the monkeys. "There are two sides to everything. Most ethical questions don't have simple, cut-and-dried answers, do they? Maybe some sacrifice is worth securing a better future for the next generation."

Charisse looked at him thoughtfully, wondering if there was an oblique message behind that remark.

Kristy turned, pointing to a tree on the island. "Look, Mummy! That monkey's got a baby!"

Charisse moved forward, placing a hand on Kristy's shoulder. "Yes, I see."

The monkey plunged from a branch, swinging with one hand, her tiny offspring clinging to her neck, and Kristy gave a dismayed exclamation. "She won't let the baby fall in the water, will she?"

"I'm sure she won't," Charisse assured her, even as the adult monkey swung to another branch. "The baby's quite safe with its mother."

"Where's the daddy monkey?" Kristy asked.

"I don't know."

"There." Joining them, Daniel went down beside Kristy and pointed. "The big fellow in the corner, watching them. He's keeping an eye on his family, making sure they're okay."

Charisse cast him a sceptical glance that he returned with a quizzical one of his own, daring her to contradict him.

Kristy seemed satisfied with the explanation. She watched the monkeys for a bit longer, then tugged at Charisse's hand. "I want to see the lions."

They saw the lions, and the seals and the reptile house and the elephants, had a late lunch, and afterwards toured more of the zoo until even Kristy's energy at last began to flag. "Carry me, Mummy?" she begged.

Daniel said, "I'll carry you, Kristy. You're a bit big for Mummy now, aren't you?"

Kristy eyed him consideringly. "Okay," she conceded. "You are bigger than my mummy too."

He bent and swung her into his arms. Kristy hooked her hands about his neck, her silky curls brushing his cheek.

An extraordinary expression crossed Daniel's face. For a moment he looked as if someone had knocked the breath from his body. His eyes went dark and his firm mouth softened. Charisse saw him swallow, his throat moving as he settled the child more comfortably on his strong forearm, his other hand splayed over her back, holding her safely.

It was the first time he'd held Kristy in his arms, Charisse realised. And she could see, with a growing apprehension, that it had profoundly affected him.

She knew the feel of that small, trusting body nestling against her own, and the melting warmth that it produced. She'd known it first when Kristy was put in her arms on the day she was born, when she'd looked into the fathomless blue eyes and been surprised and shaken at the strength of feeling that flooded her. Overwhelmed by tenderness and love and a totally unexpected and powerful protectiveness, a passionate desire to preserve this tiny human being from the harshness of the world.

She could see it happening to Daniel—see him running the gamut of emotion that caught him unaware, squeezed his heart, and changed his life forever.

Her own heart sank within her, leaving a hollow feeling in her chest. She knew with every instinct in her that from this moment he was irrevocably tied to his daughter just as she had been.

And that he would never be able to give her up.

Chapter 7

Every weekend Daniel indulged Kristy with some fresh treat or experience. One Saturday he even took her and Charisse to a matinee performance of an overseas musical show.

Kristy was entranced, her eyes shining, her mouth parted in wonder for at least half the time at the colourful spectacle on the stage, and her peals of giggles at moments of slapstick comedy ringing out uninhibited. Daniel had spent as much time watching her as he did the stage.

"You're spoiling her," Charisse said after he'd delivered them home and Kristy had gone off to her room to take off her shoes and add the glossy illustrated programme to her hoard of treasures.

Daniel gave her a long, thoughtful look. "I'm trying to make the most of our time. But if you don't approve—"

"It's going to be difficult for her to adjust later. I don't have that kind of money."

"If money's a problem, I told you—"

"There's more to being a father—"

"You think I don't know that?" he enquired harshly. "I'm working on it."

Charisse bit her tongue. She could see he was working on it. And she didn't want to antagonise him. She couldn't afford to, because if their tentative informal agreement deteriorated and a legal battle ensued everything might fall apart. Her whole world—and Kristy's. She hadn't yet broached the subject of a formal legal document, waiting for the right moment to present itself.

Half the time she wished passionately that Daniel would return to Australia and get out of their lives as quickly as possible. The other half she dreaded his going, not only for Kristy's sake but her own.

He was gentle and patient and as fascinated by Kristy's reaction to finding a small spotted spider or a new flower in the garden as she was at her discovery. He gave the little girl simple explanations of where the wind came from or how the pop-up toaster worked when she demanded to know, willingly played with her while Charisse cooked them a meal, and read her stories on demand before she went to sleep.

Seeing the growing bond between Daniel and his daughter, his absorption in her every move, and Kristy's giggly delight in his company, Charisse felt a peculiar ache of pleasure mixed with pain. And a growing, inexorable sense of doom.

When she invited him to eat with them Daniel helped with the dishes; once he insisted on cooking for them all while Charisse sat and watched him turn out a presentable pasta dish. Another day he arrived unexpectedly to find her trimming the hedge, took over the job and afterwards drove her and Kristy to a beach. He'd bought them fish and chips on the way and they'd eaten their meals out of the paper bags, sitting on the sand.

Despite the fact that he seemed to have withdrawn physically from Charisse, he had become a part of her life as well as Kristy's. When he was nearby she felt his every move even if she wasn't looking at him, her body attuned to his presence, tingling with awareness whenever he came within a few feet of her.

He was a very attractive man, she rationalised, who for a time had openly shown his interest in her. Any redblooded woman would have responded. Especially one who had deliberately cut men from her life.

And then he'd discovered Kristy's existence and everything had changed. Perhaps Charisse as a single woman without ties had been fair game, but the mother of his child was a different proposition. What an irony that was.

One day Daniel drove them over the harbour bridge to the hot swimming pools at Waiwera. Charisse's swimsuit was an old but hardly worn one-piece, and she couldn't help a faint glow of satisfaction when, holding an excited Kristy by the hand, she joined Daniel at the poolside and saw the veiled but approving look he gave her as his gaze moved from her face to her long legs and back again.

He looked good, too, stripped to a pair of swimming trunks that hugged his lean hips. It was obvious that he didn't spend all his time behind a desk.

He took her hand and led her to the edge of the pool, then waited while she dived in, following her a split second later.

Together they towed Kristy about the pool, and encouraged her to try swimming on her own while they made sure she stayed afloat. Then Daniel let the child cling to his back while he swam the length of the pool and she squealed with delight.

"Race us, Mummy!" she commanded, and chanted, "One, two, three, go! Come on, Mummy!"

Urged on by Kristy, Daniel easily won, and Charisse was panting when she reached his side, pushing wet hair from her eyes.

Kristy wriggled from her perch to sit on the side of the pool, crowing, "We won, Mummy, we won!"

Daniel grinned at Charisse. "Do I get a prize?" he asked, his eyes gleaming wickedly.

Charisse shook her head and pushed off again, backstroking away from him. He grabbed her ankle and hauled her back, and when she was level with him he let go. "Sure?"

"Sure." She splashed him and he retaliated, while Kristy giggled at them from her vantage point and finally demanded to join in.

Before returning to the city they got an ice cream for Kristy and sat at an outdoor table with drinks. The warm water and exercise had induced a pleasant lethargy, and Charisse felt more relaxed than she had for ages.

Catching Daniel smiling at her in a rather odd way, she queried, "What?"

Daniel shook his head. "Nothing. Just that I hadn't remem—realised how very…bewitching you are."

Charisse looked down at her half-empty glass. "I'm perfectly ordinary."

"No. You were nev—you never could be ordinary. There's something about you that I can't quite grasp, something almost mysterious." Tiny creases appeared about his eyes. "Hidden depths."

"Aren't all women a mystery to men?" Charisse enquired lightly. "You guys are always complaining that you don't understand us."

"Supposedly. Certainly I don't seem to be very good at reading women."

''There are things men will never understand about us, I guess.''

''There are lots of things I don't understand about you. Charisse...''

A crowd of young people passed the table, hooting and yahooing. Daniel looked up impatiently and didn't finish whatever he'd been going to say. He drained the last inch of liquid in his glass, glanced at her empty one and shoved back his chair. ''Shall we go?''

Before leaving them that evening, Daniel said, ''A friend of mine wants to try out a new nightclub. I've known Mac ever since leaving school, and he suggested we join him and his wife one evening. Maybe next Friday?''

Meeting a friend of such long standing might give her a new perspective on him. ''Will I need to dress up?'' she asked cautiously.

''Wear whatever you feel comfortable in.''

''I'll have to get a baby-sitter. And explain to Kristy why she can't come.''

That took some doing, and Kristy showed signs of rebelling when Daniel arrived early. Still in jeans and a denim jacket over a work shirt, he explained, ''I was late getting back from the site, and decided to come here first to save time. I thought we could drive on into town and stop by my place so I can change.'' He'd told her he'd planned for them to have dinner in the city before meeting his friends.

''I may take a while to get ready,'' she warned him. She'd borrowed a dress from Brenna, and planned to take care with her makeup and hair; tonight she wanted to look glamorous, to do justice to the rare chance to visit a sophisticated nightspot, and perhaps impress Daniel's friends. And deep down she knew she hoped to impress him, too. Despite her reservations about their relationship, and despite all sensible considerations, she wanted him to find her desirable.

"Take all the time you want," he said. "I just didn't want you hanging about waiting for me."

With a minor bribe of her favourite ice cream in a cone after her bath, plus Daniel's promise of a special surprise the following day, Kristy accepted that this was a grown-up outing and agreed to be a good girl and go to bed. "But I want Daniel to read me a story!" she insisted.

"All right, you hop into bed and I'll be there in a minute," he promised.

She'd probably coax Brenna into reading her another one later, Charisse supposed. Turning to Daniel as Kristy trotted off, she asked, "A special surprise?"

"There's a free family concert in the domain tomorrow evening," Daniel told her quietly. "A bluegrass band. If the weather holds good I think Kristy will enjoy it, provided you don't mind her having a late night."

"You like that kind of music?"

"You know I—" He'd stopped there and amended, "Actually, yes. And I know you do. How much longer do you intend to keep this charade up, Charisse? I can't see the point!"

She hadn't actually thought of it lately, but thank goodness he'd given her a ready excuse for her momentary lapse. "The point is," she said, feeling her way, "you never really knew me before."

He studied her in silence. "You could be right there," he conceded. "I was five years younger then, and possibly too self-centred and stupid to see beneath the surface."

Charisse tried a pale smile. "Very possibly."

"Then I can only say I'm sorry."

Daniel read Kristy her story while Charisse showered and changed into Brenna's black silk-knit stretch sheath shot with subtle silver lights. She fastened her hair with a silver clasp that had once belonged to her mother, stepped into the black suede shoes that she kept for formal occasions, and applied makeup to eyes and lips with much more care than usual. Then she called to Brenna, and the other woman came through, casting her an approving glance. "Looks better on you than on me," she said.

Charisse laughed, shaking her head.

Entering the room, she saw that Daniel was sitting on the sofa, leafing through an old magazine. She couldn't help but be gratified by the way his eyes altered when he saw her. His gaze swept over her in undisguised appreciation as he stood up. "You look lovely, Charisse."

"Thank you."

"And very sexy," he added.

Caution belatedly reared its head, and she gave him a wary look.

He grinned down at her, moving closer. "Don't tell me you don't know it," he said. His hand touched her arm. "Shall we go?"

Maybe she should have worn her old cream dress after all. But when Brenna had offered the wonderful black and silver she hadn't had the willpower to refuse, and she did feel sexy in it. It wasn't a crime, was it?

But it might be a mistake.

In his city apartment with a view of the harbour, Daniel poured her a drink of gin and lemon and told her to make herself at home while he showered and changed.

The living room furniture was leather-covered and the long coffee table a sheet of plate glass laid over a couple of big black marble cubes.

Thick, neutral-coloured carpet yielded under her feet as she went to the glass door set in a wall of windows. On a small balcony outside, a realistic fake potted palm waved gently beside a green canvas lounger. The heavy cream drapes were half-drawn, and an electrical switch on the wall swished them back when she pressed it.

Finding the door handle, she slid the glass panel aside and stepped out. The hum of traffic rose from the street, and a breeze stirred her hair. She peered over the waist-high concrete wall, fascinated by the passing cars far below, and the oblivious pedestrians on the pavement.

"Great view, isn't it?"

Charisse jumped as Daniel appeared beside her. "I didn't hear you."

He wore dark trousers and a white-on-white striped shirt, full-sleeved and open-necked, with a vest over it. It gave him a slightly piratical look.

"I was watching the people down there," she said, turning to go back inside. "This place is…"

"What?" he asked.

She supposed it would be rude to comment on the cost but he was waiting for an answer. "Well…luxurious. And you're hardly here except for weekends."

He glanced at her as if he'd never thought about it. Closing the balcony door, he followed her into the room. "The firm pays the rent."

"You're obviously pretty important to them."

"I'm good at my job," he said simply.

And highly paid. "Do they provide your car, too?"

"It's part of the deal." He eyed her empty glass. "Can I get you another drink?"

Charisse shook her head. "I've had enough for now."

He took the glass from her. "You're very abstemious these days."

"I always…I've never drunk a lot."

"Not often," he agreed. "I wasn't suggesting you're an alcoholic."

He was on his way to the kitchen, and she stared at his retreating back. Not often? Not ever. She had always been careful about alcohol. She wanted to tell him that, but instead waited in silence for him to return.

"I'll call a cab," he said, "if you're ready to go?"

"A cab?"

"If I don't have my car I needn't worry about an extra glass or two of wine or spirits," he explained, "or finding a place to park."

Minutes later they climbed into a cab and Daniel gave the driver the address of a restaurant she knew to be among the top three in Auckland.

Involuntarily she said, "That's awfully upmarket, isn't it?"

He looked amused. "In that dress you deserve upmarket," he told her. "I'm told the food's very good."

They had a light meal but it was more than good, it was superb, and the wine he ordered complemented it beautifully. By the time they left, Charisse's cheeks were faintly flushed and she knew her eyes were brighter than usual. And Daniel's hard mouth had softened into a curve that was almost a smile. When he looked at her his eyes were lit with admiration that he didn't try to hide.

It went to her head even more than the wine, that look. It said he liked her and was attracted to her, and she found herself meeting his eyes boldly, sending him reciprocal messages, the clamouring voice of caution for once stilled.

At the club he introduced her to his friends. Julia Mac-Donald wore a low-cut dress with a sequined bodice and a tight skirt that suited her exotic, dark prettiness and lush figure and made Charisse thankful she'd accepted the loan of Brenna's dress. Her husband was good-looking, slightly overweight and prepared for a good evening out. He shook Charisse's hand and said, "Just call me Mac."

After they were all seated at a table, Julia asked Charisse where she and Daniel had met.

"In a supermarket," Charisse answered.

Julia laughed. "I read something the other day about the best places for singles to meet, and supermarkets were near the top of the list."

Daniel said, "Actually I knew Charisse before, in Australia. We happened to bump into each other again some weeks ago."

"Oh, really?" The woman turned back to Charisse. "Were you in Aussie for long?"

"No," Charisse answered, her gaze flickering to the wineglass in her hand. "Not long at all."

"Almost half a year," Daniel supplied. "But then she got...homesick and came back to New Zealand." As she looked up his eyes met hers, a mocking light in the grey-green depths.

"How did you like Australia?" Mac enquired.

"I...I don't remember much about it," Charisse stammered.

Daniel was still looking at her. His eyes cooled. "It didn't make much of an impression," he said, "obviously."

"I've always wanted to travel," Julia remarked. "Have you been to England?"

Charisse shook her head. "I went on a cruise round the Pacific islands once, with...with my sister." Surely that was a safe topic. She dredged up memories of palm trees and coral beaches and markets selling bright-printed fabrics and shell goods, and was relieved when the band began playing and the music made conversation almost impossible.

Daniel asked if she wanted to dance, and she mentally took a deep breath and said yes. He took her hand in his and they joined the couples already on the floor.

It was a much bigger and less crowded floor space than there had been on the dinner cruise, where there had been no choice but to dance close and intimately.

She pulled her hand from his clasp and put a couple of feet between them. Coloured lights flashed about them and shimmered over her borrowed dress as she moved her feet and hips in time to the heavy beat. Opposite her, Daniel, too, followed the music, his eyes holding hers and a faint smile on his lips.

Charisse began to enjoy herself, smiling back at him and tossing her loose hair away from her face. She had always loved dancing and Daniel was good, his lithe body perfectly in tune with the music.

The rhythm became faster, and Daniel caught her about the waist and twirled her once before releasing her, all without missing a beat.

Charisse laughed up at him, her hips swaying as her feet tapped on the floor. Again Daniel came closer, dancing to her side, then behind her, and she cast a laughing glance over her shoulder.

His hand slid about her waist and he pulled her momentarily back against him, matching the swaying of her hips with his own, moved around her again and then he was in front, still holding her, both hands on her waist now as they danced with only inches separating them.

She followed his every variation with ease, and he became more adventurous, inviting her to join him in unexpected manoeuvres and tricky little steps. It was a challenge, a game, and as the music came to an end he drew her close and executed a neat old-fashioned turn, then let her go, retaining only a light hold on her waist as they returned to the table.

Charisse felt exhilarated and breathless, and not only from the exertion. She'd never had a more exciting dancing partner. Mac applauded as they approached, and Daniel gave a mock bow.

He exchanged a few joking remarks with Mac, and asked Charisse if she'd like another drink.

"Yes, thank you," she said recklessly.

Julia asked for a refill, too, and as Daniel went to fetch the drinks from the bar, declining Mac's offer of help, Charisse turned to his friend and began asking leading questions.

She learned that Mac and Daniel had worked together for several years before Daniel got a job overseas, and Mac volunteered that Daniel was regarded as one of the best in his field, generally respected and liked.

"He can be a bit hard on guys who've done sloppy work though," Mac said. "And even more if they try to cover up their mistakes. Hates lies and dishonesty."

A pulse began to hammer in Charisse's throat, and she felt suddenly hot, then cold. "Really?" she said faintly.

"Doesn't stand any bull. Mind, he's as likely to bawl out the boss as he is a labourer. When I first worked with Dan he put his job on the line because safety standards weren't up to scratch. Most guys just grumble a bit and go along with the cost cutting or whatever because the money's good. Not him. Had a stand-up argument with the project boss."

Julia caught Charisse's eye, a slightly derisive smile on her face arousing Charisse's curiosity. Then Daniel returned with the drinks.

Later Daniel asked Julia to dance, and Charisse returned to her conversation with Mac.

"Took off to Australia when he was just a young feller," Mac told her with a hint of envy. "Now he's his company's number one trouble-shooter. They even offered him a promotion to administration."

"He turned it down?"

Mac shrugged. "Doesn't want to be stuck behind a desk, enjoys the challenge and the change he gets in his job. Bit of a rolling stone, our Dan."

"He's never been married, has he?" Charisse ventured.

"Nope." Mac looked at her quickly, then away, to where his wife was talking to Daniel as they danced.

"Do you know why?" Charisse asked.

Mac grinned. "Not because no one'd have him, that's for sure."

"You think no woman could turn him down?"

Mac laughed. "Dan never had a problem pulling girls— I mean, he's not a bad-looking sort of sod, is he? And he's a real stubborn sort of guy. Tough, too. A good bloke to have on your side in a pinch, but when he goes after something he wants, I wouldn't like to get in his way."

"Really." Uneasily Charisse sipped at her soda.

Mac shrugged, looking embarrassed. Perhaps he hadn't realised how much he was giving away about his friend. "Um, want to dance?"

It would be rude to say no. Charisse got up and Mac followed her onto the floor. He didn't have the flair that Daniel had, but she thanked him nicely afterwards and he said, "My pleasure."

Daniel and Julia were already seated. Julia looked flushed although she hadn't been dancing all that energetically. And Daniel's face was very bland. But Julia looked up and smiled at her husband as Daniel pulled out Charisse's chair and hitched his own closer so he could drape an arm over the back of hers.

After that Charisse danced exclusively with Daniel. Hardly touching, they were increasingly aware of each other, their body movements in sync, their eyes locked and exchanging messages as old as time. She was playing with fire, but tonight it didn't seem to matter. Recklessness was in the air, in the music and the lights, and most of all in the hypnotic glitter of Daniel's eyes.

They were on the floor together at midnight when the music slowed and the lights dimmed even further.

Daniel folded her into his arms, and she realised she'd been waiting for hours for him to hold her like this.

They swayed together, barely moving their feet. The floor was crowded and most people were dancing with their arms hooked about each other, heads close together.

His cheek rasped lightly against the fine skin of her temple, and she succumbed to the temptation to rest her head on his shoulder. It seemed as if this whole evening were a dream, one from which she didn't want to be woken. She could feel the hard warmth of his chest against her breasts, and his muscular thighs tensing against hers. Her nostrils were filled with his masculine scent.

His hand moved on her waist, caressingly, then subtly tightened, bringing her closer, until she could feel the effect she was having on him.

The muted lights shifted around them, the other dancers shadowy figures in the murky bluish light. Daniel turned his head slightly until his lips touched her skin, and he murmured, "Doesn't this bring back memories?"

Chapter 8

It broke the spell. Charisse made an effort to put a little distance between them, but although his hold wasn't tight he kept her imprisoned by his arms.

He lifted his head to scrutinise her. "Charisse, what's the use of pretending? We both know what we want...just as we did the first time."

She wished now he wasn't holding her so close. It made rational thought impossible. But she couldn't afford to let this stupid, mindless desire overrule her common sense. She knew all too well where it could lead.

Besides she couldn't possibly make love to Daniel without telling him the truth, and she wasn't nearly ready to do that. She had no idea what his reaction might be.

The next time he suggested they dance she shook her head and asked him to get her a glass of soda.

Julia said, "I'm going to the Ladies'. What about you, Charisse?"

Charisse followed her, taking the hint.

They stood side by side at the basins while Julia renewed her lipstick. "Is it serious, you and Daniel?" she asked, capping the lipstick and pulling a tissue from her bag.

"He's only here for a few months," Charisse said evasively.

"Mmm." Julia blotted her lips, her eyes briefly meeting Charisse's in the mirror. "And you knew each other before. So I guess you have some idea what sort of guy he is."

"What sort of guy is he?"

Julia threw the tissue into a waste bin and laughed. "Well, Mac thinks he's the cat's whiskers, but Daniel can be an unfeeling bastard where women are concerned. At least, he was when he was younger, and I doubt he's changed that much. I've never seen him take a woman seriously."

Charisse's nerves stood on end.

Julia turned to face her. "If he's just filling in time until he goes back to Australia you could end up with a broken heart. Believe me."

Charisse enquired cautiously, "You speak from experience?"

"Yes." The word came out with a snap. "Oh, not my own. My sister was seeing him for months. This job in Australia came up and he dropped her and took off without a backward glance. She was devastated. A total mess. So if you want my advice—which you're welcome to throw back in my face, because I know this is really none of my business—be careful. If you're expecting any more from him than a great fling—and I'm sure he's quite capable of giving you that—don't hold your breath."

Charisse said steadily, "That would be some time ago that he knew your sister."

"Oh, yes. She's married to someone else now, and happy enough, but I wanted to kill him for a while. Mac reckoned it wasn't Dan's fault if she got the wrong end of the stick, but men always stand up for other men. I figured you deserved a friendly warning.''

"Thank you," Charisse said. "I'll bear it in mind."

On the way home in the cab Daniel had hailed, Charisse sat with her hands clenched in her lap. Daniel reached across and prised them apart, capturing one in his hard, enveloping clasp. "What's worrying you?" he asked her quietly.

"Nothing. I'm tired, but I had a good time, thank you." She'd liked Mac, and maybe Julia's slightly brittle air had hidden a secret worry on Charisse's behalf. Or a lingering resentment of what she said Daniel had done to her sister. "Your friends are nice."

"Mac's a good bloke, easy to get along with."

"And very fond of you."

He gave a slight laugh. "Julia doesn't quite approve of me."

"Why not?" She waited to see if he would tell her.

But after a short pause he said lightly, "Perhaps she thinks I'm a bad influence on Mac. The two of them have been together since they were in their teens—they were married as soon as they hit their twenties. I have a feeling she's always been afraid I'll lead him astray. He wants her to think about moving to Australia, but Julia's not keen."

"Is that what she was talking about when you danced with her?"

"Among other things."

Charisse's palms were damp. She hoped he wouldn't notice. She flexed her fingers and he changed his grip, but only to flatten her hand on his thigh, his own keeping it there while his thumb moved back and forth over her wrist.

Very conscious of the warmth and muscular firmness of

his flesh under the cloth of his trousers, she said, "Mac told me you'd turned down a promotion."

"It was no big deal. I make enough money as it is, and I like what I do. Anyway, the extra responsibility wasn't worth what they were offering."

"I see." He'd rather be footloose and fancy-free. He hadn't really changed much at all.

When he said good-night she didn't resist his kiss. All evening she'd been leading him on, tacitly promising at least this much. In truth, she was more than a little ashamed of herself. As he deepened the kiss her heart pounded and her blood ran hot, but somehow she retained a scrap of sanity and restraint, eventually stirring in his arms and pushing against him.

For a moment it had no effect, then he seemed to realise she was calling a halt, and let her go.

She sensed his impatience and frustration, but all he said as she turned away was, "I'll see you tomorrow."

The bluegrass concert began in the early evening. The weather was growing warmer but it wasn't yet summer. Charisse and Daniel wore sweaters and jackets, and Charisse had put Kristy into leggings and woollens and packed a picnic into a plastic shopping bag.

When they parked, Daniel hauled a checked rug and some cushions out of the back of the car. "Might as well be comfortable," he told her, handing one of the cushions to Kristy to carry.

He found a spot on a slight slope that gave them a good view of the outdoor stage. The air was crisp but not too chilly and there was no sign of rain. Kristy, pink cheeked and sparkly eyed, helped unpack the picnic and did more than her share of demolishing it.

The concert was as much fun as Daniel had predicted,

the performers expert and exuberant, the audience, many of them in family parties, applauding every item with enthusiasm. Kristy soon caught the spirit, clapping her plump little hands with gusto.

Later she drooped against Charisse, and eventually yawned, curled up on the blanket and went to sleep.

"Should we take her home?" Daniel asked.

Charisse shook her head. "She's fine." Taking off her jacket, she spread it over the sleeping child.

"Have mine," Daniel offered. "You'll be cold."

"No, I'm all right, really."

He put his arm about her shoulder though, and she let it stay there, his body warm and hard against hers.

Slanting a glance at him after one particularly lively piece, Charisse saw that he was smiling as he watched the soloist taking a bow. He looked relaxed and unguarded, obviously enjoying himself, and with heart-catching clarity she thought that was how he might have been when he was five years younger.

The smile still on his mouth, he turned to her. His eyes darkened as the smile died, and he searched her face while the scattered remnants of applause about them gave way to an expectant silence as the musicians readied themselves for the next piece.

He shifted slightly on the blanket, an eyebrow lifting in mute question. And then the music started again, breaking the spell. Charisse, her heart thumping, turned away to watch the stage.

She kept on watching although her breath paused for a moment when Daniel's palm briefly caressed her upper arm, then tightened on her shoulder.

Farther down the slope one young couple had a blanket and were lying entwined on it, kissing. The darkness probably gave them an illusion of privacy, or they just didn't care.

Charisse wrenched her gaze away.

When the bracket of numbers finished she clapped enthusiastically, but Daniel didn't move his arm.

After the finale, while people all around began packing up to go, he turned to her and leaned down until his lips found hers. Everything in the world faded except the feel of his mouth on hers, warm and firm and questing, but without the passion of last night. He seemed to be reassuring her that he wouldn't ask for more than she was prepared to give.

It was a few seconds before he lifted his head and helped her to her feet. Trying to regain her poise, Charisse picked up the cushions, while Daniel tenderly folded the blanket about Kristy's oblivious form and lifted her in his arms. Neither of them spoke on the quite lengthy trudge back to the car.

She helped him strap the protesting little girl into the back seat, and by the time they reached the house Kristy was asleep again.

Daniel carried her inside, and in the darkened bedroom laid her on the bed, stepping back to allow Charisse to remove the leggings and outer clothing and tuck her in.

As they stepped into the lighted passageway he closed his fingers about her arm. "Charisse?"

She stiffened, raising her eyes to look at him. "Yes?"

The harsh light showed her his face, leached of colour and with a frown between his eyebrows. "Can we talk?"

"It's late."

"Yes, it is. We should have had this discussion long ago."

"That isn't what I meant."

He released her and thrust his hands into his pockets. "I

know.'' But he didn't offer to postpone whatever he wanted
to say, instead standing rocklike and determined, looking
down at her.

Charisse shrugged and turned to lead the way into the
sitting room. ''Do you want some coffee?''

''No. Come here.'' Looking thoroughly exasperated, he
reached out and dragged her into his arms, and before she
had a chance to protest he was kissing her with a fierce,
concentrated eroticism. Her lips involuntarily parted, allow-
ing him to deepen the kiss until she was boneless, her body
crumpled against him as if she'd lost any will of her own.

When he lifted his head and his eyes glittered into hers,
she could hardly stand. Not that she needed to, because he
was holding her so tightly she could feel the tiny hammer
of his heart beating against her breast.

He said huskily, ''I think we both needed that, though I
didn't intend to do it. Whatever we had in Perth, Charisse,
it hasn't died, has it? It's stronger than ever. And I'm not
alone in feeling it.''

That was enough to bring her to her senses. She pushed
at his arms, her body arching away from him, and reluctantly he released her.

''It doesn't solve anything,'' she said thinly, and walked
blindly through the doorway to the other room and took a
chair, because if she didn't sit down she might just fall at
his feet.

He followed but remained just inside the doorway, sur-
veying her with a guarded expression, then abruptly moved
and sank onto the sofa opposite her. ''But it tells me something,'' he insisted. ''You haven't stopped wanting me any
more than I've stopped wanting you.''

''And how many women have there been since?'' she
challenged him.

A betraying colour darkened his cheeks. ''This discussion is about you and me. Nobody else need come into it. I want to talk about us.''

. She let the remark pass. "All right. What would you have said,'' she asked him carefully, ''back there in Perth, about changing the parameters?''

"What?''

"Supposing,'' she suggested, ''that instead of just saying goodbye the note had asked you to think about commitment and maybe even about permanence? And given you a chance to reply. Would you have got in touch?''

He stared at her in silence. ''I'd certainly have contacted you.''

"And said what? Yes, I want more than we had? Or, Sorry, I prefer to hang on to my freedom?''

"If I'd known you were pregnant—''

"But if you hadn't…. If the note said nothing about that?''

He got up, took a few steps away and turned back to her. ''It was five years ago. If you want an honest answer—''

"I do,'' she cut in swiftly. ''Please.''

"Then I don't know,'' he said finally. ''All I can say is, I would have preferred the chance to make the decision myself.''

That, she guessed, had been half the problem for him. He was used to making decisions, not having them taken out of his hands. He'd been furious and frustrated because for once someone else had taken control, wrested a part of his life away without his consent. She couldn't help a small, sad smile. ''You see,'' she told him, ''the pregnancy wasn't really the issue. It just precipitated things.''

"Then what the hell *was* the issue? What was it all about, Charisse?''

"It was all about loving you!" She looked at him accusingly. "That's what it was about."

He was silent for several seconds, taking that in. His face changed, as if he was thinking back, and he looked almost shocked. "That was what our last night together meant to you? You were...you were in love with me?"

Charisse's smile turned acrid. The familiar, deep smoulder of hidden rage and blame threatened the bounds of her control. "Didn't the possibility ever occur to you?"

He shook his head, almost in disbelief, still staring at her. "Was I such a blind, selfish oaf? Oh, my God, Charisse—I'm so very sorry!"

She couldn't doubt that he was sincere. Her eyes flickered away from the dismayed comprehension in his, and her anger ebbed. "No woman really wants a man to stay with her out of obligation because she's pregnant. Not if he doesn't love her. I suppose," she said slowly, "it wasn't your fault. As you said, you'd spelt out the terms from the beginning."

And if it wasn't his fault, should she tell him everything? Perhaps it was time.

Even as she thought about it he thrust a hand through his hair and said, "I guess I was pretty insensitive." He seemed stricken, for once caught off balance. Moving suddenly, he pushed himself to his feet. "Perhaps I *wanted* to be oblivious to what was happening, to how you felt—it was more convenient for me that way. I never intended to hurt you, but that's no excuse, is it?"

"Daniel—"

He took her hands and pulled her to her feet, his eyes scanning her face. Jerkily he said, "It's five years too late, but I do apologise. I'll get out of here now. Good night, Charisse. I'll see myself out. But I'll be here tomorrow—I promised Kristy."

He bent and kissed her cheek, a fleeting, sexless touch that she felt nevertheless right down to her toes, and left her standing there.

In the early hours of the morning Charisse was woken by a distressed wailing from Kristy's room, and hurried to see what was wrong.

In the darkness she sat down on the child's bed. Kristy was probably dreaming, perhaps affected by overstimulation the previous day. "It's all right," Charisse soothed, and put out a hand to brush back the child's soft dark hair from her forehead, then almost recoiled with shock at the heat of her skin.

"My head hurts," Kristy whimpered and sniffed, then gave a rasping cough. "Mummeee!"

Kristy had run fevers before—children were always picking up minor ailments and there was no need to fear the worst. But lately there'd been a number of cases of meningitis and doctors were warning parents to be on the look-out for the symptoms. Fever and headache had been mentioned. And a rash, but by the time that appeared it was sometimes too late. The disease was difficult to diagnose, fast-developing and often deadly.

She inspected Kristy's hot body and found no spots, but the child's distress was obvious and worrying. When she failed to settle after a dose of children's over-the-counter-medication and continued to complain that her head hurt, Charisse phoned her doctor's emergency number and was advised to take the child straight to hospital.

Hours later she found a telephone in the hospital lobby and rang Daniel's number.

When he answered she said, "Oh, thank goodness. I was afraid you might already be on your way to my place."

"What's up?"

"I'm at the hospital."

"What happened?" he asked sharply. "Have you had an accident?"

"No, it's Kristy. She's been admitted with—" she paused to steady her voice "—suspected meningitis."

He said nothing for a second, then, "That can be serious, can't it?"

"Very." She couldn't trust herself to say more.

"Tell me where you are, exactly. I'll be there just as fast as I can make it."

Charisse didn't argue. He had the right. And she wanted him to be here—wanted it with a strength that surprised her.

Brenna had driven them to the hospital. Charisse had hesitated about waking her, but Kristy had been clinging and miserably crying, and Charisse didn't want to leave a sick child strapped into the backseat alone while she drove.

When they arrived at the hospital Brenna had insisted on staying through all the admission procedures and tests, fetching Charisse a cup of coffee and a sandwich, and staying with Kristy while Charisse went to make her phone call. Kristy was now asleep in a hospital bed, looking small and frighteningly ill, an IV tube in her arm.

Charisse stopped by the nurses' station to tell them that Daniel Richmond would be arriving soon. She hesitated briefly. "He's Kristy's father."

When he arrived he looked almost as pale and worried as she felt. Brenna was still there, her arm about Charisse, when a nurse ushered him in saying, "Here's her daddy. I'll just check her temperature again."

Brenna looked startled, but said nothing until the nurse left the room. Daniel moved nearer the bed, staring intently down at Kristy.

"Her daddy?" Brenna murmured.

Daniel dragged his concentrated attention from the sleeping child and focused momentarily on Brenna. Before that he didn't seem to have even noticed her. He nodded. Then he transferred his sombre gaze to Charisse. ''Thank you for telling them.''

Brenna was looking puzzled. Charisse turned to her friend. ''Daniel is Kristy's father,'' she confirmed quietly.

''Her *real* father?''

Daniel, whose gaze had returned to his sleeping daughter, glanced up again. ''Yes.''

Chapter 9

Brenna seemed stunned. Then she rose from her chair. "I'll leave you two alone with her," she suggested. "Charisse, is there anything you need from home? I could fetch it for you…?"

"Um…maybe Kristy's Big Daddy Ted later, and Annabelle." Charisse got up, too, and said to Daniel, "I won't be long."

In the corridor Brenna turned to her. "You never said!"

"Kristy doesn't know," Charisse confessed. "Daniel's only here for a short time, and I didn't want her to meet her father and then have him take off into the wild blue yonder. But he's entitled to be here and I don't think they'd have let him in otherwise."

"He seems very fond of her."

"Yes. It's a problem."

"I suppose it could be," Brenna said slowly. "Look, if you think of anything else you want, ring and we'll bring it over. You might need things for yourself. Will you be all right now for a while?''

"Yes. You've been wonderful, Brenna. I'm sorry about dragging you out of bed and disrupting your Sunday morning—"

"Don't be silly! Anything we can do, just ask."

"Thank you." Charisse hugged her. "I don't know what I'd do without friends like you."

Daniel was still where she'd left him. When she came to stand beside him, he said, "Is it all right if I touch her?"

"Yes," Charisse assured him. "But don't wake her."

He fingered Kristy's damp, fine hair very gently, and she noticed his hand trembled. Involuntarily she slipped her own hand into his free one, and his fingers closed over hers in a bone-crushing grip. Then he turned to her blindly and his arms came about her and she slid hers about his waist, holding him as he was holding her, in a desperate mutual need for comfort and support.

I am not going to cry, Charisse promised herself fiercely. She needed to be strong for Kristy.

Daniel gradually eased his hold and guided her to the chairs that stood side by side. They sat down, his arm still about her shoulder, and he took one of her hands again and said, "Could she have picked it up at the concert? Was it too cold in the open air?"

"I don't think so. It doesn't matter where she got it, Daniel. And it may not be as serious as we...as we fear. We won't know until tomorrow."

"Tomorrow!" He sounded as if it were light-years away. Charisse felt that way, too. He said, "She was fine when I left."

"I know. It was so sudden, that's why I thought

maybe…but she doesn't have a rash. They said it's a pre-caution, really."

"She'll be all right, Charisse. She has to be."

His voice held such conviction that she actually believed him. Which was stupid, she knew. Some things were out of mortal hands, even hands as capable and comforting as Daniel's. But right now she badly needed someone to tell her everything was going to be all right. And Daniel was doing a very good job of it.

He continued to do so for the rest of the long, stressful day. Each time Kristy woke, fretful and peevish, he helped Charisse keep her occupied and even made her giggle a couple of times. When she lapsed back into sleep he fetched Charisse coffee and a snack and made her have them.

Charisse was told she could stay overnight on a mattress on the floor of Kristy's room.

"I'll have to phone Brenna," she said, "and ask her to bring some things for me."

Daniel took out his cell phone. "Use this."

Afterwards he went off to the ward's dayroom to make some calls of his own.

He didn't leave even at the end of the day, but said he'd spend the night in the public day room. Not that either of them slept much. Even if the nurses hadn't been constantly checking on Kristy, Charisse doubted if she could have slept properly, and several times she opened her eyes from a light doze to see Daniel's shadowy form at the other side of the bed. Sometimes she joined him and they sat side by side in the darkness, holding hands. She offered him the mattress, whispering, "I'll wake you if anything changes," but he shook his head silently and sat on.

When Charisse woke the following morning after at last falling into a real sleep, he was sitting by the bed again, unshaven and with his shirt half-open, watching Kristy. He stayed there while Charisse had a wash and changed, and when she returned he called his office.

"If you need to go," she murmured as he came back to Kristy's side, "it's all right."

After a moment he said reluctantly, "I should get a change of clothes, I guess. And call in at the office long enough to organise some essential paperwork and talk to a couple of people, but I'll be back."

When he returned, shaved and in fresh clothes but still looking hollow-eyed and haunted, she greeted him at the door of the ward, fell into his arms and burst into tears.

"Oh, God!" he said hoarsely. "What's happened?"

She looked up, and through the tears that blurred her eyes saw he'd gone sickly white, his face gaunt.

"It's all right," she sobbed. "She doesn't have it! Some kind of flu bug, they think. She was dehydrated and there was a bit of inflammation in her throat, but they've pumped her full of antibiotics and fluids and she's already looking better."

She realised he was gripping her shoulders hard, and said, "I'm sorry, I didn't mean to give you a fright." Scrubbing at her eyes with the back of one hand, she added, "I'm just so relieved."

His arm came around her shoulders and he pulled her to him again. "Thank God!" he said against her hair. She felt the huge sigh that shook his body. "Thank you, God!"

"I've been praying all night," she told him, her voice muffled against his shirt.

"Me, too." His hand was stroking her hair and it felt like heaven. "I've only just found Kristy and I was so afraid I was going to lose her. And you…" His hold tightened. "You've already lost everyone else. I kept telling myself fate couldn't be so cruel."

"We've been lucky this time." Someone came in

through the door and had to skirt around them. Charisse eased herself away from Daniel's reassuringly broad chest. "Thank you for being here, Daniel."

"I couldn't be anywhere else," he said. His hands captured her head, holding it gently while his thumbs wiped tears from her cheeks. Then he bent and kissed her. It was a soft, passionless kiss of comfort and promise, and the sweetness and tenderness of it shook her to the core. When he raised his head she stood staring at him, not wanting to move an inch for fear of breaking the spell.

A nurse spoke to them, and the moment passed. "The fever's come down nicely. It's just one of those nasty bugs that are going round. Doctor says you can take her home, but keep her warm and make sure she has lots of liquid, and he'll give you a prescription you can have filled at the hospital pharmacy before you leave. If you're worried at all, contact your own doctor."

"I must ring Brenna," Charisse said then. "May I borrow your phone again?"

Brenna sounded almost as relieved as Charisse felt. "That's wonderful news!" she said. "Is Daniel with you?"

"Yes, he says he'll take us home later."

"Good. Just give us a call if there's anything you'd like us to do for you."

Kristy was still flushed but she no longer complained of a headache, and her skin wasn't scorching hot as it had been. They bundled her up in the blanket Charisse had wrapped around her when she and Brenna had raced to the hospital, and Daniel carried her to his car.

When they arrived home he took the child in his arms again and followed Charisse to Kristy's room. Brenna, Charisse noticed, had changed the sheets, bless her. She pulled back the covers and Daniel carefully laid down his burden.

Charisse tucked her in, the teddy bear under the blankets beside her.

"Would you like a glass of orange juice?" she asked.

Kristy nodded. "And I want a story," she said.

"All right. After I've seen Daniel out I'll come and bring you some juice and read you a story."

"I don't want Daniel to go away," Kristy fretted.

"Darling, he has work to do. He can't stay too long." He'd already taken a lot of time off.

Tears welled in Kristy's eyes. "I want him to read me a story!"

"Kristy—" Normally she'd have nipped such behaviour in the bud, but Kristy was still sick and patience was obviously called for.

"I'll read you a story," Daniel volunteered. "Which one would you like?"

"The mouse book."

Charisse found the book on the bright red-painted shelves against the wall, leaving him sitting on the bed as she went to fetch the juice.

It was a small book, an old favourite that Kristy had been given for her third birthday, and by the time Charisse returned with a glass in her hand Daniel had almost finished it. She waited in the doorway until the story was over, then moved forward to give the glass to Kristy, helping her to sit up and drink it.

When the glass was drained Kristy ordered Daniel, "Read me another story."

"Kristy!" Charisse warned.

"Please," Kristy amended with a consciously winsome expression. "Read me the bear book."

Charisse looked at Daniel. "If you have to leave…"

But he shook his head. "It's okay. Give me the book."

She handed it to him, and took the glass back to the

kitchen. Obviously Kristy was feeling much better. She could only be thankful for that, although she foresaw a trying day or two while a fractious, imperious little madam wrung every ounce of credit out of her illness. And after that huge fright Charisse would find it hard not to allow her to get away with a certain amount of mayhem.

And there was the problem of Daniel. He'd been a tower of strength, but now Kristy was showing a definite dependence. What Charisse had most feared seemed to have happened all too quickly. The two of them had formed a bond, and Kristy was inevitably going to get hurt.

Not only Kristy. Her own feelings didn't bear examination. She rinsed the glass and refilled it, too tired to think clearly but knowing that once again her life had changed forever. If Daniel walked out of it tomorrow and never returned there was no going back to where she had been. He would live in her mind, in her heart, for the rest of her life.

Holding the glass, she stood staring out of the window, not even seeing the hedge that needed trimming again, the flowering flares of hibiscus, the old tree in the corner where the swing hung idle, waiting for Kristy.

Sighing, she turned and found a lemon in the fridge, squeezed some juice into the glass of water and stirred in a spoonful of sugar, then made her way back to the bedroom, stopping short in the doorway, her heart leaping into her throat.

The book Daniel had been reading from lay on the floor, but he still sat on the bed. And in his hand he held the picture that always stood on Kristy's dressing table, while she pointed and informed him, "That's my nana and that's my grandad, and that's my one mummy and *that's* my mummy too."

"You have two mummies?" He smiled down at her.

''Yes,'' she told him firmly, with a decisive nod.

Daniel studied the picture, then looked up at Charisse. ''Your sister was very like you,'' he said. ''You could be twins.''

''They *are* twins,'' Kristy informed him. ''Don't you *know* that?''

''No.'' He glanced at the photograph, then looked again at Charisse. ''You never told me.''

''I guess…the subject didn't come up,'' she said. Her skin felt cold, her temples damp.

Kristy coughed a couple of times, then whimpered, ''My throat still hurts, Mummy.''

''I know, honey.'' Charisse moved to her side, smoothing back her hair and noting that her temperature felt almost normal. ''I'll give you some more medicine for it soon.'' The next dose was due in an hour. She put the glass down on the dressing table. ''Do you think you could have another sleep now?''

''Stay here, Mummy, ple-ease.'' Kristy grabbed at her hand.

''I can let myself out.'' Daniel stood up and replaced the photograph. ''I'll come back later, okay?''

Charisse nodded, sinking down onto the bed.

''I'll bring dinner,'' Daniel promised.

''There's no need.''

''Please,'' he said. ''Let me, Charisse.''

She should be grateful. ''All right,'' she said. ''Thank you.''

''Fish and chips,'' Kristy suggested.

''You must be feeling better,'' Daniel commented, smiling down at her.

''I like fish and chips,'' she told him.

''Okay. Fish and chips it is.'' He switched his gaze to Charisse. ''Would you prefer oysters?''

She shook her head. "Anything's fine with me." She didn't expect to be very hungry anyway.

Soon after he'd left, Brenna knocked on the internal door and, when Charisse opened it, handed her a foil dish, still warm. "Thought you wouldn't feel like cooking," she said. "I saw Daniel leave. How is the little one?"

"Asleep now. Come in, Brenna, and thank you for this. If it's okay I'll keep it until tomorrow. Daniel's promised to bring dinner later."

"That's a nice thought." Brenna followed Charisse to the kitchen. She dropped her voice. "It's a bit of a surprise...him being Kristy's father."

"I'm sorry I didn't tell you before," Charisse said uncomfortably, putting away the casserole in the fridge. "Kristy doesn't even know yet."

"None of my business," Brenna said hastily. "You don't need to tell me anything you don't want to. And I won't spill the beans to Kristy."

Charisse cast her a grateful look. "Do you want a cup of coffee?"

"I'll make it—you look as though you could do with a cuppa and a sit-down. It's been rough, hasn't it?"

"It wasn't fun, but thank God she's going to be all right."

When they were both sitting at the table with coffee cups in their hands, Charisse asked tentatively, "Brenna, what would you do if you had a secret that someone had a right to know, but that might harm someone else in the long run?"

Brenna put down her cup. "This is about Kristy's father?" Without waiting for confirmation, she said, "I don't know what I'd do, frankly. I do know that some secrets are better kept to yourself. Unburdening onto someone who 'has a right to know' can make *you* feel better, but it could just hurt that person if they don't really need to know. If the other person is a child, then it's doubly important to be sure your motives are pure.''

''Pure?''

Brenna looked down at her coffee and picked up the cup again. ''Well, it's not the same thing, but when I was fifteen I found out my father had a girlfriend. Being at the self-righteous age, I decided my mother had a right to know, so I told her. She's never forgiven me.''

''I'm sorry. Your father…?''

''Oh, he forgave me, and she forgave *him*. But I'm the one she blames. She didn't want to know. Didn't want to have to deal with it.''

''You think she already knew?''

''Probably. And had decided to turn a blind eye. I just messed everything up and forced her to confront him. It caused a nasty row, and the repercussions went on forever.''

''It wasn't your fault. You may have made a mistake, telling her, but it was an honest one.''

Brenna shook her head. ''Maybe. Or maybe I wanted to make my parents miserable. They'd been—I thought—unreasonable about a boy I wanted to date. I'd sulked and pleaded and thrown tantrums and been generally unpleasant to live with. And then suddenly I had the means to pay them back. To make my father look like a hypocrite and cause my mother some grief. I can't say my intentions were all good. It was a pretty horrible thing to do.''

''You were only a child.''

''Oh, I'm not beating myself up over it anymore. But I am cautious about revealing other people's secrets now. And I didn't mean to go on about my teenage problems.

Your situation's quite different. I suppose I'm not much help.''

"But you are,'' Charisse assured her. "It's given me another perspective.''

How pure were her own motives? Daniel had asked her if she was jealous of him and she'd denied it. But maybe there was an element of jealousy in her reluctance to tell Kristy the truth about him.

When he got back she let him in quietly. "Kristy's asleep again,'' she told him as he handed her a well-wrapped, warm parcel.

"Will she really want fish and chips?'' he asked her, following her to the kitchen.

"I doubt it. She had soup earlier, but she didn't finish it. A little piece of fish won't hurt if she feels like it. It's just that fish and chips is a treat she doesn't often have.''

"I got oysters and some chicken pieces as well.''

He'd bought far too much, she discovered, unwrapping the parcel. "We'll never eat all this.''

"It'll keep. How are you feeling?''

"Me? I'm not the one who's sick.''

"You're the one who spent the last two nights with a sick child.''

"So did you—one night, anyway.'' She turned to get plates from the cupboard, pausing on the way back to the table to take knives and forks from a drawer.

"I'm used to broken shifts. Lack of sleep doesn't bother me too much.''

"Well, with a child you get used to broken nights. Not that this happens often, but when she was younger…''

He nodded. "I guess I missed all that.''

Charisse laid the table and then went to get a lemon from the refrigerator, as Daniel moved aside for her. He'd missed a lot, but that wasn't her fault, she reminded herself as she found the lemon. "Hand me a saucer, will you?"

She neatly sliced the lemon into quarters before placing it on the table, then waved Daniel to sit down. "Do you want bread?"

"You sit down. I'll get it," he offered, went to the bread bin on the counter and took butter from the fridge, placing both on the table, the sliced bread still in its plastic wrap. "It's not much, but a lot better than some meals I've had, believe me."

He made her laugh with stories of weird foods and eating habits in out-of-the-way places where he'd worked. Aware that he was determined to help her relax after the stressful time she'd had, Charisse was grateful.

She was hungrier than she'd thought. Helping herself to more chicken, she said, "This is delicious. Thank you for bringing it."

"It was no trouble." He finished what was on his plate and pushed it away. "Charisse—"

"Yes?" She looked up and put down her fork, because his expression was intent and probing and she knew he had something important to say.

"I'm not sure how to put this into words," he began. "But Kristy being so ill, and the thought that she might die—" He broke off there, apparently finding it difficult to continue.

Charisse's skin cooled, and she felt her heart beating in her chest. "Yes?" Her voice sounded forced.

"When I saw her lying there in the hospital, looking so sick and so little and helpless, I discovered something about myself."

"About...yourself?"

"I know you're doubtful about my commitment to Kristy, afraid that I'll leave her in the lurch when the novelty of having a child wears off. But you're wrong. You've got to understand, Charisse. Now that I've found my daughter, I'm not going to be able to go back to Australia without her.''

Chapter 10

"No!" Charisse said hoarsely. She pushed back her chair and got up. *"No!"* she repeated. Terror and a ghastly sensation of inevitability impeded her breathing. She'd seen this coming, had been dreading it since that fateful meeting in the supermarket, but now that the moment was here she found herself totally unprepared. "You can't do this. You promised you wouldn't hurt her."

"I won't! All I want—"

"You want Kristy!" Her voice rose despite herself. "You just said so."

"Yes, I do, of course I want her, she's my child, but—"

"Damn you. I won't let you do this to us, Daniel! You haven't changed a bit after all! Just for once can't you think of someone besides yourself?"

"I am!" He rose to his feet too. "Charisse—"

"No, you're not!" she disputed hotly. "Don't you realise what it will do to her, tearing her away from everything—everyone she knows? Altering her whole life for a selfish *whim?*''

''It's not a whim!''

''I'll fight you through every court there is,'' Charisse promised wildly. She would get the money for it if she had to sell her body to do it—or her soul. And somehow find a lawyer good enough to win. ''I'll never, never give Kristy up,'' she vowed. ''I don't *care* what your legal rights might be. No judge with any compassion or sense of justice would hand over a child to a father who'd never laid eyes on her until only a few weeks ago!''

''A few months, actually. And whose fault was that?'' Daniel demanded. ''I don't *have* too many legal rights, do I?'' His voice was harsh, his eyes dark with anger of his own. ''Because I was never offered the opportunity to claim them!''

The black tide of fear receded a little as common sense began to reassert itself. Biting back a renewed tirade, Charisse forced her brain into gear. Daniel didn't know what she knew. So far as he was concerned she held all the trumps—he'd just admitted it. Her heart thudding, she clamped her mouth shut and tried to open her mind.

Daniel leaned on the table, his fists clenched. ''I would never do anything to harm Kristy!'' His eyes still smouldered. ''And I deeply resent those accusations you just flung at me, Charisse.''

''You said—''

''I *said*—'' his voice overrode hers ''—I couldn't bear to return to Australia without my daughter. You didn't give me a chance to finish.''

Again the black dread threatened to overwhelm her. She shook it off, determined to keep a clear head. ''All right,'' she said shakily, suspicion in every taut line of her body. ''Go on.''

He straightened, his head held at an angle she could only see as arrogant, his mouth very determined and his eyes almost sea-green now and steady as they met hers. "I want you, too."

She could have sworn the room tilted. When it had righted itself, she said, "Me?"

"I want the three of us to be together—to be a family. Is it such a surprise?"

Maybe it shouldn't have been. If she hadn't been so obsessed with protecting Kristy she might have seen this coming.

Of course, it was impossible. There was no way she could agree. Everything was just too complex, too tangled. "I can't uproot Kristy and move to another country," she said flatly.

"It would be a big step to take," he admitted, "but I'm asking you to consider it. The trouble is, I'm contracted to the company in Perth for another eight months at least, and getting out of that would involve me in a legal wrangle that might keep me in Australia for months anyway, besides leaving me without a job. Would it be so terrible for you and Kristy to come back there with me? I take your point about uprooting her, but you'd be with her."

"And I'd still be there when you go swanning off to another part of the world for weeks and months at a time," she flashed resentfully. "You've worked it all out to your own satisfaction—to suit yourself and your lifestyle." The panic hadn't yet fully subsided, and fright still fuelled anger. "You get a daughter you can pick up and put down at will like an animated toy, and a free nanny thrown in for when you're off doing more important things."

Daniel flushed, his eyes flaring dangerously. "Cut me some slack, will you, Charisse? That isn't what I was thinking at all. I want to look after Kristy. And you. On my salary I can afford to do that very well. You won't even have to think about money.''

He must have guessed she'd had to think about it a great deal up until now. But she'd managed, and Kristy had never been deprived of necessities. ''Money isn't everything,'' she protested.

''I accept that, but it helps. I earn a very good salary and until now I've had only myself to spend it on. You could be very comfortable—you and Kristy.''

''You can't *buy* your daughter back, Daniel!''

She saw his chest lift with the deep breath he drew in. His mouth tightened. Then he said with deceptive quiet, ''You've been under a lot of strain so I'll ignore what you just said. But I warn you, another crack like that one—''

Charisse's head lifted. ''Don't threaten me!''

''Then don't goad me!''

They stood glaring at each other. Daniel took another deep breath. ''Let's discuss this sensibly—''

A sound from the bedroom caught Charisse's attention and she immediately brushed past him to the door.

By the time she reached Kristy's bedside he was right behind her. Kristy was tossing restlessly and whimpering.

''What is it, darling?'' Charisse murmured.

''Toilet.''

''Okay, I'll carry you.'' Charisse pushed back the bed-clothes and hoisted Kristy into her arms.

''Let me,'' Daniel said, but she shook her head, making for the bathroom.

''We're all right.'' She had an irrational fear of giving the child up to him even for a minute, as if he might spirit her away.

He was still there when they returned and she lowered Kristy to the bed. He stepped forward and pulled up the blankets, tucking them in securely.

"Daniel?" Kristy said sleepily. "You came back."

"Sure, sweetheart," he answered. "I brought you fish and chips too. Do you want some?"

"Not now. I want some tomorrow."

"Fine. You go to sleep now."

Charisse turned to the medicine bottle sitting on the dressing table and poured a dose. "Here, Kristy, have this first."

Kristy balked, turning away from her. "I don't like that medicine."

"It will help your throat."

"I don't *like* it!" She started to cry.

Kneeling by the bed, Charisse said, "Drink it down quickly and you won't notice the taste."

"I will so!"

"You can have a little drink afterwards."

"Orange," Kristy insisted then, sniffing pathetically.

Charisse turned to Daniel. "Would you mind…? In the fridge. I made some up this afternoon."

"Sure." He turned and headed for the kitchen.

Combining firmness and coaxing, Charisse managed to get the child to swallow the medicine, and by that time Daniel was standing by with the orange juice. He bent and helped Kristy drink while Charisse replaced the top on the medicine bottle; then she slipped into the bathroom to rinse the plastic measure.

When she came back Daniel was straightening, the empty glass in his hand. "Good girl," he said. "Do you think you can sleep again now? Your mummy's very tired from looking after you. She needs a good sleep, too."

"Will you stay with me then?" Kristy asked.

"If that's what you want."

"Mmm." Kristy snuggled down, holding her teddy.

He'd made her dependent on him, Charisse realised,

watching him settle on the edge of the bed and take the trusting hand that Kristy extended to him. He'd infiltrated their lives and now he wanted to disrupt them.

Daniel glanced up at her. "I'll stay until she's dropped off again."

But Kristy whimpered, "I want you to stay all night."

"Kristy," Charisse said, "Daniel can't stay."

"Yes I can," he argued. "As long as Kristy needs me. I'll sleep on the sofa."

"You can't!"

His lifted brows made it clear he thought her objection absurd.

"It's too small," she said.

"I'll manage."

"*Please,* Mummy? I want Daniel to stay."

Kristy sounded as though she was getting ready to cry again. Normally she knew crying wouldn't help her get her own way, but normally she wasn't so sick.

"We have a camp bed," Charisse said grudgingly, "that Kristy's friends sometimes use. I'll put it up in the sitting room for you."

"A mattress on the floor will do," Daniel said. He turned back to Kristy. "I'll be right next door all night, okay?"

Charisse stalked out of the room. They didn't need her. In the kitchen she began viciously clearing the remains of the meal, scrunching up the greaseproof wrappings and clattering dishes together, guiltily conscious that, yes, she *was* jealous, and that it was a totally unworthy and despicable emotion.

And mixed with it were other emotions, even more complex and unwelcome. Dimly she was aware that at the basis of her fury with Daniel was something very personal—a suspicion that he was manipulating her feelings for him to get his own way. To get Kristy. She recalled his friend Mac admitting that he wouldn't want to be in the way when Daniel wanted something. And Julia's warning.

Julia had known him for a long time, and didn't trust him.

There was all that time when his sexual interest had seemed to abruptly switch off after he found out about Kristy. Then he'd kissed her after the night club, and again the next evening with passion and something that was almost anger.

Yet she'd melted in his arms like ice cream on a summer day, totally and completely capitulated. Let him know he had only to crook a finger and she was his for the asking, she reflected scorchingly as she dumped a pile of dishes into the sink and began running hot water on them, reaching for the detergent. And she'd blurted out exactly why he'd been left high and dry in Perth, why he had never been told he was a father. For love, she'd said when he'd asked her what it was all about. *It was about loving you.*

It had seemed to pole-axe him. He'd gone away then, obviously rethinking their whole relationship. .

Was that when he had decided that he could persuade her to let him have Kristy, and that it might be a good idea to take her along as well?

It would beat trying to obtain his daughter through time-consuming and expensive litigation that he might not even win—and that could do irreparable harm to Kristy and to her relationship with him.

No, surely he couldn't be so devious.

But he knew Charisse wouldn't let Kristy go without a fight. And he saw no reason not to marry the mother of his child. After all, he liked Charisse and he'd left her in no doubt that he wanted to make love to her. She would be a kind of bonus. The ideal solution from his point of view.

And why should she want more? At least, as he'd said about that time in Perth, he was being honest.

If she was honest, the prospect of sharing her life with Daniel was infinitely alluring. If only…

She turned off the tap and began scrubbing at a plate. Everything had been so much simpler before that fateful meeting. Why had Daniel had to be in the supermarket at that particular time?

If she'd had the sense to stay away from him after that she wouldn't be in this dilemma now. And Kristy would be safe and happy as she had been before. And unknowing. Never having had the chance to meet her father.

Her hands stilling, Charisse watched the bubbles of detergent settle and pop one by one. There was the crux of it. She hadn't had the right to deprive Kristy of that.

And did she have the right to refuse Daniel's wish to have his daughter with him?

Never had she missed her sister and her parents so much.

What would Gabrielle have done? What would her parents advise if they were here? The piercing grief and loneliness that had attacked her less often as time passed filled her without warning, and she clenched her teeth tightly and shut her eyes against its impact.

It will pass, she told herself, weathering it as best she could. It always passes.

Then Daniel's hands were on her shoulders and he said, "What is it, Charisse?"

Shuddering, she opened her eyes. In the window over the sink she could see their shadowy reflections like a couple of strangers—a woman with a pale face and tragic eyes, and the man behind her, his head inclined toward her in concern, his hands cupping her shoulders protectively.

It was a tempting picture. A seductive one, even. For so long she had been the protector, the one who had to look after Kristy, who had to be strong and dependable, often putting aside her own needs and wants because Kristy's needs must come first. Trying to be a good parent although she'd been totally unprepared for such a huge responsibility, frightened at her own inadequacy, missing terribly the wisdom and experience her own parents had brought to Kristy's first two years, and with a great gaping hole in her life left by their deaths and that of her sister.

"What were you thinking about?" Daniel asked her. "Your family?"

"How did you know?" Astonishment made her turn round, and his hands slid away from her, leaving her feeling oddly vulnerable. She clutched at the counter behind her to support herself.

He said slowly, "You looked so…forlorn."

"I'm not forlorn." It sounded spineless. And she couldn't afford to be spineless. There was far too much at stake. She swung about and went on with her task, lifting a plate onto the drainer.

"Not usually," Daniel agreed, moving to lean on the counter so he could see her down-bent face. "You seem very self-sufficient. I suppose having a child to care for has made you that way." He lifted a strand of hair away from her eyes. "I can't believe you never told me you were a twin."

No, she couldn't afford to be spineless. *Wake up, brain.* Feeling her way, she said, "Are you sure I never mentioned it?"

"I knew you had a sister, of course, but identical twins…" He shook his head. "Even Kristy seems to have had difficulty telling you apart. When your sister died you must have felt as if a part of yourself had gone."

"It still feels that way," she acknowledged huskily, surprised by his insight. "Even though—"

"What?" he asked as she hesitated there, concentrating on rinsing soap from a glass.

"We tried not to be too interdependent." At least she had. Asserting their individuality had never seemed quite as important to Gabrielle. She put the glass on the drainer. "Of course we looked the same and we shared a lot of likes and dislikes. We never dressed identically and hardly ever chose clothes together, though sometimes we wore each other's, and quite often we bought the same thing when we were apart. But our personalities were different. People don't realise."

At school people who couldn't tell them apart would hail either of them by calling, "Hey, twin!" or "Twinnie!" Charisse had hated that. Gabrielle had thought it a bit of a giggle—she was the one who had sometimes persuaded Charisse that it was fun to swap identities and fool people.

Daniel said, "I had the impression Gabrielle was a couple of years younger."

"She... I told you that?"

"Not in so many words, but you said she was younger and I definitely thought there were more than a few minutes between you."

Sometimes it had seemed like that. Charisse shrugged, attacking the last greasy plate. "I don't know where you got that idea. I don't want to talk about it anymore. Do you mind?"

"I didn't mean to upset you." Daniel took a tea towel from its rail. "You've had enough worry and trauma in the past couple of days."

"Yes." A little stiffly, she added, "I appreciate your help. You've been wonderful with Kristy."

"She's my child, too," he said. "Charisse—"

She could have done without the reminder. Hauling on

the plug, she let the water out of the sink with a noisy gurgle and turned to dry her hands. "I'll fix your bed."

"You don't need to go to that trouble."

"It's no trouble." She left him drying the last of the dishes while she pulled the camp bed from the hall cupboard, and was setting it up when he joined her.

"I told you there's no need—"

"I've almost finished." She unfolded the metal frame to jerk it into place—and caught her finger, giving a gasping squeal of pain.

"What have you done?" He grabbed her hand as she instinctively made to put the abused finger in her mouth, and inspected the damage. It looked pinched and red.

Unexpectedly he lifted it to his own mouth and sucked.

A jolt of pure sexual energy stiffened her body and made her lips part with shock. "Don't!" she choked, dragging her hand away.

"It's what you were going to do, isn't it?"

She couldn't now. Folding the bruised finger inside her other hand, she held it tightly. "You didn't need to do it for me."

"I wanted to." His eyes were hooded but gleaming. "I enjoyed it—didn't you?"

"It was...it was inappropriate."

Daniel grinned. "Big word," he murmured admiringly. "Sucking on a hurt actually does make it less painful— something to do with providing another stimulus and blocking the pain message out of the brain."

"Is that so?" But her sarcasm sounded weak. He'd certainly provided her with another stimulus. For a second she'd forgotten entirely about the pain, swamped in equally intense pleasure.

"I saw it on TV once," he told her. "It's true."

"You can't believe everything you see..."

"On television? No, I don't. But it seemed authentic."

"I'll get you some sheets and a duvet."

She went off to fetch them, and after removing them from the shelf stood there, forcing a couple of deep breaths into her lungs, before returning with the bedclothes.

He took them from her and insisted on doing the job. "I'm sorry to put you to this bother, but I couldn't turn Kristy down."

"If you're going to be a real father to her," she advised him, leaning against the door frame and folding her arms, "you'd better learn."

He glanced up from tucking a sheet under the thin foam mattress. "This is not the right time, is it? She's sick."

"No," she admitted. "But you can't expect that she'll always be sweet and biddable when she's well."

He shook out the other sheet. He'd made a bed before, she thought. His movements were sure and economical, and he mitred the corners with army precision before throwing the duvet on top. "I do know that no child is an angel. And I think I'm capable of exerting discipline without going overboard about it. After all, I'm used to handling teams of men."

"It's not the same," she told him. The remark gave her pause though. Administration wasn't the only field that demanded accountability and care. His vaunted reluctance to accept responsibility for other people didn't apply in his work. Maybe she should have taken that into account before. "I don't suppose your labourers try to influence you by bursting into tears or giving you a kiss and saying they love you best in all the world."

He laughed. "Kristy does that?"

"It can be difficult to resist."

"But you do."

"If what she wants isn't going to be good for her. And I don't encourage her to use those methods."

"I'll try to remember that."

Charisse came away from the wall. "We'll have to work something out."

"Yes, we will," he agreed. "You didn't seem impressed with my suggestion."

"That Kristy and I up sticks and move to Australia?" Charisse shook her head. "Taking her away from everything, everyone she knows—"

"Except you. And me. Her parents. Would that be so terrible? Lots of children don't live in one place all their lives. My family had dozens of shifts. My mother went wherever she could find work and cheap rent. We made new friends, learned about new places."

"You weren't in a different country," Charisse protested.

"True. They do speak English in Australia though, with a slightly different accent. Surely the most important stabilising influence in a child's life is people, not places."

That was no doubt true. And it was true that plenty of well-adjusted people had moved frequently as children.

Maybe she was being selfish. He hadn't suggested separating Kristy from Charisse, wrenching them apart. This wasn't her very worst nightmare, after all. If she were to look at this rationally it actually did make some sense.

"When my contract runs out," Daniel offered, "I could hunt for a job here in New Zealand if you don't like it over there, or Kristy isn't happy. I'd be lucky to find anything that would pay as well though, and with a family to look after…"

A family he didn't want to leave while he fulfilled the rest of his contract. Reluctantly she couldn't help but see his point of view.

"I know you're fond of this place," he said quietly, looking about the room. He hesitated. "I don't mean to sound callous, but Charisse, what do you have to keep you here now? Your family's...gone, and you have no career ties. I know you don't have a lot of money..."

She looked about them, at the wallpaper that still showed faint signs of Kristy's two-year-old artwork when she'd run amok with crayons, the sofa that sagged slightly in the middle, and the cheap mat covering a bald patch on the carpet. Through the doorway she could see a corner of the kitchen cupboard, in need of a fresh coat of paint, and part of the fridge, stuck in an inconvenient corner too far away from the work counter.

It might not look much to Daniel but this was her home, where she'd been happy as a child and where Kristy was happy now.

"I have a life!" she said. "And so does Kristy. A home, friends and neighbours who've been kind to us. I couldn't have survived without them after my parents and Gabrielle died. We might not have much money but Kristy's secure here, among people I can count on for help if I need it. People like Brenna and Baz."

He blinked, apparently at a loss for a moment or two. "And they're important to you," he said slowly. "I guess I hadn't thought about all that."

He wouldn't have. Relationships had never meant as much to him as his career, and he'd never been in dire need of help and advice and emotional support as she had. "It's *very* important," she told him. "And you expect me to leave it all behind without a thought and follow you to Australia on your say-so, because you've discovered you like having a daughter to spoil. You have no idea what it's like being a long-term parent, needing people you know will be there when you need them. Like Brenna, getting out of bed at an ungodly hour to take Kristy and me to the hospital.''

"You could have called me."

"Brenna was closer. And if she hadn't been here it would have been quicker to get a taxi, and hang the cost."

"If we're together," Daniel said, "I'll be closest."

"Not if you're on a job, you won't be!"

"I've thought about that. You didn't give me a chance to finish what I was saying before. I could probably get myself moved into an administrative job so I wouldn't be travelling all the time."

"But you'd hate that," Charisse objected. "You've already turned it down."

Daniel shrugged. "Plenty of men endure a bit of boredom for the sake of their families."

And he'd be willing to do that? Could she believe him? It seemed such a complete turnaround. "You might not be able to stand it. How do I know you won't get tired of being a daddy when the initial thrill wears off? And then where will we be—Kristy and I?"

That was mean and harsh, but surely realistic, she justified herself. He was shooting down her reasons for refusal one by one. Soon she'd have no more arguments left.

Daniel's eyes darkened. "It won't wear off," he said with conviction. "I'm in this for the long haul, Charisse. Forever. You seem to believe I have trouble making any sort of commitment."

"Do you blame me?"

He looked at her broodingly. "It's true that five years ago I wasn't looking for a permanent relationship, but things have changed since then. *I've* changed. And so have you. A lot. You grew up, you said. Well, can't you give me credit for doing a bit of maturing, too?"

Charisse hesitantly opened her mouth, but before she

could speak he went on, "I was intrigued to meet you again, and to find the old attraction hadn't died, that it was more potent than ever. From the first I badly wanted to make love to you again and assumed it would happen in time, but further than that..." He stopped there and gave a small shrug. "I admit I hadn't thought it through that far until recently. When I saw you'd come looking for me I knew that it wasn't all over for us after all and it gave me a hell of a buzz, but I was prepared to take things as they came and see what developed. Then I discovered Kristy, and later you told me you'd been in love with me in Perth. That was a bit of a bombshell."

Charisse moistened her lips. "Before you met Kristy I thought you'd walk away."

He shook his head. "I can't walk away from you, Charisse. I thought I still could, when you told me to leave after I kissed you. I found I couldn't turn my back without one more attempt at getting through to you. Only Kristy was here and...a lot's happened since then."

Yes, it had. He'd discovered his daughter, and Kristy was the reason he'd been unable to walk away after all.

"I hope to God you can forgive me," he said, "for being so obtuse and self-centred in Perth that I didn't notice your feelings had changed."

"I suppose," she conceded, "there were faults on both sides." She'd misjudged Daniel—he wasn't the lightweight she'd always assumed he was. Even five years ago he couldn't have been as shallow as she'd believed.

"This time I'm serious," he said. "And just so there's no misunderstanding, when I suggested you and Kristy come and live with me, I wasn't talking about a loose arrangement. This time I'm asking for a long-term promise. The real thing, for keeps."

"What do you mean?" What other plans did he have in mind that might complicate things even further?

"This isn't the way I meant to broach the subject," he said, giving her a rueful half smile, "but we sort of got off on the wrong foot before. And I'm sorry if it seems unromantic after all we've gone through but...when I said I wanted us to be a family, I was asking you to marry me."

Chapter 11

In seconds Charisse ran the gamut of emotions from astonished hope to adrenaline-rushing panic to black despair. "I…can't marry you!"

"Can't?" His expression went wooden, then bewildered. "Why not?"

She couldn't even begin to tell him. The reasons were myriad and mixed and increasingly seemed insurmountable.

"I don't understand," he said when she didn't answer. "You said you loved me. You had my baby."

"That was *then!*" she said hurriedly, her brain whirling.

She was very tired, Charisse realised, trying to arrange her thoughts logically. What was happening felt surreal, as if she were caught in a dream world where nothing made sense. She put a hand to her eyes and then dropped it, but the room seemed to sway.

Daniel came round the camp bed and his hands lighted on her arms, stroking them. "You're exhausted. I won't press you for an answer right now. Why don't you go to bed? If Kristy wakes I'll deal with her if I can, and otherwise I'll call you.''

''If Kristy wakes I'll hear her.''

''Then don't get up unless we need you.''

Could she do that? Lie in bed when Kristy was calling for her?

But maybe Kristy would call for Daniel instead. And after they told her who he was, maybe next time she needed someone she would call for her daddy….

Everything would change.

''Go to bed,'' Daniel urged her, and his lips brushed her forehead. ''Sleep on it.''

Yes, that would be best. In the morning her mind would be clearer and she'd be better able to see if there was a way out of this maze of deception and fear.

She slept in. It was years since she'd done that, and when she threw on her thin old robe over the T-shirt she wore at night and stumbled to Kristy's room the bed was empty.

Her heart leaped straight to her throat before she heard voices and went flying to the kitchen, only to stop short in the doorway.

Kristy was seated at the table with a plate in front of her, a fork clutched in her fist. She wore a dressing gown and slippers and was rosy-cheeked and clear-eyed, although her hair was unbrushed and tangled. And Daniel, unshaven but otherwise looking remarkably fresh, stood by the toaster, a couple of pieces of bread in his hands.

''She got out of bed,'' he said, ''and told me she wanted breakfast. I thought if she was hungry I should feed her.''

Charisse leaned on the door frame to steady herself. ''Fish and chips?'' She looked at the plate in front of Kristy.

"I heated it." Daniel sounded slightly defensive. "It's what she asked for."

Charisse pushed back her tumbled hair. "You *must* be feeling better," she said to Kristy, and walked over to put a hand to the smooth, childish forehead. Slightly warm, maybe. But certainly the raging fever had gone.

"Better, Mummy." Kristy lifted her face for a kiss.

"Can I make you some coffee?" Daniel asked.

"Thanks," Charisse said. "I'll go and have a shower and put some clothes on." She was suddenly conscious of her dishevelled state, straight out of bed. She hadn't even fastened the robe, and it had fallen open when she ran to the kitchen, displaying the faded T-shirt and the length of her legs.

"Pity," Daniel said. "You always look luscious in the mornings, like that."

Charisse met his eyes and felt her heart thump. She pulled the robe across herself and backed to the door.

When she was dressed in jeans and a loose shirt and had combed her hair, she followed the smell of coffee back to the kitchen and Daniel handed her a steaming cup.

Kristy had left her half-eaten fish and chips, and was busy lining up all her stuffed toys on the sofa, talking to them in a continuous patter.

"An amazing recovery." Daniel joined Charisse at the table with a cup of his own. He pushed a plate of toast toward her.

"In a day or two she'll be back to normal. You didn't give her any medicine?"

Daniel shook his head. "Should I have?"

"It's okay, I'll do it soon. Don't you have to go to work?"

He consulted his watch. "I should, shortly." With a hint of reservation, he said, "Will you think over what I asked you last night? If I can get back here this evening, maybe you'll have had time.''

She was cowardly enough to welcome the few hours' respite. But because she desperately needed to know, she asked, ''What if I still believe Kristy's better off as things are?''

His face took on a determined cast, his eyes darkening. ''We'll work it out, Charisse. Somehow I'll find a way.''

Charisse thought again of the kindergarten child who was shunted between homes weekly, of the social worker saying some cases required the judgement of Solomon. Daniel turned his coffee cup, studying it, then looked up at her. ''Why don't you and Kristy come over to Perth with me anyway—call it a holiday. If you like it you can stay, and if it doesn't work out…well, we could cross that bridge should it ever come up. After all, you loved the place before.''

Charisse saw the opening, knew she should take it, but her heart failed her and she retreated, framing her reply carefully. ''Living there with a child would be quite different from visiting as a young single.''

''Granted. But it's not a bad place to bring up a family, and the climate's great. I could sell the apartment and buy a house out of the city centre—someplace where there'd be other families, children for Kristy to play with. I think we could be happy there. And if you're not—or Kristy's not—I promise I'll bring you home again. Just say you'll think it over while I'm gone, okay?''

She'd have a job thinking of anything else. Slowly she nodded. ''Yes, I will.''

The cell phone in his pocket burred, and he excused himself to answer it. She could hear his voice in the next room—terse, impatient.

Folding the phone into his pocket as he came to the door

again, he said, "Something's gone wrong at the site." He had picked up his jacket and hooked it over his shoulder by one finger, hesitated and looked at her apologetically.

"You have to go, then," Charisse said.

"Will you be all right?"

"Of course."

His eyes searched hers. Slowly he closed the space between them, raised a hand and curved it about her nape, an explicit question in his eyes. "While you're thinking things over, remember this," he said when she didn't attempt to pull away, and then he bent his head to kiss her.

And she let him. More than that, she returned the kiss with eager abandon, her lips parting beneath his persuasion, her body subtly leaning toward his. His mouth moved over hers, seductive and frankly arousing, and then his hand was on her waist, clamping her against him, while the kiss deepened and his hand slid from her nape to the front of her shirt, and cradled her breast in its warmth.

Charisse's response was instantaneous and shocking. Her whole body tensed and flooded with sudden heat, her blood singing.

And then she heard Kristy's clear young voice demanding, "Why are you kissing my mummy too?"

Charisse jerked away in reaction, but Daniel let her go quite slowly before turning to Kristy, who was standing just inside the doorway. "I like kissing her," he said calmly. "Do you mind?"

Kristy thought a moment, then shook her head. "So do I like kissing her, but not like that!"

Daniel said gravely, "Grown-ups sometimes kiss differently."

"Like mummies and daddies."

He gave Charisse a rueful look and returned to Kristy. "That's exactly right."

"Are you going to be my new daddy and stay with us?"

Charisse caught her breath. Daniel gave her an unreadable look, and she said quickly, "Kristy, Daniel lives in Australia. Remember, I explained to you he's got to go home sometime."

Kristy nodded, looking crestfallen. "My one daddy lives in Australia," she told Daniel. "And I haven't *never* seen him!"

The tragic tone of the last pronouncement would normally have made Charisse smile, but at this moment it made her profoundly uneasy. And Daniel looked stricken. When he turned back to Charisse, there was accusation in his eyes, but to her great relief he remained silent.

Quickly Charisse said, "Daniel's going now, Kristy."

Kristy turned to him. "Why do you have to go away?"

"I have to work," he told her. "I'll come back as soon as I can."

"When?"

"I can't promise, but maybe tonight." He looked up at Charisse.

"Say thank you to Daniel for staying," Charisse instructed.

"Thank you," Kristy said, holding up her arms for him to swing her into an embrace. She kissed his cheek, then wriggled down. "You dropped your jacket," she pointed out, and picked it up for him, gathering it with some difficulty into her rounded arms.

"Thank you, Kristy." Daniel took it from her and slung it over his shoulder again. He ruffled her hair with his free hand. "See you."

Kristy skipped beside him as he went to the door. Charisse watched it close behind him and remembered she had to give Kristy another dose of medicine. That accomplished, she made the beds and straightened the kitchen, firmly vetoing Kristy's desire to play outside, because a cold wind was whipping about the trees and shrubs. Instead she took out some puzzles kept for just such occasions.

As she'd expected, Kristy was fractious and sometimes whiny, demanding help with the puzzles and then curling up on Charisse's lap, although denying any need for an extra sleep. She had half a sandwich at lunchtime and afterwards became heavy-eyed and lethargic, and Charisse put her to bed over only a token protest.

While Kristy slept Charisse sat on the sofa, absently smoothing a stuffed rabbit's ears, and tried to come to some sensible decision.

One of the kindergarten mothers phoned to discuss preparations for a fund-raising fair and check why Kristy hadn't been to a session that week, and Charisse told her about Kristy's illness.

Later the woman came round with a toddler in tow to deliver a get-well card made by some of Kristy's playmates. Accepting Charisse's invitation, she came inside, the toddler perched on her hip, and stayed to chat for an hour.

Soon after her visitor left, Daniel phoned. Just hearing his voice made her heart lift in the most absurd way. "How's Kristy?" he asked. "And you?"

"Kristy's sleeping again, but she's lots better. And there's nothing wrong with me. Now that I know she's going to be okay, I'm fine."

"Thank heaven for that. All hell's broken loose at the dam site."

"You don't need to worry about us, Daniel. We're not your responsibility."

"We'll talk about that when I get back," he said. "I'm not sure at this stage when that might be. You've got the number of my cell phone. Call me if you need me."

Charisse didn't answer that. If she needed him, he could hardly come running while he had a problem at the dam.

She'd weathered all sorts of crises before without his help, and she probably would again.

"I'll let you know as soon as I'm back," he promised. "Give Kristy my love."

"Yes," she said. She would do that.

When Kristy woke she wanted to know where he was, and Charisse explained that he'd had to return to work but that he'd sent his love.

"Will he come back tomorrow?" Kristy wanted to know.

"He isn't sure yet. But soon." He'd certainly be back, and wanting his answer from Charisse.

Instead he phoned, the reception fuzzy and indistinct, to check that Kristy was still on the mend and to tell Charisse, "There's a major problem here. The excavators have come across an unexpected soft spot in what should have been solid ground, and now it's raining. It may be a few days before I get back to Auckland. How are things with you?"

"Fine, and even if they weren't, I can cope. I always have."

"Yes," he said. "I know." At least he didn't stress that if she'd had to do so alone it had been her own choice.

Overnight it rained in Auckland, a downpour made worse by the fierce wind. In the morning it was still pouring and Kristy, much better but restless at her continued incarceration in the house, was difficult to deal with. Charisse was relieved that after lunch she went to sleep on the sofa, wrapped in a blanket.

When the phone rang Charisse ran to answer it.

"Is anything wrong?" Daniel's voice demanded. "You sound…odd."

"I just raced to get to the phone," she explained. "Kristy's sleeping." Peeking through the doorway, she could see the little girl hadn't stirred.

"Sorry. How is she?"

"Much better, only it's raining hard and we can't get out of the house."

"Here, too. It's causing us a hell of a lot of trouble."

"You won't be coming back here yet, then."

"I wish I could be."

It might be as well that he wasn't. When he was about, her mind tended to go on holiday while her emotions took over. And she really needed to be able to get a few things straight in her head before he returned. "How's the dam?"

"In trouble," Daniel answered grimly. "It's a race against time and the weather. We'll be working round the clock."

"I'll tell Kristy you rang," she promised.

"Yes, do that and—hang on a minute." He broke off and she could hear a muffled conversation, then he said quickly, "I have to go. Take care."

Charisse often missed the television news. But tonight she had switched on the set so Kristy could watch the comedy programme that preceded it, and when the headlines began she perched on the arm of the sofa where Kristy was huddled in a blanket, caught by mention of the dam site where Daniel was working.

The rain had begun to ease in Auckland, but apparently it was still pouring down there. A TV journalist wearing yellow oilskins and a hard hat stood under an umbrella, reporting that work on the giant dam had been halted while engineers inspected a newly excavated area that they feared was unstable.

The heavy rain, he explained, had further complicated matters, and workers were labouring in the dark and in filthy conditions. This could put the whole project back by months.

"There's Daniel!" Kristy pointed excitedly at the screen.

He had appeared on camera, and tersely gave the reporter a rundown in layman's language of the problem. Then the picture switched to another man who was in overall charge of the project, talking about containment of costs, and saying that he hoped to keep the delay minimal.

Charisse made a point of watching the late news, too, after Kristy was in bed, fast asleep and looking perfectly healthy.

The studio presenter soberly read an item just to hand that there'd been a mud slide at the site of the new dam and several men were believed to have been caught under it. No information was available.

"Oh, God!" Charisse raised horrified hands to her face. "Daniel!"

It felt like a scream but came out as a whisper. "Oh, my God," she prayed. "Please let Daniel be all right."

The phone. She could phone him. She ran, her fingers trembling as she dialled. A calm recorded voice informed her that the mobile phone she had called was either out of range or turned off.

She tried other numbers—the office in Auckland, the firm he was working with, the number of his flat. Nobody answered. What about his friend Mac? He used to work with Daniel. Maybe he'd know someone…

She hunted through the phone book for MacDonalds and found three and a half pages of variations. She didn't know which spelling Mac used. Mac was a nickname, of course. She had no idea of his first name or where he lived, and she could hardly ring every one of the MacDonalds in the phone book at this hour. Besides, if she was using the line and Daniel tried to contact her he wouldn't get through.

She stood with her forehead against the wall, thinking, coming up blank. There was nothing she could do but wait.

Eventually she went to bed, switched on the radio alarm clock that had been her father's, and lay awake listening for further news.

She learned that rescue teams had been sent in, but for fear of further landslides everyone else had been removed from the area.

Then if Daniel was all right why hadn't he called her? And why was his phone out of commission?

Chapter 12

Her stomach churning, Charisse tried to listen to the music following the bulletin, telling herself that Daniel *was* all right. He must be. No one had mentioned his name as being among those trapped, possibly killed.

But then no names had been mentioned. She wouldn't be the only one waiting and dreading and hoping through this long, long night. Other women, families, were in the same horrible predicament.

Or maybe not. Maybe wives—relatives—were being kept advised of what was happening, not wholly reliant on public radio bulletins.

Charisse was neither a wife nor a relative. She had no formal claim on Daniel and no one would think to alert her if he was in danger.

She couldn't even get there, drive through the dark and the rain to be on the spot—supposing her battered old car would have made the journey—not with Kristy to look after. All she could do was pray.

She dozed fitfully with the radio still on, and got up at dawn when the announcer told her that the rescue operation was severely hampered by the weather conditions and the possibility of further slides. Three men were believed trapped inside a temporary building under mud and rubble. It was hoped the building might have partially withstood the onslaught, giving them a chance of survival overnight.

There was still no response from Daniel's phone.

Maybe his brother had been told something. She got a number from directory service, but when she rang it the call went unanswered. She didn't know if that meant anything or not.

At eight, eight-thirty and nine o'clock she tried the Auckland office again, and at last a woman with a harried manner listened to her plea for information and enquired if she was a relative.

Charisse said no, but couldn't the woman just tell her if Daniel was one of the men trapped?

"I suppose that can't hurt," the woman admitted cautiously. "No, that name isn't one of them. But everyone down there is involved in the rescue."

"Thank you." Charisse replaced the receiver with shaking fingers, tension draining away in a wave of relief.

Of course the rescuers were still at risk, but she tried not to think about the possibility of another slip. And surely they'd be extra cautious now?

The weather outside had totally changed, the day summery and clear and the leaves on the lemon tree and the shrubs bordering the garden shiny and clean. Kristy ran out to play and Charisse didn't even try to stop her. Opening the fridge, she realised it was almost empty, and the remaining milk had begun to smell suspicious. They would have to go to the dairy.

Kristy skipped alongside her as if she'd never been ill at all, chattering happily.

Looking down at her, Charisse felt a deep pang of regret and foreboding. Supposing Daniel had been in that hut when the mud slide hit, and supposing—she flinched inwardly—supposing he hadn't survived. And Kristy had never known who he was.

It didn't bear thinking of.

Unusually, she bought Kristy an ice-cream cone, and on impulse splurged on a bag of chicken pieces, even more expensive at the small shop than in a supermarket.

Every time the telephone rang she jumped to answer it, her heart hammering. There were several calls, but none from Daniel.

And then, as she was preparing Kristy's bath before bedtime, the bell shrilled again. She leaped up and then stopped to hurriedly turn off the taps so there was no chance of Kristy burning herself with hot water, all the time praying, "Don't hang up, don't hang up, don't…"

"Can I get in the bath?" Kristy asked.

"Yes, all right," Charisse answered. "But be careful." And then she ran to the phone, lifted the receiver, took a shaking breath and said, "Hello?"

"Charisse."

"Daniel!" The hallway darkened, spots swam before her eyes and she sank down against the wall to sit on the carpet. "Daniel."

She closed her eyes dizzily, and said again, "Daniel."

"Charisse, are you all right?"

"Am *I* all right?" she repeated. "Yes. I was worried sick about you all night!"

"You were?"

He sounded both surprised and pleased, and reaction

made her sharp. "Well, what do you expect," she demanded shrilly, "when the news was full of the fact that a hillside fell on the dam and I knew you were there, and you weren't answering your phone!"

"I was with the rescue team and I switched off the phone because I couldn't afford the distraction."

"Couldn't you at least have let me know you were all right?" she snapped.

There was a surprised silence and she heard, with the ear that was automatically attuned to the sound, Kristy splashing in the bath.

"I'm sorry," Daniel said finally, and she realised he was tired, his voice slow and indistinct, not just blurred by the imperfect cell phone reception. "I'm sorry, Charisse. Really. It never occurred to me you'd be worried. As a matter of fact I did try to call you a couple of times earlier on. The first time the phone was engaged, and then later there was no reply."

She'd been trying to find out if he was safe, and later she'd been at the shop. And that was a bit late, anyway. "One phone call last night would have helped," she said, wanting to shout at him.

"I thought you'd be asleep. You needed an early night, and I didn't want to wake you."

She swallowed her fury. Maybe she was being unreasonable. After all, what claim did she have on him? And he had tried—if not hard enough. "Did you find the men?" she asked.

"Yes. They've just been taken away by ambulance. Two are injured but they should be okay. The other one seems fine but they've put him in for observation. Thank God we got them out in time."

"I'm glad," she said coldly. "Now I have to go. Kristy's in the bath and I don't like to leave her for too long."

But after she'd hung up she sat slumped against the wall for minutes longer, listening to the vigorous sounds of Kristy enjoying her bath, and taking several calming breaths before she went into the bathroom.

Daniel didn't get back until Sunday. He phoned at midday and said, "We've worked like mad to stabilise the site and I'll have to be back there again tomorrow. I'll snatch a couple of hours' sleep, and then is it okay if I come round?"

"Yes. Have you eaten lunch?"

"Thanks, I've had something. I'll be there later this afternoon."

She was on tenterhooks until he arrived, and when she opened the door to him all she could think about was how wonderful he looked despite his recent lack of sleep. There were faint signs of strain about his eyes but, freshly shaved and casually dressed, he could have stepped out of a magazine cover, the epitome of a rugged, sexy male.

Kristy ran to him and he hugged her, told her she looked much better, and then put her down, his attention going back to Charisse. "Have *you* got over it?" he asked, his eyes searching her face.

"I told you, I'm fine." She turned away. "Can I make you a cup of coffee?"

But Kristy was clamouring for his attention, and he shook his head and let himself be led to Kristy's room to examine her latest treasure, a coloured feather she'd found in the backyard. Then she demanded a push on the swing outside, and he obliged with apparent willingness. Watching from the kitchen window, Charisse wondered if he would always demonstrate this level of patience and entrancement with his daughter.

As she watched them he looked up, and through the glass

his gaze met hers. He caught the swing, stopping it, and went down on his haunches, talking earnestly to Kristy.

Kristy seemed to listen intently, then she nodded a couple of times and Daniel gave the swing another push, straightened, and came toward the house.

Charisse went out to meet him. She had to face this, and now was the time.

"I've bribed her," he said. "Fifteen minutes for us to talk, and then I promised to give her a surprise."

"Do you have one?"

"I've got a chocolate bar in the car. I did mean to ask you before I gave it to her, but I'm getting desperate."

"It's okay." Though she doubted if Kristy would last the fifteen minutes. "Shall we sit down?"

She led him to the terrace, where the vine-covered trellis sheltered the old park bench. As they sat down a starry, faded bloom dropped into Charisse's lap, and Daniel involuntarily glanced at the entwined pandorea and clematis, smothered in pink and white, over their heads.

"It's very pleasant here," he said.

Charisse absently picked up the flower, twisting it in her fingers. "We always spent a lot of time here in the summer when my parents were alive. On hot days we'd picnic here instead of eating inside, and sometimes neighbours or friends came over for a barbecue."

"You've always lived in this house?"

"We moved in when Gabrielle and I were eight. I remember how excited we were. It was the first time my parents had owned a home of their own." She smiled. "Their very own home with their very own mortgage, and they worked so hard getting the house and garden just right. We had a wonderful childhood here. I've tried to do the same for Kristy."

Both she and Gabrielle had moved out for a time, trying

their wings and learning to be independent of their parents and later even of each other, although the bond between them remained strong. And they'd known they could always come home if things went wrong.

Daniel looked at her thoughtfully. "Doesn't it sadden you, living here? There must be so many memories. Your parents, your sister…"

"They're mostly happy memories. I don't want to lose them."

"And you think you would if you left this place?"

Charisse thought about it, and somewhat reluctantly shook her head. "Memories are always with you, I guess. After the accident that killed my family I inherited the house, and it did hurt for a while, having all their things around. But it was a comfort too, in a way. And Kristy needed a stable home. She'd been here since she was born, never lived anywhere else."

"That's something I never had," he admitted. "Not in the sense of a house. My mother did her best for us—she was the one constant in our lives—but she was so busy feeding and clothing us we had to fend for ourselves to some extent. It made us independent at an early age and I always thought that was probably a good thing, but I guess we missed out on a sense of permanence."

"You were quite young when your father…?"

"About Kristy's age when he left. Haven't I told you this before? I hardly remember him." His eyes went to Kristy, now off the swing and absorbed in examining something that had caught her attention at the foot of the tree. "But I missed having a father. I will never do that to any child of mine. I can't." His eyes returned to Charisse, and her heart turned over at the bleakness in them. "I know I've turned your life upside down, and I admit you've done a wonderful job with Kristy. But there's no way I can turn my back on her…or you…now. Ever.''

Charisse bowed to the inexorable. Knowing this was a fateful decision, and one she couldn't go back on, she said, ''I know. And I think it's time we told her who you really are.''

He was so still she wondered if he'd heard her. Then she saw his chest move and he momentarily closed his eyes. When he opened them again he regarded her with a steady gaze and said simply, ''Thank you, Charisse.''

''It's your right. And hers.''

Daniel looked at her soberly. ''Like I said, I couldn't bear to lose you both again. I meant it when I told you I couldn't leave without her. Certainly not without knowing that I'll see her again—and you—soon. If you still won't come to Perth I'll find a way to move back to New Zealand eventually.'' He paused. ''I should have said this before— I love you, Charisse. I asked you to marry me. Have you come to a decision?''

He loved her? Perhaps he thought he did, but his feelings for her were all tied in with his feelings for Kristy—and with the lover he remembered in Perth all those years ago— and he didn't realise how much had changed.

Charisse was silent, trying to shape words. Fantastically, she wondered for a second or two if she could keep quiet and let events take their course. When he found out the truth it would be too late to change things.

But he must find out ultimately. And of course it wouldn't do. There were some things that were simply beyond decency.

Surely when he knew everything at last he wouldn't, as she had feared, separate her from Kristy? He'd assured her he didn't want to do that.

He took one of her hands in his, frowning down at it. ''I

wish you'd just say yes. It's such a simple little word." He gave her a fleeting, whimsically hopeful smile.

"It's not as simple as you think. Daniel, there's... something I have to tell you."

The smile died and he released his hold on her hand. "There's someone else?" he queried sharply. "You said there was no one."

"It isn't that."

"Mummy!" Kristy came running up to them. "Daniel, look what I found!"

Daniel's stormy gaze stayed on Charisse's face a moment longer. Then he turned to Kristy. "It's not fifteen minutes yet, honey. Give us a bit more time, huh?"

Kristy's face fell. "But isn't it *nearly* fifteen minutes? I want to show you what I found! Look!"

She opened her carefully folded fingers, her face alight with the wonder of discovery as she leaned against Charisse's knee and held out her palm, displaying the delicate, empty amber shell of a cicada larva. "It's got little legs and they prickle."

"So it has," Daniel agreed, giving up with a resigned glance at Charisse.

Kristy turned to her. "What's its name, Mummy?"

Charisse explained briefly, and suggested, "If you want to keep it you'd better put it away inside."

"Later," Kristy said firmly, and climbed up on the seat between the two adults.

"Hey," Daniel reminded her. "You promised you'd give me fifteen minutes to talk to your mother, remember?"

Kristy sighed and wriggled off the seat. "*What* are you talking to her about?"

"Grown-up things," Charisse said.

"What kind of grown-up things?"

Daniel laughed.

"Is it a secret?" Kristy demanded.

Charisse looked over her head into Daniel's questioning, smiling eyes. She wrenched her attention back to Kristy and said with all the calmness she could dredge up, "It...it was a secret before, but we just decided it was time to tell you about it. Daniel...is your daddy, Kristy."

Daniel's gaze changed, then fixed almost painfully on his daughter. Charisse saw his throat move as he swallowed.

"My real *one* daddy?" Kristy asked, her eyes growing rounder.

Charisse said, "Yes."

"Like my real one mummy?"

Charisse's voice was husky as she confirmed it. "Yes, like your real one mummy."

Daniel raised his brows at Charisse, his smile puzzled, a little strained. "Does she understand?"

"Yes I do!" Kristy told him indignantly. "You are my one daddy. And my one mummy died and went to heaven with Nana and Grandad, but *this* is my mummy too!" Triumphantly she launched herself at Charisse and hugged her. "My mummy too is my bestest mummy now! And you can be my bestest daddy."

Daniel cast a bemused look at Charisse over the child's head. "A bit muddled, isn't she?" he murmured.

And Charisse looked back at him and said despairingly, "No, she isn't muddled. That's what I've been trying to tell you, Daniel. Kristy is your daughter—and Gabrielle's."

Chapter 13

Daniel's expression went totally blank. He sat in stunned silence.

Charisse dropped a kiss on Kristy's sun-warmed hair. Her voice not quite steady, she instructed, "Go and put your cicada shell away, okay? Find one of your little boxes that I gave you, and make sure it's safe. And maybe you can find a box for your feather, too."

As she trotted off, Daniel continued to stare at Charisse. Finally he said, "I never met your sister."

"Yes, you did." She moistened her lips. "Only you thought she was me."

He blinked, and shook his head as if to clear it. "I don't follow. What the hell is this?"

"I know it must be a shock. But when we first met—when you saw me in the supermarket—I told you I'd never been to Perth. It was true."

Daniel got up, took a couple of strides away and then swung to face her. Hoarsely he said, "But Gabrielle had?"

''Yes. She spent several months there and came home pregnant. I guess she was calling herself Charisse when she met you.''

''You guess?''

''She never told me she'd been using my name over there.''

He gazed around him as if hunting for some clue to this bizarre twist, then looked frowningly back at her. *''Why?''*

''She probably didn't realise at first that the two of you might develop a serious relationship. And having begun as…as Charisse, she just didn't know how to change things.''

''That doesn't tell me why!''

Charisse looked down at her hands. ''Twins often exchange identities. As kids we did it for a bit of fun.''

''Fun? She did it as a *joke?''*

''No! I don't think so. I told you, I didn't know about it, so I'm guessing.'' She took a deep breath. ''Gabrielle was always getting into trouble when we were younger because she didn't think things through. When we were quite little she used to say she was me if she'd done something wrong. Our parents got wise to it, and usually I didn't mind. As we got older she'd look to me to get her out of whatever mess she was in. Maybe those few minutes between us did make me feel more responsible or something, being technically the elder. I used to cover for her.''

Charisse blinked to stem stupid tears at the memories that she'd evoked. ''Then, when we were teenagers,'' she went on, ''I was forever being accosted by strange young men convinced that they knew me. She said it was just for a laugh, but I think that when she was being me she adopted a different personality—not hers, but not mine, either. It made her more confident and outgoing. More reckless, I often thought.''

"The girl I knew was certainly an extrovert," Daniel commented.

She glanced at him, saw he still looked rather dazed. "I missed her terribly when she went to Australia alone, but I thought it would be good for her, that she'd find it easier to assert her own identity and...value herself more. Because I think that's what she needed—to have confidence that she was a real person in her own right, that people would like her for herself, not just as one half of 'the twins.' Or...or as me."

"I'd never have picked her as lacking in self-confidence," Daniel said sceptically.

"She was playing the role."

"How could she keep it up for that long? Months!"

"She was very good at it by then."

"And you..." he said accusingly. "You must have been aware that I'd mistaken you for your sister, and yet you let me go on believing you were her! Why didn't you tell me?"

"I did try to, that first time I came looking for you," she reminded him. "You didn't believe me."

"I might have if you'd mentioned you had a twin!"

Charisse looked away. "When I realised who you were I was scared."

"Scared?" He thrust a hand over his hair. "What have I ever done to scare you? Or...or your sister? She didn't say I was *violent?*"

"For all I knew you might have been. She said very little about you—one of the few things she never shared with me." That had hurt—and worse, had made Charisse worry that Gabrielle might be hiding something even more traumatic than an unplanned pregnancy. "She seemed certain Kristy's father wouldn't have been interested in knowing about the baby, because he'd made it very clear that he wanted no ties. But I could tell she was in love with him.''

Without ever having met him she'd despised and almost hated Daniel for that—for taking advantage of her sister's trust and naivety.

Daniel winced. ''I might have said something like that. All right, I did. But she wasn't looking for a permanent relationship any more than I was. And I certainly would have stood by her if only she'd told me.''

''Gabrielle didn't know that.'' And yet Gabrielle must have known him for longer—and much more intimately— than Charisse had.

Daniel said, ''Why did you go on pretending to be her? What were you afraid of?''

''I was afraid for Kristy,'' Charisse said tensely. ''I told you in the beginning she was my sister's child—''

''But she calls you Mummy now.''

''She'd always called both of us Mummy. I was her 'mummy too,' her mother's twin. It was a family thing. I've never claimed to be her mother. I didn't tell you I was.''

His brows drew together. ''You made no attempt to persuade me otherwise. For God's sake, *why?*''

If she didn't tell him he'd guess, eventually. ''Because if you knew,'' Charisse said at last, her mouth drying, ''then you might take her away from me.''

''Take her away?'' Daniel repeated blankly. ''I would never do that! I couldn't.''

''Legally you could—maybe. Or at least you might have tried.'' Her voice unsteady, she explained, ''I never formally adopted her—it didn't seem necessary, and legal fees cost money.''

He stared at her. ''And you thought I'd drag her away from the woman who's been her mother since…I suppose it must be almost ever since she can remember?'' He heaved in a breath. "That's why you got so emotional when I said I couldn't leave without her.''

Charisse nodded. "I was terrified that if you found out I wasn't really her mother you'd try to get custody. But I *am* her mother in every way that matters. The only one she has. I can't give her up, Daniel. I won't.''

Daniel stood staring at her. "I swear it never crossed my mind. That's why I asked you to marry me. One of the reasons.'' He paused there, complicated emotions playing across his face as he looked at her. "Why didn't you just say yes? It would have secured your future with Kristy.''

Marry a man who thought she was her sister? Spend the rest of her life letting him think she was Gabrielle, the woman he'd once had an affair with—who had borne his child? She lifted her head. "I couldn't!''

His eyes darkened. "Weren't you even tempted?''

Tempted, yes. "I *couldn't* do it,'' she reiterated vehemently. "Anyway, everything was complicated enough without adding a deception like that. Sooner or later you were bound to find out. There was no way I could have kept it from you forever.''

"You seem to have done fairly well so far. I'd never have guessed. It's still almost impossible to believe.''

"I'm sorry. I really am. But at first I was desperate to protect Kristy. If you'd been a different sort of man…'' She made a helpless gesture. If he'd been a different sort of man she might not have told him at all.

"I suppose I should be glad you decided at last to trust me.'' He looked away from her, then back into her eyes, his expression bleak. "It's difficult to take in the fact that…the woman I knew in Perth—the woman I made a baby with—is dead. Especially when I can see her face right here in front of me.''

"Not hers." Charisse's skin prickled. "Mine."

"Yes—yours." He briefly passed a hand over his eyes, rubbed at his temples. "I'm sorry if that was…tasteless." He couldn't seem to remove his gaze from her, perhaps trying to detect any subtle difference from the girl he remembered in Perth.

"It's all right. You'll need time to get used to this."

"Yes, I will." He stared at her a few moments longer, swung away from her again and stood a few feet off, one hand in his pocket, the other massaging the back of his neck. Then he dropped his hand and stood there for several more minutes.

He must be utterly confused. And perhaps he was grieving for the lover he had known. A lump rose in Charisse's throat.

Without turning round, Daniel said, "All this doesn't change the central problem, does it?"

Charisse swallowed. "Kristy."

"I want my name put on her birth certificate." He did turn then, and his face looked drawn, his eyes sombre. "I want legal recognition that I am Kristy's father."

This was what she had been afraid of all along—that Daniel might establish a stronger claim than hers. Fighting a desperate rearguard action, she said, "Gabrielle's gone. It's too late for that." Thank God she hadn't named him.

"You can do it," he insisted. "As her sister. I'm sure I recall my lawyer saying something about a deceased mother's close relative signing a declaration that they know a man is the father of a child. I wasn't listening properly because I didn't think it applied, but I'll phone him and check."

"And I'll phone mine."

"Your lawyer? What about?"

Charisse moistened dry lips. "About applying for an

adoption order.'' She had to do this, for both Kristy's sake and her own. In her heart she trusted Daniel, but she couldn't let her emotions override common sense. She needed to be absolutely sure that if she was mistaken after all, Kristy could never be a casualty. ''If I'm to sign a declaration that you're Kristy's father, I want my legal rights taken care of, too. I hope you won't oppose it now that you know the situation.''

Daniel's eyes had narrowed. ''Is that a condition?''

Charisse hesitated. ''A safeguard. Just to make sure that Kristy can't be taken from me.'' She wasn't at all certain that she'd be allowed to adopt her niece if Kristy's father were to oppose the move, but it was no use now trying to do it without his knowledge. She had to secure his cooperation somehow.

A faint look of hostility crossed his face. ''If you refuse to make the declaration a DNA test should be sufficient proof.''

She'd hoped he wouldn't think of that.

''Please, Daniel,'' she said, her hand crushing the delicate bloom she still held, ''for Kristy's sake, let's not fight each other. The two of us warring over her is the last thing she needs.'' It was what she'd tried all along to avoid.

''It's the last thing any of us needs,'' Daniel agreed grimly, and Charisse felt a cautious relief. ''You'd better come with me to see my lawyer,'' he said. ''I think we should begin by getting some advice together rather than separately.''

Charisse sat nervously at Daniel's side while he asked questions and the lawyer quoted from the relevant statute.

Eventually Daniel said, ''Okay, let's get this straight. If I can prove I'm her father, I could have a legal claim to my daughter. But if…her aunt…adopts her, then I have no rights?''

The lawyer nodded. ''Adoption is very final. And if Ms. Lane were to marry at some time in the future her husband could also apply to adopt the child.''

Charisse's heart sank like a stone. Daniel wouldn't risk that.

''You could contest it, of course,'' the lawyer continued.

Daniel had said he wouldn't take the child from her, but she knew he wouldn't give up his all-too-tenuous rights and lose any hope of influencing Kristy's future well-being.

And equally she couldn't separate him from his daughter. Not now. ''Isn't there some way we might share custody?'' she asked, although dreading some arrangement where Kristy would be shunted from one of them to the other.

The lawyer looked at her thoughtfully. ''That would be unusual, and possibly create some difficulty.''

''Suppose we were married?'' Daniel said abruptly.

The lawyer looked from him to Charisse and back again. ''To each other?''

''Yes.''

''Certainly as a married couple you'd be able to apply to adopt the child jointly. That's quite commonly done.''

''We'd both have to apply for adoption, even though I'm her father?'' Daniel demanded.

''Even so, I'm afraid. An interim adoption order would be made, then a social worker would assess the situation and keep an eye on it. If they see no problem, in six months the adoption should be finalised.''

Daniel turned to Charisse with a strange, almost febrile light in his eyes. She stared at him dumbly. Surely he wasn't thinking…?

''Thank you,'' he said to the lawyer. ''We'll talk this over and get back to you.''

The man looked at them curiously as he stood to usher them out. Charisse let Daniel lead her to where he'd parked his car, and not until he'd let her in and slipped into the driver's seat beside her did she speak.

"There must be something we can do," she said. "Both of us have Kristy's interests at heart. We have to think of what's best for her."

"My thoughts exactly," Daniel concurred. "And we've just been given a very obvious solution." His voice was soft but a harshness underlaid it. "I've already asked you to marry me, Charisse. The offer is still open."

Marriage as a pragmatic answer to an insoluble problem? The notion seemed unreal. And it would put her into a situation she instinctively recoiled from. Mothering Kristy in Gabrielle's place had been a natural, instinctive thing— she'd never even contemplated not doing it. But taking her sister's place as Daniel's wife was a totally different proposition, even though now he knew who she really was. She shook her head. "There must be another way."

His face took on a grim expression. "You heard what the lawyer said. It's the only option to give us both equal rights."

Charisse's thoughts scattered. She looked blindly through the windscreen in front of her. "Shouldn't we give it some thought?"

"I've given it all the thought I need. Take as much time as you like, but I don't see any other way round this. You're still the only mother Kristy has. And I'm her 'one daddy,' aren't I? I certainly don't intend her to have another. Or you to have another husband. I still want you, Charisse."

"But…" Was it really *her* he wanted?

"And I want my daughter. That hasn't changed."

He'd said before that he wanted them both. A package

deal, she reflected wryly. Except that part of it had come in false packaging.

"And this hasn't changed, either," he said, his hand reaching out to turn her face to him, before he bent and kissed her, with warmth and restrained, persuasive passion.

She couldn't help responding, her lips parting for him, desire for a few moments taking over her body, hope and longing warring with doubt.

When he tipped her head further and his hand lay caressingly on her throat she made an effort to resist the tide of sweetness that threatened to engulf her. She pushed against him until he released her, and then she looked away from him, taking a deep, shuddering breath to steady herself.

"What is it?" he asked, his voice low. He took one of her hands in his. "What's the matter?"

She pressed her lips together. "When you suggested marriage to me before," she reminded him, "you thought I was my sister."

His hand tightened, and her fleeting glance at him showed her he was frowning down at their entwined fingers. "Now I know you're not, and I'm asking *you*—Charisse." He seemed to hesitate, his gaze quizzical. "Of course, if you can't stand the thought of being married to me, you'll have to say no." His voice became deeper, husky. "But if the way you kissed me just now is any indication, would it be such a hardship?"

Charisse shook her head very slightly. It wouldn't be a hardship at all, if he meant just the sexual component. But marriage entailed a whole lot more than that.

How could she put her reservations into words? She wanted nothing more than to capitulate, tell him yes, she wanted to be with him, to share their delight in watching Kristy grow, to have him by her side in sickness and in health—hers, his, Kristy's. That increasingly she couldn't bear the thought of life without him.

But his feelings for her were unclear. He'd thought it was Gabrielle he was proposing to the first time—his lover of long ago, the girl he'd made love to and lost, and believed he'd found again.

And in a couple of days how could he have made the transition from one to the other? It wasn't possible. Perhaps he still had them mixed up in his mind.

"I know you love Kristy just as much as her mother did," Daniel told her. "And people do marry all the time for reasons other than being wildly in love."

They did. Of course they did. It used to be a given that if a woman was pregnant with a man's child they married for the sake of the baby. Even now many couples stayed in an unsatisfactory marriage for the good of their children.

And she was not deceiving him anymore. Whatever confusion there might be in his heart, intellectually he knew she wasn't her sister, that Kristy wasn't biologically her daughter. But because he wanted Kristy, and Kristy needed her, he wanted her to be his wife. For the sake of the child they both loved. And surely that was a bond that two people of goodwill could build a marriage on?

"If...if you're sure it's what you want," she said, hearing the words come out as if someone else were saying them, "then yes."

He blinked, almost as if he'd expected her to say no. "Thank you." His hand briefly touched her cheek again. "Would you like a church wedding?"

Her parents had been devout and regular churchgoers, and she was a believer, although not as punctilious as they in attendance.

"I know the minister at my local church, but—"

"Then we'll go and see him. I guess Kristy will want to take part in her...her mummy too's wedding."

The next two weeks seemed unreal. When Charisse finally stood in the church and exchanged the age-old vows, she felt she was walking through a dream.

She wore a simple short-sleeved white silk street-length dress that she'd found at a bargain price, and had embellished by sewing a border of heavy guipure lace and seed pearl beads around the scooped neckline and adding a row of tiny pearl buttons at the back. With a small hat that featured the suggestion of a veil just over her eyes, and a modest bouquet in her hands, she hoped she looked bridal but not elaborately so.

Kristy, in a pretty new dress and with a wreath of flowers on her hair, had preceded Charisse down the aisle, solemnly holding a posy.

A couple of dozen of their friends were there, and Daniel's mother sat in the front row alongside his brother, his brother's wife and Kristy's newly acquired cousins. She'd been intrigued at having a grandmother again, but the two of them would hardly have time to get to know each other before Daniel whisked his daughter and his new wife off to Australia.

After checking that the New Zealand adoption procedures could be completed even if they were living in Australia, Charisse had agreed to move to Perth with him after their marriage, and when she broached the subject to Kristy, the little girl had reacted with excitement at the prospect of flying to another country. Charisse had no more excuses.

As Daniel slipped a gold ring onto Charisse's finger she became suddenly aware of his hand under hers, his fingers sure and steady, and his voice firm as he repeated his promises to her. She looked up and into his eyes, and his serious, determined expression reassured her.

Brenna had offered to look after Kristy overnight while Charisse and Daniel stayed at the luxury hotel where Daniel had paid for a celebratory meal for their guests. She'd made the offer to them both, and Charisse had been casting about for a tactful way to decline it when, to her astonishment, Daniel said, "That would be great, Brenna. We won't have a chance for a real honeymoon before we fly out to Perth."

After the other guests had departed, Brenna and Baz took a still excited but tired Kristy home and Daniel ushered Charisse into an elevator that whisked them to an upper floor, and then led her along a carpeted corridor to a room with a view of downtown Auckland and the Waitemata Harbour.

Her overnight bag already sat on the luggage rack next to his, and the sight seemed to underline the intimacy of the bond she and Daniel had entered into.

She had tacitly accepted that he intended a real marriage with all that implied. And she was prepared to fulfil his expectations, had even fantasised about making love to him. But over the past few weeks he had been almost aloof, his kisses limited to greetings and farewells.

There were two queen-size beds in the room. Daniel loosened his tie and strolled over to the window, glancing at the beds as he passed. "Which one do you want?" he asked casually.

Charisse didn't answer for a moment. Lifting the veiled hat from her head, she laid it carefully on top of the over-night bag.

When he half turned to her, enquiring, she said, "I'm not fussy." Her feelings were a mixture of relief, surprise and letdown.

He looked away from her, seemingly admiring the view.

Then he moved and faced her. "I'm assuming you don't want to share one."

Charisse gave a breathy, nervous laugh. "I was assuming you *would* want to share."

There was a small silence. His eyes held a deep glitter. "It's entirely up to you. I certainly have no objection, but I thought you might want a bit more time."

He continually caught her off guard. "We're married," she said huskily. "And when you accepted Brenna's offer, I thought…"

"I figured you didn't want everyone to know that this isn't the usual kind of marriage. If you'd told Brenna, she'd never have made the offer."

She'd told no one, through a kind of humiliation and embarrassment at the pragmatic, essentially unconventional nature of this marriage. Brenna had accepted the news of their engagement at face value. She'd been thrilled and delighted for her friend, and Charisse saw no good reason to disillusion her.

"I suppose…" Charisse said slowly, "…we should have discussed this before."

"Do you want to discuss it now?" Daniel stepped from the window, coming toward her. "Or…"

He strolled closer and almost casually cupped a warm hand under her chin, lifting her face to his intent inspection. "Or shall we skip the discussion and go with action instead?"

Maybe he picked up on the sudden acceleration of her pulse when he touched her. She saw lambent desire in his eyes, and he must have read an answer in hers, because his voice had slowed and changed in timbre, and the last word was murmured against her mouth, and then he teased her lips apart with his own, his free hand finding her waist and drawing her to him, fitting her body to his as he deliberately deepened the kiss.

It seemed such a long time since he had kissed her properly. And yet there was a feeling of rightness and inevitability about his mouth persuading hers to open for him, the strength of the arm that kept her imprisoned as he freed her chin and skimmed his hand to her throat, gently probed the shallow hollow at its base with his thumb, then circled her nape and supported her head when the insistence of his kiss forced it further back.

Charisse clutched at his sleeves, then her balance gave way and she hooked her arms about his neck, yielding to the sensations that his mouth and his lithe male body brought surging through her.

Her eyes were closed, the room about them disappearing in a dark haze of increasing desire, her whole being concentrated on the fierce possessiveness of Daniel's embrace, the increasing passion of his mouth and the response that it evoked from hers, the waves of pleasure that threatened to engulf her.

His hand moved from her nape to cup her shoulder, cradling her head in the curve of his arm, and his other hand went to her breast, stroking it until she shuddered and made a tiny, agitated sound in her throat.

Daniel marginally lifted his head, leaving her mouth bereft. His eyes slits of fire, he studied her flushed face and dazed eyes. "Did I hurt you?"

"No," she whispered. "No."

His hand still lay on her breast. He shifted his feet a little, his hold altering as he looked down, his expression absorbed. Then he moved his hand again, shaping the soft flesh underneath the silk, his fingers brushing the telltale peak that showed clearly through the fabric. Charisse drew in a choking breath, bit her lip, and breathed out unsteadily.

He smiled, shooting a burning glance at her, and for a moment one finger lingered tantalisingly, then again brushed over the taut bud. He murmured, "You like that?"

She could hardly speak. "Yes." The sensation was exquisite, although his touch was featherlight.

He bent his head, and without thought she leaned hers back, closing her eyes as his mouth wandered along her throat, his tongue dipping into the small indentation, tasting and teasing, and then he lifted his head again, his palm cherishing her breast as he said, "Did I tell you what a beautiful bride you are?"

Charisse swallowed. "Thank you. I'm glad you like the dress."

A faint twist of humour showed on his mouth. "It's a lovely dress. But I want to take it off. Do you mind?"

Unable to form the word, mesmerised by the unmistakable desire in his eyes, she simply shook her head.

Unexpectedly he kissed her forehead—a fleetingly tender gesture that melted her insides, making them liquid and warm. Then gravely he stepped back, firmly turning her, and began undoing the row of buttons at the back of the gown.

He took his time over it, prolonging the suspense as each carefully sewn loop gave way. When he undid the last one at the base of her spine she was shivering with nervous anticipation.

She felt his fingertip on the back of her neck, slowly, slowly tracing the curve of her spine all the way down. Her breath caught, and she could hear him breathing, too, evenly but a little faster than before.

"You have a gorgeous back," he told her.

She laughed unsteadily. And he slid one hand about her waist inside the dress, his fingers warm and intrusive on her bare skin, pulling her back against him. "Feel what it does to me?'' he asked, his cheek pressed to hers, his other hand pushing the dress from her shoulder while he ran a hard, exploring palm down her arm.

She did, but only for a second, as he removed the other sleeve and the dress dropped silently to the floor, pooling about her feet.

Then he was swinging her into his arms, her satin pumps falling with two small thuds to the carpet as he carried her to one of the beds and lowered her onto it.

He leaned down and turned the covers back, smiling at her. ''Move over.''

She sidled across the sheet, and Daniel pushed down the covers, hauled off his tie and bent to remove his shoes and socks. He was still undoing his shirt with one hand when he dropped beside her and began kissing her again.

Eventually she helped him, pulling the last button apart as he fumbled at the hook of her lacy bra.

After that she wasn't capable of helping him with anything, because the way he looked at her exposed breasts made them tingle and grow taut and then he touched them and kissed them, and when she felt the tender tug of his mouth on her, the erotic charge was so piercing she could only moan under his ministrations and hold him to her with her fingers raked into his thick, sleek hair.

She moaned again when he stopped, twisting restlessly under his hands, but soon he began kissing her everywhere, tasting her with his tongue, finding new areas to tease with his clever, exciting fingers. And she reciprocated, stroking his chest, his back, watching with eager eyes as he shucked off his trousers, and taking the opportunity of exploring the enticing male musculature of his calves and the tautness of his behind, so different from the rounded curves of hers that he found equally fascinating.

She wanted to prolong the exquisite buildup, but her

body was clamouring for release. ''Now,'' she heard herself begging. ''Oh, please, now!''

''Yes,'' Daniel agreed, the word coming from deep in his throat. And then he surprised her by turning over onto his back, his strong arms holding her close, hands going to her hips to guide her onto him. ''Okay?'' he queried huskily. Darkened hair lay on his forehead and his eyes were brilliant.

Charisse gulped and nodded. She was beyond speech, and as she felt him glide into her she almost sobbed with relief and pleasure.

His hands shaped the twin curves exaggerated by their position, and inch by inch moved up her sides to find her breasts.

She lifted herself to give him better access, bracing her hands on his shoulders, and he smiled up at her.

''This way I can see you better,'' he told her, his gaze shifting lower as he played with her breasts, his thumbs and forefingers forming two small, framing circles. ''Rosebuds,'' he murmured, gently squeezing. ''Perfect.''

She rocked slightly, felt him echo the movement. Her teeth bit into her lower lip. ''If you keep doing that,'' she gasped, ''I—''

''Yes?'' His eyes blazed, his face suddenly tautly expectant. He repeated the movement, tightened his fingers again ever so slightly.

''I—'' She sucked in a breath. ''I—*oh!*''

''*Yesss!*'' he hissed, and bucked beneath her so that she cried out again, then he rocked her, entering deeper and deeper, his eyes holding hers, alight with triumphant knowledge as her lips parted and her body went rigid, another cry torn from her throat before her eyes closed and she lifted her head back, racked by spasms so intense she thought she'd die.

And when they began to abate at last Daniel turned so she was under him, and rhythmically thrust into her again and again, until the pleasure began to build once more, higher, higher—and this time his voice mingled hoarsely with hers while the pleasure crested and she was hurled a second time into the vortex.

Minutes later she returned to reality, her head tucked against Daniel's shoulder, his arm still cradling her as they lay on their sides. With his free hand he smoothed a strand of hair back from her face. "That was fantastic," he told her, his voice low and vibrant. "Magical, Charisse."

A faint unease stirred somewhere far inside her, but she was too sated and sleepy now to bother tracing its source. For her the experience had been shattering, the depth of her emotions unsuspected until this moment.

Always before she had forced herself to firmly keep Kristy's interests to the forefront. But now she had to acknowledge why she had responded so completely, so ardently, so unreservedly to Daniel's lovemaking.

Oh sure, he was obviously not inexperienced at giving a woman pleasure—Charisse quelled a shaft of pure jealousy that threatened to overwhelm her at the thought—but his undoubted proficiency wasn't the only reason he had drawn that cataclysmic reaction from her. Something within her had been awoken at his very first touch, and had flowered into full bloom in the unremitting light of his lovemaking.

She had to face what she had deliberately tried to blot out of her mind. She was completely and irrevocably in love with a man who had married her not because he loved her and desperately wanted to share his life with her, but because he couldn't bear being parted from his child. A man who might subconsciously still be confusing her with her dead sister.

Chapter 14

"What are you thinking?" Daniel's lazy voice slurred in her ear. His hand stroked her shoulder.

"Nothing." Charisse suppressed a sigh. If she told him she was bothered at the idea of being a substitute bride he'd deny it anyway. No man in his right mind would admit to thinking of one woman while he was in bed with another.

"It was all right for you, wasn't it?" He propped himself up on one elbow, looking at her questioningly.

"You mean you didn't notice?" she asked him dryly.

Daniel grinned. "You were pretty vocal."

She looked away, her lashes sweeping down to hide her eyes. "It's been a long time since I did this."

"Really?" He regarded her curiously.

"I've been too busy looking after Kristy to…to have time for anything else."

"Well…we'll have to see what we can do about making up for what you've missed." His hand moved slowly down her arm, pausing as the thumb idly explored the fine skin inside her elbow.

"A charitable project?" Charisse enquired with a wry smile.

His eyes lifted, gleaming with humour. "What else?" he asked. "I'm a real philanthropist, me."

"Yeah," she gently scorned, her heart lifting in response as she pushed away the insidious misgiving. Daniel was her husband and she was his wife—she, not Gabrielle. And hadn't he often said she was different from the girl he'd known?

Soft laughter shook him. "You don't believe me?"

"Not hardly." Charisse turned her head aside to hide a yawn.

"Tired? It's early yet." Outside the window the sky was darkening, but it was only dusk. "Do you want to go and eat?"

"I'm not hungry." She hadn't eaten very much at the reception, but despite that she felt as though she'd had a meal. "Are you?"

"I could do with a sandwich," Daniel admitted. "But I can get that in the hotel. Sure you don't want to dine out or sample the nightlife? The casino's not far from here."

"Doesn't appeal to me," Charisse answered. "I guess I've got too used to having to watch my finances with an eagle eye to enjoy throwing away money." She'd taken a spectacular gamble in marrying him, though. Perhaps even more so than when she'd decided on an impossible deception to get to know Kristy's father.

"If there's anything else you'd like to do…?"

"Not really. Unless *you* want to go out on the town?" And when he shook his head, she added, "Wallowing in this luxury is enough for me, truly. It's a holiday in itself."

"Suits me," he said. "We could ring room service and get them to send up a snack."

"Okay," Charisse agreed. "You do that while I have a shower."

She slipped out of the bed, a little self-conscious at her nakedness and the blatant way he lay staring at her, his own now quiescent body unabashedly on display.

"Do me a favour," he suggested as she rummaged in her bag before making for the bathroom. "Don't put on too many clothes."

When she left the bathroom she was wearing a peach-coloured satin robe. She saw that her crumpled wedding dress no longer lay on the floor and the bed had been roughly straightened. Daniel sat at the small round table near the window with a tray before him. He'd put his shirt and pants back on and smoothed his hair.

Looking up, he smiled. "I ordered sandwiches and a salad for two, some cake, and champagne. Sound okay?"

"Sounds wonderful."

Perhaps it was the shower, or the sight of beautifully presented food, but suddenly she was hungry after all. She took the chair opposite him and picked up a glass that he'd already filled with champagne, the bubbles lazily chasing each other to the surface. "I'm not used to this," she said, her gaze sweeping the darkening harbour, the lights beginning to switch on about the waterfront below, and returning to the simple but obviously expensive fare before her.

"We won't be doing it every day," he promised, and raised his own glass to her. "Here's to our future, Charisse. Let's make it a good one."

"Yes." She wanted to for all their sakes—her own, his, and above all Kristy's. "We will."

The champagne fizzed on her tongue as she took a sip.

Daniel drank some of his and put down his glass. "Want

a sandwich? There's smoked salmon, or avocado and chicken.''

Between them they ate most of the sandwiches and half the salad. By that time the bottle of champagne was close to empty and Charisse felt pleasantly muzzy, filled with a sense of well-being.

Daniel must have switched on some lights while she was in the bathroom. A mellow glow lit the walls and gave just enough illumination for them to see each other, while not overpowering the night view outside the windows.

But Daniel didn't seem terribly interested in the view. Every time Charisse took her eyes from it she found him studying her, with a lazy light in his eyes and a half smile on his mouth. When his gaze wasn't on her face it lingered on the swell of her breasts that the flimsy robe scarcely concealed, or the shadowy cleft framed between its lapels. He was spinning an unseen web of tension between them just by looking at her. She could feel it shimmering in the air, being drawn tighter and tighter.

''Had enough?'' Daniel asked after they'd sat in silence for some time, finishing off the champagne.

''Yes.''

He gathered the used dishes and utensils back onto the tray and stood up. ''I'll put this outside the door.''

Charisse watched him cross the room, admiring the smooth play of muscle under his clothing. She knew now what his body felt like without the civilised covering, when he was naked and trembling with desire.

He closed the door on the tray and turned to go into the bathroom. ''I won't be long,'' he promised.

Minutes later Charisse heard the sound of the shower running.

She took the blouse and new hopsack trousers she planned to wear tomorrow from her bag, opened the wardrobe and saw her wedding dress hanging there. Somehow the thought of Daniel carefully putting it on a hanger touched her.

You're getting sentimental, girl, she told herself. But she was glad he'd thought of tidying away the evidence of their hasty passion before the person from room service arrived with their meal. Opening a drawer, she discovered her undies neatly folded. Recalling the way he'd made up the camp bed, and the near-sterility of his rented apartment, she wondered if he was a stickler for neatness.

That could be a problem.

He'd never shown signs of disliking the inevitable clutter of Charisse and Kristy's home. And he loved Kristy. He wouldn't expect to maintain a pristine household with a small girl in it, would he?

When he came out of the bathroom, wrapped in one of the hotel's white towelling robes, she was seated on the bed, her legs curled under her, flipping through a glossy magazine she'd found on the night table.

Coming over to the bed, he sat facing her, a hand on the coverlet. "Mind if I wallow with you?"

Charisse laughed. "Do you want to look at a fashion magazine?" She let it fall to her lap.

He skewed his head sideways, trying to see the double page spread, a man and a woman provocatively posed on gold satin sheets, the man fully dressed in evening clothes, the woman wearing a sheer black lace dress over nothing but a triangle of black fabric, her feet bare and her toenails painted scarlet. A single word was scrawled in looping letters across the lower part of the picture.

"Fashion?" he queried. "What are those two advertising?"

"Perfume."

"Ah." He turned the magazine, looking at the picture fully. "Well, they have the right idea."

"The right idea?"

"About what to do in bed. They don't look to me as though they're talking about perfume."

"They don't look to me as though they're talking about anything," Charisse agreed.

"Exactly." He closed the magazine and dropped it onto the bedside table, then smiled at her. His hand closed about her thigh, just below the hem of her robe where it had ridden up. "You look so sexy in that thing."

She'd seen the peach robe at sale price and bought it on impulse. It was opaque and perfectly plain, not particularly provocative, but the material was sensuously smooth against her skin and she'd hoped she'd look nice in it. Sexy hadn't entered the equation, she told herself virtuously, but she was glad that Daniel found it so.

He hitched himself closer, his hand gliding further up under the hem of the gown, and his lips touched her cheek, slid to her jawline, and along it to the sensitive skin just below her ear. Charisse closed her eyes.

He was stroking her, evoking shivers of delight that danced over her skin. His hair brushed her chin as she lifted it to allow him to trail small kisses down her throat and further, nudging aside the satin from the tender slope of her breasts.

Charisse let out a shuddering sigh, and he raised his head. "Is it too soon for you...again?"

Not too soon at all. She wanted him with a fierceness that shocked her. "No," she managed to say.

He smiled, and kissed her mouth, taking it fully under his, while his wandering hand found her inner thigh, curling around it briefly, then stroking again, all the way down to her knee and upward again, but not quite far enough.

Her head going back to rest against the pillow, Charisse gave a whimper of protest and scrunched farther down on the bed, felt him shift his position to lie beside her, one of his strong thighs coming between hers as his hand stopped its lazy movement and tugged at the tie of her robe.

When it gave under his fingers and the robe fell apart, cool air wafted over her breasts. Then his mouth was there warming them, warming her all over, and once again his hands, his mouth, his body, brought her to the brink of ecstasy and at last, a long time later, flung her with him into the dancing dark.

Kristy was as thrilled to see them the following day as if they'd been away for a month. She ran into Charisse's arms, then turned to Daniel to be picked up and hugged. After he'd put her down, she took his hand and dragged him into the kitchen to see what she'd made of pink Play-Doh, and Brenna smiled at Charisse. "I can tell marriage agrees with you. I haven't seen you look so glowing since I've known you."

Charisse laughed, willing the colour from her cheeks. "Thanks for looking after Kristy. It was great of you to offer."

"I enjoyed it. Baz and I will miss her when you're gone. Oh, there was a phone call from the rental agency to say they have someone interested in looking at the flat."

"I hope they've found someone you and Baz can get along with. Thanks for taking care of this business for me."

"Well, it suits us to pick our fellow tenants. You know we could be interested in buying if you ever decide to sell."

"I'll keep that in mind," Charisse promised as Daniel came back into the room.

Brenna said, "I'll leave you to it. Remember, if you need

any help packing or want Kristy out of the way while you do it, Charisse, call on us anytime.''

After she'd left, while Kristy was still working away at the kitchen table, Daniel said, ''Brenna and Baz want to buy the place?''

''If I decide to sell eventually it would be easier than seeing it go to strangers. Meantime the rent will give me an income.''

Daniel was looking pensively at her. ''I told you, I can well afford to keep you.''

''I'm accustomed to having my own money.'' With Kristy to keep, as well as herself, she'd had to watch her finances, but she was proud that they'd managed without going onto a state-funded benefit.

''Finished!'' Kristy called from the kitchen. ''Come and see my wedding cake, Mummy!''

Charisse went to admire the three rounds of dough piled on top of each other, and provided candles when asked without pointing out that wedding cakes didn't usually feature them.

Later they filled in the adoption papers and pinned a copy of their marriage certificate to them. The department would liaise with their Australian counterparts, they'd been told, who would make any necessary visits to check on Kristy's well-being, before the adoption could be finalised.

Daniel spent the night in Charisse's bed. In the dark hours they made love, and Charisse determinedly pushed away the occasional insidious thought that maybe when he kissed her and touched her and brought her to a mindless pitch of need and delight, he was reliving that long-ago love affair.

In the morning Kristy came pattering in and climbed over to ensconce herself between them, chattering and singing and demanding stories and games. And Daniel still seemed enchanted by her, his patience endless.

''We have some more packing to do,'' Charisse reminded them after a while. There were last-minute arrangements to be made, and Kristy had to be persuaded to temporarily part with some of her treasures so they could be sent separately in boxes.

When they finally boarded the plane at Mangere and took off for the long flight to Perth via Sydney, Kristy was pink-cheeked and wide-eyed with excitement. By the time they arrived she was exhausted, and slept in the taxi that took them from the airport to Daniel's apartment.

Charisse felt foggy, too. She hardly noticed what they passed en route to the city, only gathering a general impression of spaciousness and flowering gardens and elegant buildings.

Symmetrical Norfolk pines and tall decorative palm trees were reflected in the calm waters of the Swan River, and skyscrapers reared above other buildings in the central city.

Daniel's apartment was in a multistorey building, with a view over part of the city and a stretch of the wide river.

While Daniel took his and Charisse's bags to his room, Charisse put Kristy into a bed in a smaller, twin-bedded room where she went instantly back to sleep.

When Charisse came out the big living area was empty. She gazed around at the comfortable pale yellow leather chairs and matching sofa, a long, low table of some light, satiny wood, wall-shelves that held books and a number of exotic artifacts.

On the broad window ledge stood a large glass sculpture—a fluid inverted triangle of sparkling colours made translucent by the late sun shining through it.

She went over to examine it, her finger tracing the smooth curves of glass, warmed by the sun.

Daniel came into the room and Charisse half turned, her finger still on the sculpture. "This is lovely," she said. "Where did you get it?"

"Don't you remember—" He stopped abruptly. Across the room their eyes met, and she saw the stricken apology in his. "I'm sure I mentioned your sister left me a farewell present."

Charisse removed her hand from the glass. Her heart had gone cold, a hard lump in her chest. "Yes, you did. I remember now." Her voice sounded lifeless, distant. She knew, damningly, that deep down he hadn't yet separated her and her twin. "I'm a bit tired," she said. "Do you mind if I lie down for a while? You could wake me in an hour or so." Right now she wanted to be alone, if not to actually sleep.

But she did, wakening to the brush of Daniel's lips on her forehead, then her lips. "You said to wake you," he reminded her.

Consciousness returned, and with it memory. She opened her eyes and he lifted his head, looking down at her. "Kristy's still sound asleep," he told her, and smiled, his lids lowering as he flicked a languid gaze over her. "You look very tempting lying there—on my bed."

Where Gabrielle had once lain. She remembered with obscene clarity what he'd said the day she tracked him down, when he thought she was Gabrielle. That he remembered her calling out his name, *when you were going wild in my arms—in my bed. You can't have forgotten…*

He still remembered that night.

No, don't think about it. That way lay torture. But when Daniel began to lean toward her again she turned her head aside and levered herself up. "It's not dark yet."

"So…?" He glanced out the window and then back at her, amused.

"I should adjust to local time." Charisse sat up fully, forcing him to move and allow her to get off the bed.

She pushed back her hair. "I have to unpack, and find a hairbrush."

Unpacking and making room for her things occupied them both for the next hour, and then Charisse familiarised herself with the kitchen and offered to make a meal.

"I'll do it," Daniel said.

"It'll keep me awake," she insisted, "and I need to find my way about the place."

She found spaghetti and a jar of ready-made sauce and some cheese, and learned how to work the stove-top set into the bench. They ate at a small table near one of the big windows and watched the lights of the city, and the ceaseless lines of headlights on the roads.

Kristy began to whimper sleepily, and Charisse picked her up and took her to the bathroom, then changed her into pyjamas and tucked her back into bed.

"Maybe I should sleep in the other bed in her room," she suggested, going into the kitchen where Daniel had just finished cleaning up. "In case she wakes in the night. Her sleep pattern is disrupted, and she might be disoriented and frightened."

"We can leave the doors open. But please yourself." He straightened from putting away a pot in the cupboard and looked directly at her, but she couldn't read his eyes.

She spent the night with Kristy, hardly sleeping at all herself. Instead she watched the hours crawl by, her brain ceaselessly gnawing at thoughts, memories and fears, and an increasing sense of dread growing like a lump of lead in her chest. So far away from home, she felt alone in a strange land, and suddenly very afraid of what she had done, of what the future held.

Chapter 15

The following day Daniel made a few phone calls and, after collecting his car from the garage that stored it when he was away, took Charisse and Kristy on a short tour of the city, before driving them to Cottesloe on the coast.

The sand was white and the sea an astonishing blue, and Kristy had a wonderful time making sand castles, splashing about in the shallows and admiring the surfboarders riding the breakers onto the beach.

As they entered the apartment building again a fortyish couple was just leaving. They greeted Daniel by name, and the woman smiled delightedly. "Charisse! How nice to see you again!"

Charisse froze. Daniel's fingers, lightly encircling her arm, tightened. For a moment no one spoke, and then Daniel said, "Pete and Sally O'Regan, darling. They have the apartment right below ours."

"We're still here!" Sally stepped forward and gave

Charisse a hug. "You haven't forgotten us, surely! And who's this little one?" she enquired, seeing Kristy.

"This is our daughter, Kristy," Daniel said woodenly. After the briefest hesitation, he added, "Charisse and I got married a couple of days ago."

Sally's eyes widened. She looked from him to Kristy and then at Charisse, her expression changing from surprised curiosity to perfect understanding. "Married! Oh, I'm so glad for you both—for all three of you!"

Pete held out his hand to Daniel. "Congratulations." And, casting a glance at Charisse, he said, "I'm sure you'll be very happy."

She swallowed, and managed a smile. "Thank you," she murmured.

"I was my mummy too's flower girl," Kristy informed them proudly.

"Really?" Sally beamed. "You must have been a very pretty flower girl!"

Kristy giggled at her, hooking a finger into her mouth and fluttering her long lashes. "I was too!"

"Oh, she's gorgeous!" Sally cooed. "You must all come to us for dinner one night. We'll catch up."

"Thanks, we'd like that." Daniel urged Charisse toward the elevator. "See you two again."

They rode up to the apartment in silence. While Kristy went to her room to take off her shoes, Charisse followed Daniel to his, closing the door behind them and leaning back against it. "Why did you do that?" she asked, keeping her voice level.

"Do what?" His expression was very controlled.

"Let your friends think I was my sister!" She straightened. "What did you think you were doing?"

His mouth tightened a fraction. "What was I supposed to do?" he asked. "I didn't know how you'd want to handle it. Do you intend to tell everyone we meet that your sister lived with me masquerading as you, and you married me because of her child?''

Put starkly like that it sounded preposterous. And certainly a fertile field for gossip and speculation.

''It was stupid of me,'' Daniel confessed, ''not to realise this would happen. We should have talked about it earlier, but just now it seemed the best thing was to say as little as possible. We can give Pete and Sally the whole story if you like—and tell all my other friends. Personally I feel it's none of their business.''

More deception, Charisse thought, her mind rebelling at the thought. But equally her heart quailed at baring the reality of this marriage to the curiosity of strangers. Letting everyone think—*know*—she was a kind of second-best clone. A stand-in wife. ''I won't recognise anyone,'' she pointed out. ''People who think they know me.''

''After five years people will understand you may have forgotten their names. And it won't occur to anyone that you're not the person they knew. You fooled *me* and I knew your sister better than anyone here.''

''I'm not her!''

The fierceness of her denial evidently surprised him. ''I know,'' he said. ''I just don't see that everyone else needs to.''

A wave of anger swept over her. Anger with Gabrielle, who should surely have grown out of such childishness at twenty-two. Who had left a legacy of lies that had unwittingly entangled Charisse and from which she seemed unable to escape.

Guilt swiftly followed the anger. Gabrielle was dead, and whatever mistakes she'd made in her short life, she had never deliberately hurt anyone. Least of all her twin. Or her daughter. And how might it affect Kristy if it was common knowledge that her mother had deceived everyone here, pretending to be her own sister?

Inevitably there would be speculation. Children picked up on that sort of gossip and some teased. "You're right," Charisse admitted reluctantly. "It's no one's business but ours." Eventually people would get to know her and accept her for who she was, herself. "But Kristy knows Gabrielle was her mother."

"If we have to, we can explain that she's your sister's child and we've adopted her. That's simple enough, and it's the truth. Given the way Kristy puts it, I don't think anyone will twig there's any more to it. I doubt if we'll need to go into detail."

Wanly Charisse said, "I suppose you're right." Maybe, if they did have to divulge that much, other people would think it just coincidence that Kristy's eyes were so strikingly like Daniel's. And they'd hardly be crass enough to express any doubts aloud.

"Then we keep it to ourselves?" Daniel asked.

Charisse nodded, against an obscure resentment that she knew was unwarranted.

Daniel reached out a hand and touched her cheek. "What's the matter?"

Her smile was strained. "This is going to be more complicated than I'd realised."

"We'll weather it," he promised, his fingers lingering, then moving to lift her chin as he came closer. He bent his head and kissed her but she didn't reciprocate, held back by a multitude of conflicting feelings.

Daniel looked at her questioningly. Before he could say anything, Kristy called, "Mummy?" And Charisse pulled away, turning to open the door.

"Here, darling. What is it?"

"I couldn't find you!" Kristy told her reproachfully. "I want to play with my tiger puzzle. Where is it?"

It was in one of the boxes that hadn't yet arrived from New Zealand. Explaining that and finding an alternative puzzle among the limited number of toys and games they'd brought with them took some time.

Charisse and Daniel weren't alone again until she'd put Kristy to bed and he had read her a story.

Charisse was in the kitchen, clearing crayons and an activity book and a scattering of interlocking plastic blocks from the worktable while coffee percolated on the counter, when he came up behind her and slipped his arms about her waist.

His lips nuzzled her neck. "I missed you last night." He turned her in his arms and kissed her lips softly, then her cheek, gliding his mouth down the side of her neck while he held her snugly.

Charisse sighed soundlessly. Her body instinctively responded to him, a faint warmth beginning to spread through it, but her mind was jittery.

"Let's go to bed," he whispered against her skin.

"It's too early," she objected. "I'm making coffee."

Daniel raised his head, his eyes laughing at her. "Coffee."

She slid her gaze away from his. "Do you want some?"

"I just told you what I want," he said, his voice low and seductive, his head cocked to one side as he smiled down at her.

"Yes—well, even *you* can't always have what you want just when you want it!" she said, shattering the mood.

As his arms dropped away from her, his expression changing as though she'd slapped him, she was appalled at the sharpness of her reaction, wanting to take back the words.

"I'm sorry," he said stiffly. "I guess you feel I'm pressuring you." Then he swung round and left her.

The coffee gurgled in the machine and she turned back, watching blindly as the droplets fell into the jug and the rich aroma filled the room.

With shaking fingers she poured two cups and put them on a tray, then carried it to the other room. "I made some for you," she said. A peace offering.

Daniel was standing with his hands in his pockets, staring out of the window, the curtains still drawn back although it was dark now.

It was a moment or two before he turned.

Charisse straightened from putting the tray on the low table. "I didn't mean what I said in there."

When he offered no response she took one of the cups and sank down onto the sofa.

At last Daniel moved, slowly crossing the carpet to pick up the other cup. He seemed to hesitate before seating himself opposite her, and took several gulps of the hot drink.

Charisse sipped at hers, tasting the pungency of the coffee on her tongue, welcoming the warmth as it entered her stomach. "I'm still a bit tired," she said.

Daniel regarded her across the narrow table. "If you don't want to make love all you have to do is say no. I won't force you."

"I know you wouldn't." She glanced up at him. "It's more involved than that."

"So tell me."

She hesitated. "I'm feeling a bit…disoriented. As if I've lost control of my life—and Kristy's." It was true, although not all of the truth.

"You haven't," he argued. "We're married, Charisse. Any decisions from now on are joint ones, that you and I make together. I won't be riding roughshod.'' Smiling a little, he added, ''As if you'd let me.''

''I'm not used to consulting anyone else.'' And yet how often she had wished for someone close to help her make crucial decisions, share the responsibility.

''Neither am I. You might have to remind me sometimes that you've a right to have your say, tell me if I'm taking too much for granted. I wouldn't have thought that would be difficult for you. You're a very strong woman.''

''Is that how you see me?''

''How else could you bring up Kristy alone after what happened to your sister and your parents?''

''I had no choice.''

''There's always a choice. Just as there was a choice between contacting me again and letting it go, never giving Kristy the chance to meet her father. I'm glad you decided to take that chance. That you made that choice. And glad you chose to marry me.''

''There didn't seem to be any real alternative to that either.''

He said nothing for a few moments, his expression coolly inscrutable. ''Perhaps not. But it has compensations, doesn't it? I don't think you found our wedding night too disappointing?''

''Not disappointing at all,'' she agreed huskily. She wondered if he had found it so. With stark, unwelcome suddenness she recalled again those haunting, insistent words...*when you were going wild in my bed*...

And weeks later he'd told her that the night before Gabrielle left him, there was *something magical about the way you made love to me*...

Her hands clutched at the cup between them, trying to take comfort from its heat. On their wedding night he had used the same word about her. About their lovemaking. Magical.

"Gabrielle was in love with you," she heard herself say, her voice remote, as if coming from another planet.

If Daniel was startled at the shift in focus he didn't show it. His eyes turned dark and a faint flush appeared on his cheekbones. He said, "I know that now. It's something I have to live with. I never meant it to happen."

"I don't suppose she did either. Gabrielle was vulnerable when she came here…to Australia."

"She never showed it."

"No. She took on another personality, used my name, to help her cope. Help her forget."

"Forget?"

"That's why she left New Zealand, ran away. Why she went as far as Perth, I guess."

"She was running away from what?"

"Herself," Charisse said slowly. "But something else, too."

"A love affair?"

"She was in love with her boss. He was married, had a family, and she respected that. She thought she could handle it, but then she discovered he felt the same way. So Gabrielle took herself away from temptation."

"I had no idea."

"I don't suppose you wanted to."

She might have flicked him with a whiplash. He went white about his mouth. "You think I took advantage of her."

"No," Charisse said fairly. "I did think that, when she came home pregnant and so obviously unhappy. But I know you never deliberately hurt her."

"Thank you for that."

"You liked her and you wanted to sleep with her. Did

sleep with her. And now—'' she took a quick breath ''—you want to pick up where you left off…with her sister.''

Daniel frowned. "It isn't like that."

"Even when you found out I wasn't Gabrielle you were quite happy to marry me instead of her."

"What are you getting at?"

"We're not interchangeable!" she said baldly.

Daniel leaned forward, put his cup on the table and stood up. "I never thought you were. What's this all about, Charisse? You didn't have these objections before."

She wanted to yell at him, but that was irrational. Still, when she spoke her voice was strained with the effort to keep it level. "I don't know," she said honestly, bewildered herself by the force and suddenness of her rage. "It's being here." She looked about distractedly. "Where you and Gabrielle…" She couldn't go on. "I can't help thinking of her. And I know when you look at me you see her. What am I but a handy clone-wife?"

"That's not true!"

She looked at him directly. "You gave yourself away last night—when I admired the sculpture she gave you."

He couldn't deny it. "A momentary slip," he said uncomfortably. "I apologise."

Charisse lifted her shoulder. "It doesn't matter."

But it did. She knew he couldn't help it, only understanding why he found it difficult to separate her from her sister in his mind didn't make it easier to accept. And his apology, however sincere, didn't alleviate anything.

He moved impatiently. "It does matter," he said, echoing her inner turmoil. "You've made that very clear." His glance went from her to the glass sculpture on the window ledge. "Shall I get rid of that?"

"No, of course not." She turned to look at it, and the

vaguely triangular shape from this angle looked like a sur-
realistic heart, the colours bleeding through it. "You can't.
Gabrielle wanted you to have it."

"If it's going to remind you of her—"

"I don't need any reminders," Charisse said harshly.
"Even if I didn't have Kristy, I'd remember my sister every
day of my life."

"I see."

Daniel's brooding gaze had darkened. He, too, must be
thinking of Gabrielle. Whenever he looked at Charisse he
would be reminded of the woman he had once lived with
and laughed with, and held in his arms. And who looked
exactly like her.

No wonder he had trouble differentiating them.

"Is it any use telling you I don't think of you as any
kind of substitute?" he asked her.

"It's...difficult to believe."

He moved restlessly, looked out of the darkening window for a moment, then back at her. "The sooner we move
out of here the better. I have to show my face in the company office tomorrow, but you could go house-hunting. I'll
get hold of an agent, tell him we need to buy a place."

"Buy? Not rent?" It crossed her mind that buying a
house would somehow cement her decision to live in Perth
with him, make the shift permanent despite his promise to
send her and Kristy home if they weren't happy.

"I'd rather buy. Do you have any reason not to?"

"Not really." Logically it would be no more difficult to
return to New Zealand than it was already.

"I'll send the agent round to see you. If you find anything you like, let me know when I get home from the
office and we'll go and look at it again together."

"You'll have to tell me what price bracket you can afford. And what areas of the city I should be looking in."

"You might try Dalkeith. It's an established suburb. I think you'd like it." His gaze rested on her in a slightly wary way, and she dipped her head to avoid it, staring into her coffee. "I'm not sure where the good schools are. When you find a house you like I'll make enquiries among my friends and colleagues who have children."

Charisse nodded and drank some more of her coffee. Daniel's half-empty cup still sat on the table but he made no attempt to retrieve it.

The phone shrilled, and Daniel answered it. After a short conversation he put down the receiver and turned back to Charisse. "Will you be all right if I go out for a while?"

"Yes, of course. What's happened?"

"Nothing to worry about. I don't know how long I'll be. Don't wait up."

She didn't wait up. She got ready for bed quite early and went into the main bedroom and stood just inside the doorway, trying to block out a mental picture of Daniel and Gabrielle sharing it.

In the end she turned her back on it and went to the room she'd shared with Kristy the night before. She pulled the covers over the sleeping child and kissed her forehead, then sat on the bed for a while just watching her. Whatever happened, she told herself, keeping Kristy safe and happy was paramount. And whatever sacrifices she had to make— or force from Daniel—Kristy was worth every single one.

When Daniel came home Charisse was fast asleep in the other single bed.

Daniel said nothing about it before he kissed Kristy goodbye in the morning, only shooting Charisse an unreadable glance as she poured milk on Kristy's cereal.

He arrived home later than she'd expected and picked up and hugged the small pyjama-clad tornado—fresh out of the bath—that met him at the door. He admired an elaborate construction of coloured-block enclosures and plastic animals on the living room floor, and then stepped over them to go to the refrigerator in the kitchen and get himself a cold beer.

"A hard day?" Charisse guessed.

"A long one." Daniel lowered the glass in his hand and wiped foam from his mouth. He lifted his eyes to her and she almost shivered, because they were cool and nearly expressionless. "How was yours?" he enquired.

"We went house-hunting. There was one that looked promising. It's a bit late to go and look at it now."

She'd tried not to sound snappish but he gazed at her thoughtfully before he spoke. "Sorry. Next time I'll try to let you know if I get held up. Tomorrow afternoon I could take an hour off."

"I'll tell the agent. What time?"

"Will three do?"

"I'm sure it will." Charisse made a pretence of checking the oven temperature. "Dinner's ready."

"Thanks." He crossed to the sink and put the glass in it. "Mind if I have a shower first?"

"I'm keeping the food warm anyway."

He paused on his way out of the kitchen. "I don't usually eat this early. Have you been waiting for me?"

Charisse shrugged. "It doesn't matter. Kristy had to be fed, though. She's used to having her meal before six."

Daniel nodded. "I'll try to get home earlier in future. Is there anything I can do?"

"You could persuade Kristy to clear her toys off the floor."

He looked at the colourful arrangements. "Seems a shame after all the work she put into it. Can't we leave it?"

"I thought it might annoy you. You're not used to having a child's clutter about your home."

Daniel glanced up at her. "It's her home, too. I like seeing her things about. Makes me feel like a real daddy. Anyway, I want you both to feel comfortable here."

Kristy came running with a couple of books. "Read me a story, Daddy Daniel!"

"Please," Charisse reminded her.

"Ple-ease!" Kristy wheedled, giving him her most charming smile.

"Wait until I've cleaned up, honey," he suggested, his big hand on her cheek. "And it'll have to be short. Your mummy's been keeping dinner for me."

They ate after Kristy was settled into bed with the light out. Charisse described the house she'd found and Daniel said, "Is it what you want?"

She hesitated. "It has everything I told the agent we needed."

"Mmm. Well, I'll have a look."

He helped her clear up, and stack the dishwasher, then said, "I've got some paperwork to do. If you want me—" a brief gleam lit his eyes before he looked away "—I'll be in my study."

He went off to the small room next to the master bedroom. Charisse checked the bathroom, wiped splashes, straightened Kristy's towel and hung up the bathmat.

In the living room she picked up a small-size discarded sweatshirt, folded it absently and left it on the table.

She looked through the bookshelves and took a *National Geographic* over to the sofa, desultorily turning some pages before switching on the television. Finding a film on one of the channels, she settled down to watch, ordering her mind to stop jumping about and concentrate on the unfolding drama before her. A couple of times the telephone rang, but Daniel must have answered it, because each time the sound stopped after the first ring.

When the film ended she turned off the set. The apartment was very quiet. No sound came from behind the closed door of Daniel's study. She looked at the thin line of light showing beneath it, then went and knocked gently.

"Yes?"

Charisse opened the door. The desk was facing her, and Daniel was frowning at the screen of a portable computer. After a moment he looked up. "What is it?"

"I thought you might like some coffee or something. I can bring it to you here if you like."

"Thanks. Coffee would be good, if you're making some for yourself."

She made two cups and carried one to the study, placing the steaming mug on the desk beside the computer. "I'll say good-night," she said.

"You're going to bed?"

"Yes, soon. You're busy anyway. I'll see you in the morning."

She couldn't meet his eyes, instead keeping her gaze fixed on the polished wood of the desk.

As she was about to leave, he said, "Do you intend to sleep with Kristy for the rest of our married life?"

"No, of course not." Charisse bit her lip, flushing. "I'm sorry, Daniel. I can't…not in that bed!" She lifted her eyes.

He looked back at her. "I shouldn't have brought you here. One of my more obvious mistakes. We could have gone to a motel, I suppose."

She'd probably have vetoed that for Kristy's sake. "It doesn't matter."

"It matters to me." He paused. "There are other places besides bed where people can make love."

"And I suppose you've used all of them!"

His gaze was steady and ironic. "You don't really want to know."

Of course she didn't. There was no point in tormenting herself any further. "When we find a house…"

"Is that a promise?" A glimmer of humour lightened his expression.

Charisse flushed. "The furniture here—is it yours?"

"No, most of it goes with the apartment. So when we find a place we'll have to do some shopping. You'll enjoy that."

A faint knell rang in her brain. She'd never been shopping with Daniel, never told him it was something she liked doing. Gabrielle had enjoyed it, too. "Why do you say that?"

He seemed at a loss. "I'm assuming that most women like choosing stuff for a new home. Is that sexist or something?"

"Probably." She kept her voice calm. "But I'll try not to hold it against you."

He grinned at her. "I'm relieved. The only thing I want you to hold against me is your sweet, sexy self. And as that seems to be off-limits for now, perhaps you'd better take yourself off to your little bed."

His tone was light, lifting her spirits, although his eyes held a disturbing glow as he let his gaze linger on her, and his mouth took on a sardonic curve.

She turned to the door, then looked back over her shoulder. "Thank you, Daniel," she said. "For understanding."

The house she had seen was, as she'd said, everything she had asked for. Spacious and modern with adequate grounds, it was decorated in neutral colours that wouldn't clash with anything she and Daniel wanted to put in it. Even the price was within the range Daniel had specified.

And Daniel reported that the nearest school had a solid reputation, according to his information. The place was exactly what she'd told the agent they were looking for.

When Daniel had looked it over thoroughly, he told the agent they'd get back to her about it, and escorted Charisse and Kristy to his car.

Inserting the key in the ignition, he turned to Charisse. "What's wrong with it?"

"I didn't say anything was wrong with it!" she protested. "It's probably perfect."

"Probably?" His brows arched. Turning to Kristy, strapped into the backseat, he asked, "What do you think of that house, Kristy?"

"It's very big."

"Too big?"

Kristy hunched an indifferent shoulder. "Don't know."

Daniel looked from her to Charisse. "Shall we make an offer?"

She chewed her lip. "I suppose we shouldn't let it go. It does have everything, really. Do you like it?"

He was watching her face. "It seemed…empty. I figured you'd probably fix that."

He meant soulless. That was what she'd felt—that the house was a stylish shell, without warmth. Not welcoming. And maybe he was right. With the right family in it the house might achieve that elusive quality that distinguished a home from a mere dwelling. She said, "It doesn't feel like a happy place."

Daniel looked at her a moment longer. Perhaps he was thinking that wasn't a particularly sensible thing to say.

But unexpectedly he said, "I think I know what you mean. Well, none of us seem to be very keen. We'd better pass on this one."

On Sunday they looked at some houses and then drove

out into the country to admire the wildflowers that made the state famous. That night they were to have dinner with Sally and Pete in the flat below.

Charisse gave in to Kristy's plea to wear her flower girl frock. It wasn't totally unsuitable and she'd grow out of it before she had a chance to be a bridesmaid again.

The temperature was very warm, even after sundown, and Charisse put on a sleeveless blue cotton dress with a wide neck and flared skirt. She'd bought it at sale price, taken by its cool cut and the colour that echoed her eyes. This was the first time she'd worn it.

When they came out of the bedroom Daniel was waiting. His eyes kindled as he put aside the newspaper and looked at Charisse, then stood up. A strange, surprised expression flickered over his face. "That dress looks as good as new."

"It is new. I bought it a week ago."

"I thought you—" He stopped abruptly. "I thought it was one that Gabrielle used to wear," he said flatly. "I beg your pardon. You did tell me that you sometimes swapped clothes, and I suppose she left hers…"

"Yes." She didn't remember a dress like this but it was a classic pattern and she and Gabrielle had always worn a lot of blue. Now she recalled Daniel talking about a blue dress that he'd liked when Gabrielle wore it. "I'll change," she said.

"No—"

"Daddy," Kristy interrupted. "What about my dress?"

"It's very pretty," he said distractedly. "Charisse—"

"Can't we go now?" Kristy demanded. "We're ready and they're 'specting us." She tugged at Charisse's hand.

It was true, they should be downstairs by now, and she didn't know what she'd put on if she didn't wear this damned thing now. "All right," she said.

Throughout the evening Charisse spent a lot of time

steering around the subject of her supposed previous friendship with the O'Regans. She was glad that Kristy's presence gave them an excuse to leave early, and when she came out of the bedroom after tucking in the sleepy child, Daniel turned from where he'd been fiddling with the dial of the stereo and said, "I'm truly sorry I've put you in this position, Charisse. I hadn't realised how awkward it would be for you."

"Actually, neither did I." They'd both been thinking about Kristy, first and foremost.

"If you want to go back to New Zealand I could ask around, see what's available there in the way of jobs, and try to find some way to get out of my contract early."

"No." Charisse pushed aside the temptation to retreat to the known and familiar. "We're here now." Better to go forward. "I'll cope."

He came closer and lifted her chin with his hand. "Remember, I want you to be happy. You and Kristy."

His kiss was light at first, but then his lips lingered, caressed, firmed. His hand came about her waist and pulled her close, and her mouth opened for him. But when he slid his fingers inside the neckline of her dress she pulled away.

"I'm sorry," she whispered. "Please."

Reluctantly Daniel released her. "I hope you find a house that you like soon."

Chapter 16

At last Charisse found the perfect house, overlooking the Swan River. Set in broad lawns and well back from a quiet road, it was spacious and gracious and near a good school. Even Kristy declared, "I like this one, Mummy!"

There was already a swing hanging from one of the trees that edged the lawns, and an old playhouse that enchanted Kristy, despite its need for paint and a good clean-out.

"The people who own it had a family," Charisse relayed to Daniel, phoning him at the office. "But their children have grown up. The agent said you could come and view it this evening if you like."

He did view it, looked about wordlessly, knocking on walls and peering into cupboards. "It needs some repair work," he decided, after inspecting the foundations and squinting up at the roof. "It's quite a lot older than I'd thought of."

Charisse and Kristy must have appeared crestfallen. Daniel looked at them and laughed, then turned to the agent and said, "Okay, we'll make an offer."

They moved in two weeks later, following a hasty buying spree for the necessary furniture, and Kristy was ecstatic at being allowed to help unpack the boxes that had finally arrived from New Zealand.

The weekend was an orgy of unwrapping and sorting and arranging.

Charisse took the glass sculpture from a carton and removed the layers of paper. She was looking about the big front room for a place to put it when Daniel came in, another box in his arms. "This one's labelled 'lounge'," he said.

"Put it over there in the corner," Charisse requested.

He did so and straightened, looking at the beautiful, glowing thing in her hands. "Why don't we wrap that up again and keep it for Kristy until she's older," he suggested quietly. "A memento of her mother."

Relief and gratitude flooded her. "That's a lovely idea," she said. "Thank you, Daniel."

On Saturday night, with the house still in chaos, they returned to the flat to sleep. But by Sunday the place had begun to look like a home, and Charisse had made up the brand-new queen-sized bed in the master bedroom with equally new sheets and a duvet that she and Daniel had chosen together.

When Kristy had finally gone to sleep with her beloved Big Daddy Ted on one side and Annabelle on the other, Daniel opened the new refrigerator and took out a green bottle with a foil top. "I've been saving this," he said. "Real champagne. Where did we put those glasses?"

Charisse found them while he opened the bottle, the cork leaving it with a sigh, a wisp of vapour rising in its wake.

"Let's be comfortable," Daniel said, and led the way into the front room, as yet sparsely furnished with a big, deep sofa and a matching pair of two-seaters.

They sat on the sofa, facing the view across the garden to the river, and Daniel filled the delicate crystal flutes with the pale gold, bubbling liquid.

Placing the bottle on the floor, he raised his glass. "To our new home, and our future."

Charisse matched the gesture, the crystal flute kissing his with a small clink. Crisp bubbles burst in her mouth as she savoured the slightly tart flavour of the wine.

Daniel leaned back and lifted an arm to place it about her shoulders. "I hope you won't have any regrets, Charisse."

About marrying him? Coming to Perth with him? "I have no regrets."

"I've taken a new position in the company," he said. "Starting next month I'll be spending most of my time here in the city."

Because she'd accused him of wanting nothing more than a nanny for his daughter? But that seemed ages ago now. "You like moving about," she worried. "Variety."

"When I was single I liked it. But I *love* my daughter, and I love—well, I've missed out on a big chunk of her life already. She's grown and changed so much in these last few months, it just amazes me. I don't want to miss any more. And…I have a wife now. Someone to come home to every night."

"You had someone to come home to before," she reminded him huskily, "for a while."

"A short while. That was different. I was away quite a lot even then. It was nice having…having Gabrielle here when I was around, but our affair was…intermittent."

Charisse cast him a fleeting look, noticing his small hesitation. Her hands tightened a little on the glass flute. "Was Gabrielle the only woman you've lived with?"

"Actually, yes. Not that we planned it that way, but we met at a party and she was looking for a place. She loved Perth and wanted to stay longer, only her waitressing job didn't pay much and she couldn't afford expensive accommodation."

That much Charisse knew.

"I was going away on a job for a few weeks," Daniel went on, "and I offered her my place, rent-free. It suited me to have someone to look after it."

"Yes, she told us about it."

Until that point Gabrielle had been perfectly open about her plans and hopes. At least, she'd seemed so. Later, when Gabrielle had come home pregnant and unwilling to talk about the previous several months, Charisse and her parents had wondered just how much she'd been keeping from them.

"After I came back there seemed no reason to ask her to move out. I was still being sent off for days at a time, sometimes a week. We got on well when I was home and…one thing led to another, in time."

"So you were flatting together before you slept with each other?"

"We were friends before we were lovers. And after…"

"You said you and she had something you valued. And that you'd made promises to each other."

"I valued it very much." His eyes had gone darker. "I didn't think it was leading to marriage and happy-ever-after, and as far as I knew neither did she, but it shouldn't have ended the way it did. She could have trusted me."

Another memory surfaced and Charisse gave him a searching look, perhaps betraying doubt.

"What is it?" he asked.

She shook her head. "It's not my business."

"Tell me."

Charisse hesitated a moment longer, then said, "Julia told me about her sister and you."

His mouth turned down at one corner. "What, exactly, did she tell you?"

"Just that you'd been seeing her, but when a job came up overseas you went off without a backward glance."

"Leaving her weeping on the shore?" he enquired, and followed that with a small laugh. "It wasn't quite like that." He returned his gaze to the view outside the window.

"What was it like then?" Charisse asked, when he didn't seem inclined to say any more.

Daniel drained his glass and picked up the bottle to refill it, topping up hers, as well. "I was twenty years old and I thought she was the love of my life. And I was just arrogant enough—and blind enough—to think she felt the same about me."

"How do you know she didn't?"

He drank some more of the wine. "It took awhile to figure it out, and in the end I had to be bludgeoned with it. We'd been seeing each other for months but she wouldn't sleep with me. I assumed she was a virgin and of course I respected her choice. I was willing to wait, even though she drove me wild with half measures."

Drove him wild, did she? Charisse fought a flare of jealousy and said, "So?"

"Eventually I discovered she'd been seeing someone else all along. Someone who wasn't nearly as patient—or stupid. She lived in a flat with a couple of friends, but she had a key to her sister's house. Julia and Mac went away for a long weekend, and I wanted to go over some stuff he had on his computer at home. Julia picked him up from work so he handed me his key and told me to go round to the house and transfer the data to a disk so I could take it away.''

Daniel paused there to take some more champagne, and Charisse said, ''You don't have to tell me—''

''You asked,'' he reminded her. ''After I got there and let myself in I heard someone in the bedroom and thought the place was being burgled. I opened the door of the room—'' He stopped and shrugged.

''She was there with someone?''

''Very much so. The position, shall we say, could hardly be more compromising. In a split second it became very obvious that the love of my life didn't feel the same—not about me anyway—and that furthermore she was no virgin.''

Charisse felt sick. ''I'm so sorry.'' No wonder he hated lies, deceptions.

''I got over it years ago, though at the time I thought my world had ended. So I did the nearest thing I could find to joining the Foreign Legion.''

''Got a job overseas, you mean.''

''Right.'' He grinned. ''Best thing I ever did. It took me awhile to realise that my pride was probably more bruised than my heart. The girl had been using me, and that's what hurt most of all.''

''Using you?''

''The other guy was married. He worked for the same company that Mac and I were with, on the management side, and being with me meant she got to see him quite easily. I was a blind—a convenient smoke screen.''

''Julia never knew?''

Daniel shook his head. ''When I found them they begged me not to tell anyone, and I was young enough to feel sensitive about admitting I'd been made a fool of, anyway. Besides, why risk hurting the guy's perfectly innocent wife? I gather the secret relationship didn't survive long after that. I don't know how serious it was for him, but she must have really loved him, because she never gave him away. Though apparently she was devastated, an emotional mess. Julia's still convinced I broke her sister's heart. If it wasn't for Mac refusing to take sides she'd probably never have spoken to me again.''

He might make light of it now, but the episode had obviously been painful at the time. Charisse stared at the tiny moving bubbles in her glass, the little explosions on the surface. ''When you thought I was Gabrielle,'' she said, ''what did you mean when you said her promises weren't worth much? Because you hadn't made any lasting commitment, had you?''

''No, but we had promised we'd always be honest with each other, and we wouldn't sleep around in between the times we were together. That might not seem much, but when she left so suddenly I felt betrayed. Especially after the way she…we'd…been, the night before. I figured that had been a lie. And I couldn't help wondering how much else in our relationship was a lie, too. It left a sour taste.''

That explained those flashes of bitterness that had troubled and confused Charisse after their first meeting. ''Gabrielle didn't lie to you,'' she said soberly. ''Only she didn't tell you the truth, either. And that was a huge mistake.''

He'd been flung right back into a reprise of a past defection. Charisse suspected that after his first love's deceit he'd tried to protect himself from possible further hurt, laying down ground rules and conditions. And Gabrielle had accepted them, playing the role of sophisticate that she had adopted for herself along with her sister's name. Because she too was trying to protect herself.

It hadn't stopped her falling in love with him, and the

charade had faltered when she found herself pregnant with Daniel's child. For one night she had dropped all pretence and honestly shown her feelings for him—feelings that he had subconsciously recognised, had even, perhaps, been on the brink of reciprocating. If he had known about the baby that might have tipped the balance, sent him soaring into real, lasting love.

Only it hadn't happened, because Gabrielle had never given him the chance.

Her throat aching, Charisse forced down some more champagne.

"Charisse?"

She looked up, somehow bringing a smile to her lips, but he wasn't fooled.

"This was supposed to be a celebration," he said. "I didn't mean to make you sad."

Charisse shook her head. "I asked the questions."

"Maybe they needed to be asked."

"You're not used to answering to anyone, are you?" She smiled faintly.

His smile was enquiring. "What do you mean?"

"You don't explain unless you're asked. You could have told me this that night we met Mac and Julia."

His expression hardened. "I had no idea Julia had been making mischief."

"I don't think she meant to. She wanted to warn me."

"Warn you not to trust me? You *can* trust me, Charisse, I promise. Anything you want to know, just ask."

She took him at his word. "Where did you go the night after we arrived in Perth? You had a phone call and went out, without telling me why."

He looked surprised. "The call wasn't important—just a colleague with a minor query. I made it an excuse to go and fetch a file from the office for him, because you'd just accused me of confusing you with your sister and more or less told me you couldn't bring yourself to share my bed. I dropped off the file and went for a long walk. Partly because I needed to think, and partly because I figured by the time I got back you'd be asleep, and I might be able to resist the mad urge to sweep you off to bed and make love to you anyway.''

He moved his hand, brushing her hair away from her cheek, lifting a strand in his fingers. Small tremors of pleasure feathered her skin.

"Like I want to now," he said quietly. "I love your hair. It's as soft and silky as Kristy's.''

And as Gabrielle's. Exactly the same. Charisse pushed the thought away, closing her eyes, concentrating on the sensation that his caressing fingers evoked. She felt him take the glass from her, and his arm curved her closer, his lips finding her mouth.

The kiss began gently, but as her lips parted under the questing pressure of his it became eager and seeking and passionate. Daniel's free hand skimmed down her body, and then he lifted her onto his lap, holding her close as she hooked her arms about his neck.

They kissed for a long time, until her whole being was on fire and her heart pounded with excitement, and at last Daniel raised his head, looked down with glittering eyes at her flushed face and said, "Shall I take you to our bed?''

Charisse nodded wordlessly, and he gave her a fierce smile and rose from the sofa to carry her to their new bedroom.

There were no ghosts here. The new duvet yielded under her as Daniel lowered her to the mattress. He left her while he closed the curtains, and in the shadowy light he undressed her slowly, each fastening a teasing revelation, every touch on newly bared skin a lick of erotic fire. When she reached up to unbutton his shirt he stood and stripped it off. It was swiftly followed by the rest of his clothing.

Then he lay down beside her and she put a hand on him and felt the heavy beat of his heart. She smiled and kissed his salty shoulder, then his chest, and heard him make a sound like a deep purr as her tongue flicked his nipple.

''My turn.'' He eased her onto her back and returned the compliment, sending her into mindless delight.

Desire built and ebbed and built again, higher and brighter, until neither of them could wait any longer and she took him into her body, sighing with satisfaction as he gave himself to her, filled her and sent ever-stronger ripples through her, finally breaking on the shore of fulfilment just before he too reached the soaring crest and fell panting to the other side.

He draped the crisp sheet over them as they lay together in the lovely aftermath, her head on his shoulder, his arm holding her safe and warm. His lips nuzzled her forehead and he whispered her name.

Charisse didn't answer. Nothing must spoil this moment. She didn't want to talk.

Sometimes Charisse missed Brenna and her other friends, and felt a tug of nostalgia at the thought of the home she'd left behind. But that home had also held daily reminders of her family, and this totally different environment helped her forget the ache of loss. More and more she had days when she scarcely thought of Gabrielle and her parents, and the memories were less grief-tinged.

Kristy was settling well too, the acquisition of a real daddy going far toward making up for moving away from her friends and the home she'd lived in all her life.

She started school, soon making new friends, and Charisse met some other mothers, finding common ground and beginning to acquire friends of her own. Daniel too became part of the suburban social life. They met people who had never known Gabrielle, with whom Charisse could be at ease as herself, and she began to feel less like an impostor.

Everyone simply accepted her as Daniel's wife, Kristy's mother. And although she never wanted Kristy to forget her birth mother, if no one asked there was no need to explain the exact relationship.

That made it easier to deal with Sally and Pete when Charisse invited them to dinner, and with meeting colleagues and other friends of Daniel's who "remembered" her as her sister. She smiled a lot, said little and relied on hints from Daniel to get her through, pushing aside the lingering suspicion that Daniel sometimes forgot she wasn't the same woman they had all known before.

If someone mentioned an incident or a person from the past and he turned to her without missing a beat to say, "Of course we remember, don't we, darling?" she invariably murmured agreement, trying not to clench her teeth.

Their lovemaking was intense and satisfying, and Charisse told herself she had no reason for discontent. Yet sometimes she longed for something she couldn't name. Something as unattainable as the cold, distant moon.

Daniel did some of the repairs on the house himself, while Kristy importantly handed him nails and fetched tools. Charisse busied herself with redecorating, and then turned her attention to the garden, trimming shrubs and pulling out untidy plants.

They visited nurseries to choose replacements from the lush tropical shrubs and flowers that thrived in the warm climate, and Daniel helped Charisse dig them in.

"I know why you wanted this place," he said, looking about as he rested on the spade. "And why I liked it, too.

It has the same feeling about it as your old house in New Zealand.''

Increasingly they shared a warm glow of companionship as well as the more exciting but transitory heat of a successful sexual relationship. They were like a real family.

''Maybe I should look for a part-time job,'' she said one night, lying quietly in Daniel's arms in the aftermath of lovemaking. ''Soon I won't have enough to do, with Kristy away at school all day.''

''I'd have thought after so long looking after a child on your own, you'd relish some time to yourself.''

''You don't want me to go out to work?''

''I want you to do whatever makes you happy.'' His hand was playing with her hair. He shifted so he could look at her. ''Are you happy?''

''Yes,'' she said truthfully. If there was a small cloud lurking at the edge of her horizon, she should ignore it. Very few people could claim perfect happiness.

One of Kristy's neighbourhood playmates had just acquired a baby brother. Charisse helped her choose a small present for the baby, and on Saturday afternoon they delivered it and were allowed a peek at the new arrival.

Standing on tiptoe to peer into the crib where the baby slept, Kristy whispered, enchanted, ''I can see him breathing!''

When the baby stirred and woke, the mother changed him, and then said, ''If you sit down on that chair, Kristy, you can hold him if you like.''

Kristy held him with great care, while his bigger sister let him close his tiny fingers about one of hers, and they both talked earnestly to him.

On the way home Kristy chattered with excited envy about her friend's little brother, and bombarded Charisse with questions about how to go about securing one of the fascinating creatures for herself. When they reached the house, she rushed inside to tell Daniel all about it.

That evening Daniel came out of her room after reading her a story and found Charisse in the living room, mending a pair of Kristy's jeans.

"She wants a little brother or sister," he said.

Charisse's teeth sank into her lower lip. "I know," she said shortly. "She'll get over it."

"You're not keen?" Daniel queried, perching himself on the arm of a chair opposite hers.

"It's not like buying her a doll, Daniel!"

"Of course, although I suppose that's how she's viewing it." He studied Charisse's down-bent face. "You don't want another child?"

"I didn't say that. I…I need time to think about it." She'd been on the pill since before their wedding, deciding it wouldn't be sensible to get pregnant when so many changes were taking place in her life and Kristy's.

She did want babies of her own sometime. In fact, seeing the baby had set up an ache inside her to have Daniel's child, but a small core of caution deep inside warned her to hold back from this momentous decision, not to rush into it. "I don't think we're ready for that."

"It's up to you," Daniel said. "But why do you feel we're not ready?"

"I…can't explain." She found it impossible even to articulate for herself, much less to him, her ambivalence about bringing a new life into their marriage. Maybe she was being greedy, even selfish, but she wanted him to love her for herself before she gave him more children to dote on.

Kristy's school sent an invitation to an end-of-term Family Day. Parents, grandparents and siblings were invited to come along on a Saturday morning and see special displays of the children's work.

Kristy wanted to know if her new grandmother could come, but Charisse explained it was too far for Daniel's mother to make the trip. "She'll be here at Christmas, though." She'd sent a present for Kristy's birthday, and said she was looking forward to getting to know her and Charisse.

"But my daddy's coming," Kristy said stoutly. "He promised. I'm going to show him my ball that I made out of paper, and my big elephant that I drawed all by myself."

"Drew," Charisse said. "And of course he's coming." He'd needed no persuasion to accept the invitation Kristy had painstakingly made, saying, "Try and keep me away!"

On the morning of the Family Day, Kristy got up early, wildly excited. She kept asking impatiently if it was time to go yet, and Charisse referred her to the kitchen clock, helping her work out how many hours, then minutes, there were to go before they left.

"It's a big thing for her, isn't it?" Daniel grinned, watching Kristy's anxious hopping from foot to foot as Charisse flipped a couple of butterfly hair ties around the child's ponytails.

"Yes." Charisse straightened the second hair tie and kissed Kristy's forehead. "All right, you can put on your shoes now."

As Kristy scampered to her room, Charisse's gaze followed her. "It *is* a big thing. At kindergarten she never had a father to show off at days like this. She wasn't the only one, but most of the children had granddads or their mother's boyfriends to compensate. She had no one. I hope you realise *you* are her prime exhibit. She'll be dragging you around, introducing you to all the teachers and her little friends."

Daniel grinned. "I guess I can stand it."

He turned as his phone, sitting on the dressing table, began to ring. He picked it up and flicked it open impatiently. "Yes?"

Charisse saw his face change, his eyes lifting to her as he frowned. Then he said, "Yes, yes, I'm still here. Where is this? Look, can't they get someone else?"

As the other person spoke, Daniel's frown deepened. "I know that, but—" His lips clamped shut.

Charisse mouthed, "What is it?"

He shook his head, listening intently. "I'm not the only—"

Kristy came back into the room, her shoes on her feet but unfastened. "Help me, Mummy?"

Charisse took her gaze from Daniel's face and bent to fasten the shoes. Kristy was looking at her father. "Who's Daddy talking to?"

"I don't know."

"Try Webber," Daniel said. "He's good…damn, I see."

Charisse stood again and Kristy took her hand. "Can we go now? Daddy!"

"Shh." Charisse put a finger to her lips. "Wait."

Kristy gave an impatient little jump and said in a stage whisper, "Daddy! Hurry, ple-ease!"

Daniel was staring at her, his face taut, his eyes dark and worried. "I can't," he said curtly into the phone. "No. Tell them I'm sorry but I'm not available."

He paused a few seconds longer. "Because I have something important on here…you wouldn't understand." Pressing the Cutoff button, he put the phone back on the dressing table.

"Aren't you going to take that with you?" Charisse asked him.

"No." His face had an oddly blank look now. "No. Let's go."

"Who was that?" she asked him. "What's it all about?"

"Nothing. Just a job they wanted me to do. Come on." He walked forward and took Kristy's other hand.

"Something important?"

"Never mind. Kristy's the important one today."

It was nice that he thought so, but the set look on his face as he ushered them out and shut the door troubled her.

In the car he checked that Kristy was strapped in, then started the engine. The radio burst into life, playing a popular song. Kristy began to hum.

A few minutes later, as they were driving toward the school along now-familiar streets, the music stopped for a news bulletin. The announcer told them unemotionally that a landslide in the Pilbara region had engulfed a former mining town, trapping dozens of people in their homes, and it was feared some were dead. Emergency services were hampered by the weather in the area and the danger of further slides.

"It's like the dam," Charisse commented. "It must be awful."

"Yes." His mouth hardening, Daniel leaned over and switched off the announcer in midsentence.

"Why did you do that?" she asked in surprise.

"You don't want Kristy to hear it all, do you?"

Kristy was singing to herself in the back. Charisse glanced at her, then back at Daniel's drawn face, his cheeks looking hollowed, his jaw tight.

A ghastly suspicion entered her mind. "Daniel, is that what the phone call was about?"

He fleetingly looked up at the rearview mirror, and didn't answer.

"Was it?" Charisse insisted. "Did they need you to go

and help?'' Not just a job. An emergency. A disaster where lives were at stake.

A muscle moved in his cheek. He said harshly, ''Don't worry about it, Charisse. I'm not going to break my promise to Kristy.''

Charisse stared through the windscreen without seeing anything, foreboding clenching at her heart. ''Who's Webber?'' she asked.

''A geological adviser. He's very good.''

''Are they sending him? Is he as good as you?''

He slowed at an intersection, checked and then pressed the accelerator. ''He's in Sydney. They'll contact him.''

''But that's…that's *hours* away!'' Charisse turned. ''Even if they can get hold of him. Where is this Pilbara place?''

''North of here, a bit.''

She stared at him. ''You're the closest, aren't you? The nearest person with the knowledge they need, the expertise.''

Daniel's shoulder lifted. His eyes remained on the road ahead of them in fierce concentration.

Kristy was still singing. ''Twinkle, twinkle, little star…''

''Stop the car,'' Charisse said.

''What?'' His head jerked round as he looked at her, then he returned his gaze to the road.

''Daniel, *stop!*''

He shot her a glance and hit the brake, drawing to a clumsy halt at the side of the road. ''What do you want?''

''I want you to find a phone and tell them you're on your way.''

''Kristy—''

''Let me deal with Kristy.''

''I promised her…'' It was the first time she'd seen him look so uncertain, so indecisive.

"Daniel, you can't leave people to *die* because Kristy might be disappointed! I'll explain to her later."

"Twinkle, twinkle...'splain what?" Kristy asked. "Why are we stopped, Daddy?"

"Daddy forgot something important," Charisse said. "Go *on*, Daniel."

He tightened his lips and released the brake, making a fast U-turn. "We might as well go home. I'll phone from there and they can arrange a plane while I pack a few things."

Charisse turned to Kristy. "Now, I want you to be a very good girl and very patient. We can't go to your school just yet."

"Why?"

"Because Daddy has to help some people who are hurt."

"How did they get hurt?"

Charisse tried to explain.

"Why does Daddy Daniel have to go?"

"Because he's very clever and he's the only one who knows what to do to get all those people out."

Daniel's brows rose in a fleeting look at Charisse, but he didn't contradict her.

By the time they arrived home Kristy was crying, and Daniel looked at her helplessly as he unclipped his safety belt. "Kristy, honey—"

Charisse said ruthlessly, "Go and phone. We'll follow."

Before she entered the house with a sniffing Kristy, Daniel had an overnight bag open on the bed and was hauling a couple of shirts from the wardrobe.

"I'm sorry, Kristy," he said, looking wretchedly at her tearstained face.

Kristy sniffed again and clambered onto the bed. "Mummy says some kids' mummies and daddies might die if you don't help them, like my one mummy and my nana and grandad did. And kids might too, and then their mummies and daddies will be very, *very* sad."

"Yes," he said. "That's right."

Kristy sighed, looking martyred. "I s'pose you better go and help them, then."

"Yes," he said, and cleared his throat. "I suppose I'd better."

Charisse took the shirts from his hands. "I'll pack those while you get your things from the bathroom. What about socks and underpants? Have you got those?"

"No, they're still in the drawer."

In five minutes he was ready to go. "There's a helicopter standing by for me," he said. "I'll get a cab. You take Kristy to her Family Day. God—I'm so sorry I won't be there."

"Don't worry. She can tell everyone her daddy's a hero."

Daniel gave a choke of scornful laughter. "I'll keep in touch this time. I haven't forgotten how furious you were when I didn't phone you from the dam."

"I'd been worrying myself sick all night."

"I wasn't used to anyone doing that over me. I'll try not to put you through that again." He pressed a kiss on her mouth. "Take care," he urged her, and turned to Kristy to kiss and cuddle her. "I'll be back as soon as I can."

Chapter 17

The disaster was relayed on the TV news that evening. Rescue efforts were being hampered by the danger of further rockfalls and landslides, and anguished relatives were accusing the authorities of cowardice and timidity, but Daniel didn't appear on the screen.

Soon afterwards the telephone rang, and Charisse answered to Daniel's voice. "I'm not the most popular person here," he said soberly. "I had to tell the coordinator that heavy machinery or even too many workers moving around the site could trigger a secondary slide and kill the rescuers. It's a very tricky situation."

"I saw it on the news," she said. "It looks horrific."

"Has Kristy gone to bed yet?"

"Yes, but she isn't asleep. I'll take the phone in and you can talk to her."

After Kristy had chattered at length about her day, and told him the teacher had allowed her to bring her precious artwork home for him to see when he returned, Charisse took the phone back to the living room.

"Kristy's teacher asked if you could come and speak to the class later," she informed Daniel.

"What about?"

"Well, why you weren't able to be there today, and about the rescue. The disaster is all over the radio and TV news, and Kristy told everyone where you'd gone and that you were going to save all the poor hurt people."

He laughed, but she picked up a slight unsteadiness in the sound. "Single-handed, I suppose."

"Something like that. I said I was sure you'd agree to talk to them."

"You dropped me in it?"

"You'll have to do it to make up for not being there today or Kristy may never forgive you. You can look forward to adoration from a horde of five-year-old hero-worshippers."

"Sadist," Daniel accused. His tone altered. "It's so good to hear your voice, Charisse."

But all too soon he had to go, promising that he'd phone again tomorrow.

When he did, he told her several bodies had been recovered, and two survivors found almost uninjured. "We hope there'll be more, but it's a hell of a delicate job getting them out, and the longer we take the less chance there'll be of finding anyone else alive. Are you and Kristy okay?"

"We're fine," she assured him. "Missing you, but we know those people need you."

"*You're* missing me?" His voice warmed, deepened.

"Of course," she said huskily.

"This will be over in a day or two," he told her.

Each night Daniel phoned, sounding increasingly tired. Then, one afternoon while Charisse was sitting at the dining room table writing to Brenna, she heard something and looked up to see Daniel standing in the doorway and watching her with hollowed eyes.

"Daniel!" She dropped the pen and jumped up. "I wasn't expecting you! Why didn't you phone? Are you all right?" She almost ran into his arms.

"I'm all right," he said. "You look so good, Charisse. Feel so good." His unshaven cheek rasped her skin but she didn't care. "God, but I love you!"

The world stilled for a single golden instant.

Into her hair he said, "I've had this stupid, irrational fear that before I could get back you'd have left me without a word like your sister did, or—" He suddenly swayed on his feet, and Charisse steadied him, realising how exhausted he was.

"You need to rest," she said. "I'll never leave you like that. *I'm not Gabrielle.*"

"I know, I know," he said, holding her tighter still. "You're Charisse—the real Charisse—and you're alive. Thank God." He breathed in as if inhaling the scent of her neck, where his face was pressed against her skin. "And I love you more than my life."

"You should go to bed." She drew away, her arms still holding him as she guided him to the bedroom. "You need to rest."

"Bed," he groaned, "sounds wonderful. You did hear what I said, didn't you?"

"Yes, I heard."

"I've been giving you time, but what if there isn't any time? Am I making sense?"

"Not a lot," she answered, concentrating on getting him through the bedroom doorway and headed for the bed.

"Pulling those people out—people who had been killed, some of them instantly—I couldn't help thinking they hadn't known there was no time left. I need to tell you how I feel about you. It's too important to leave it unsaid. And I don't give a damn if you can't love me back, if you don't want to know."

What did he mean, if she couldn't love him back? Hadn't she been showing him with her every movement, every look, every breath, these past months? "Of course I love you!" Charisse snapped, immediately aware that it was hardly the way to make a declaration like that.

They reached the bed and he fell onto it, dragging her with him so she collapsed on top of him. His words slurring, he said, "No, not you—Gabrielle loved me. I felt guilty about her, and I thought it served me right that now the boot was on the other foot—that every day I was falling more and more deeply in love with you when you'd only married me for Kristy's sake. Because you were afraid of losing her and you thought—thank God—that she had a right to a father."

Charisse stirred, trying to sit up, but he clamped his arms about her. "Please," he said, "don't go away. I've been dreaming of this for days." He gave a heavy sigh, his eyelids drooping.

"I do love you, Daniel."

He sighed again, and his eyes closed completely. "But..." His eyelids fluttered and opened again. "When I asked you to marry me that first time, you said you couldn't do that, as if the thought horrified you."

"You thought I was Gabrielle," she said urgently, into his glazed eyes. "Even when we got married you were still confusing me with my sister. You only asked me because you wanted your daughter."

His eyes were fully open now, awareness seeping into them. And shock. "No," he said. "You wouldn't have stopped me from seeing her. I didn't need to marry you for that. But I knew it would be torture to be a part of Kristy's life and have no real place in yours. I told you I wanted you both because I couldn't separate the two of you—not physically, and never in my heart.''

Charisse shook her head. ''You wanted the woman you thought was Gabrielle.''

''It was you,'' he argued, ''from the moment I saw you. I had to know that there was no other man for you, and never would be, that we'd be together forever. Because this time I couldn't let you go.''

''Gabrielle…''

His eyes had drifted closed, but they opened again. ''I believed you were one and the same. Well, you didn't tell me you had a twin, so what could I think? You were so like her and yet so different. I thought we'd both changed and matured in five years and that's why the emotion felt stronger, deeper, why it hit me like a wall full of bricks when I saw you that day in the supermarket, and grew more powerful every time I saw you.''

She searched his face, wanting to believe him but half afraid to hope.

''I was coming to know *you*, Charisse. Your strength and your gentleness and your humour and your love for…for my daughter. I couldn't let either of you go out of my life.''

He paused, took her hand in his and held it tightly. ''When I realised who Kristy was, that you'd been lying to me all along, I was stunned. And angry that you—or Gabrielle, as I thought you were then—had kept my daughter's existence from me. Of course it was at least partly my own fault, and whatever you…or your sister…had done, you'd done it for Kristy. And I tried to focus on her while I sorted my feelings out. I soon realised it made no difference. I loved you and nothing could change that. So I asked you to marry me. And then you dropped another bomb-shell.''

That she wasn't his ex-lover and Kristy's mother after all.

Daniel's chest rose and fell as he heaved a breath. ''After you told me who you really were I had to wonder, did I really know you at all—the real Charisse. You'd deceived me from the start, and maybe those kisses we'd shared had been part of the act. You'd only been seeing me for Kristy's sake, you told me.'' Daniel closed his eyes again. ''When you agreed to marry me for the same reason I knew that you weren't in love with me. Gabrielle had been, not you. I hoped that if I worked on it I might earn your love, as I'd earned your trust. Only...''

''When you asked *me* to marry you, after we visited your lawyer, when you knew who I really was, you never mentioned love.''

He lifted heavy lids. ''I didn't think you'd want to hear it then.''

Only two days after he'd thought he was asking her sister, perhaps she wouldn't have. And she wouldn't have believed him. ''Oh, Daniel,'' she said helplessly.

His sleepy eyes half opened, and she saw a flicker of pain in them. ''You hold back from me. Even when we make love I can feel this...this glass barrier between us. It drives me insane but I can't crack it. I thought...maybe if I gave you a child, but you don't want my baby. That hurts in a way I can't...describe. You love Kristy because she's Gabrielle's, not because she's mine. And I love her, too, so much I could never have imagined it, and nothing can alter that. But I love you just as much, in a totally different way, more and more each day, and I would like so much for you to have *our* child, to love it because it's mine...and yours. Is that monstrously selfish of me?''

"No, it's...natural," Charisse protested. "Daniel, I was afraid. That's what the barrier was."

"Afraid? Of what? You still think I'll get tired of Kristy? Of you? Or are you afraid I'll love Kristy less? That's not possible! She'll always be precious to me. But if we have other children they'll be just as precious. One thing I've learned from loving you and Kristy—love can take in any number of people, it's infinitely expandable but unique to each person."

Unique, yes. "I was afraid that you were still confusing me with my sister. I've never been sure you don't still get us muddled in your mind."

He stared at her as if he had trouble taking that in. Finally he said, "Not for a long time. At first...I might have sometimes. But you're not the same. Not at all. I think deep down inside I always knew it. And I know it now as surely as I know my own name."

"You do?" She smiled tentatively, willing herself to believe.

"It's not just that you're more mature, as I suppose Gabrielle would have been by now. The longer I lived with you the more I knew you—loved you—for yourself. Gabrielle would never have cut through the dilemma I was in and made me see what I had to do the way you did. She'd have accepted that I'd made the decision not to go. That isn't a criticism—she wouldn't have stopped me, either. But she'd have cried about the tragedy, been sorry for the people involved—and got in the way. It wouldn't have occurred to her to help me pack."

Charisse couldn't help a small, choking laugh. "You're right, that's exactly how she would have reacted." Her sister's way of coping with drama had always been to create more.

"And I don't know how she'd have handled Kristy's

disappointment.'' Daniel's hand stroked her hair. ''That wasn't her, it was you—typical of you. I was fond of your sister. I'll always regret that I hurt her—and regret even more that she wasn't able to trust me—but I never felt this way about her. About anyone. If *you* had left me like that I'd have followed you to New Zealand, to the ends of the earth if necessary, and found you and begged you to come back. I have no pride with you. Only love.''

She looked into his eyes for a long, long time and saw that he meant it, that the hunger and need and passion was for her. Only her.

Happiness began to spiral up from somewhere deep inside her. ''Yes,'' she said. ''You do love me.''

His eyes squeezed tightly shut, then flickered open. ''I want terribly to make love to you, Charisse.''

''You're exhausted.''

''Not too exhausted.'' He moved, turning on his side, and gathered her close to him.

''You're crazy,'' she murmured, beginning to smile.

''About you, yes.'' His lips touched her cheek. ''One thing, would you mind undressing me?''

She didn't mind, finding it intriguingly sexy to take off his clothes while he lay apparently half-asleep, scarcely helping at all. When she'd stripped him she could see that he certainly wasn't asleep, and he watched with gleaming eyes from under drooping lids as she shed her own clothes and then knelt beside him on the bed.

He reached for her, but she pushed him down against the pillows. ''Let me. I'm beginning to enjoy this.''

He sighed and surrendered to her seduction. Sometimes she thought he'd gone to sleep after all, but after ten minutes he muttered, ''Enough torture,'' and grabbed her and turned her over on her back, his eyes alight and very much awake.

Charisse laughed at him, confident in her power, assured in her responses, no longer doubting his. Then the laughter abruptly died in a flare of passion as his legs parted hers and he came home to her with sureness and skill that stole her breath and made her gasp with delight.

"Tell me again that you love me," he demanded.

Her eyes wide open, she said, "I love you, Daniel."

"And I love you, Charisse, the one and only," he said huskily. "Heart of my heart, love of my life."

Then he took her into that territory where there is room for only two. One man, one woman. For all of their lives.

*   *   *   *   *

SILHOUETTE
SENSATION ®

AVAILABLE FROM 19TH NOVEMBER 1999

CHRISTMAS LONE-STAR STYLE Linda Turner

Enter Single, Leave Wed

Rich executive Mitch Ryan offered Phoebe Smith and her orphaned niece a home for the holidays… in exchange for secretarial services. The only catch: the apartment came fully furnished—with Mitch!

IT CAME UPON A MIDNIGHT CLEAR
Suzanne Brockmann

Tall, Dark & Dangerous

Agent 'Crash' Hawken was faced with a deadly conspiracy and he had just one person on his side—Nell Burns, the only woman who'd ever tempted him to change his dangerous lifestyle. But now, supporting him had endangered her…

HOME FOR CHRISTMAS Patricia Potter

Through smoke and mayhem two strong arms and a firm voice urged Julie Farrell and her precious son to safety. To everyone else Ryan Murphy was a killer, a bad cop. To her he was a hero. Her lawyer's mind wondered about that…

FOR CHRISTMAS, FOREVER Ruth Wind

Zane Hunter arrived at Claire Franklin's B&B just before Christmas. Then, one starry night the bullets started flying…and Claire wondered if the mysterious stranger had put more than her heart at risk.

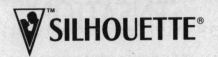

Men who can't be tamed by just *any* woman!

We know you'll love our selection of the most passionate and adventurous Sensation™ hero every month as the Heartbreaker.

HEARTBREAKERS

FREE!

2 Books
and a surprise gift!

We would like to take this opportunity to thank you for reading this Silhouette® book by offering you the chance to take TWO more specially selected titles from the Sensation™ series absolutely FREE! We're also making this offer to introduce you to the benefits of the Reader Service™—

★ FREE home delivery
★ FREE gifts and competitions
★ FREE monthly Newsletter
★ Books available before they're in the shops
★ Exclusive Reader Service discounts

Accepting these FREE books and gift places you under no obligation to buy; you may cancel at any time, even after receiving your free shipment. Simply complete your details below and return the entire page to the address below. *You don't even need a stamp!*

YES! Please send me 2 free Sensation books and a surprise gift. I understand that unless you hear from me, I will receive 4 superb new titles every month for just £2.70 each, postage and packing free. I am under no obligation to purchase any books and may cancel my subscription at any time. The free books and gift will be mine to keep in any case.

S9EB

Ms/Mrs/Miss/Mr ....Initials ....

BLOCK CAPITALS PLEASE

Surname...

Address...

....

....Postcode ....

Send this whole page to:
UK: The Reader Service, FREEPOST CN81, Croydon, CR9 3WZ
EIRE: The Reader Service, PO Box 4546, Kilcock, County Kildare (stamp required)